"I think I have the right to know the name of the person making demands of me."

The Nubian's lips tightened. "My name is Kevin. Kevin Lambert."

Kira snorted. "I find it hard to believe that 'Kevin' was a common name four thousand years ago."

He remained silent while their waiter brought their drinks and left. Then he leaned forward. "My name is Khefar, son of Jeru, son of Natek. And yes, I was born more than four millennia ago. Now that the introductions are over, may I have my dagger back?"

"I need you to answer some questions first."

A muscle in his right cheek ticked. "I want my blade back."

SERESSIA GLASS

SHADOW BLADE

POCKET BOOKS
New York   London   Toronto   Sydney

Pocket Books
A Division of Simon & Schuster, Inc.
1230 Avenue of the Americas
New York, NY 10020

This book is a work of fiction. Names, characters, places, and incidents either are products of the author's imagination or are used fictitiously. Any resemblance to actual events or locales or persons, living or dead, is entirely coincidental.

First Juno Books/Pocket Books paperback edition February 2010

JUNO BOOKS and colophon are trademarks of Wildside Press LLC used under license by Simon & Schuster, Inc., the publisher of this work.

POCKET and colophon are registered trademarks of Simon & Schuster, Inc.

For information about special discounts for bulk purchases, please contact Simon & Schuster Special Sales at 1-866-506-1949 or business@simonandschuster.com.

The Simon & Schuster Speakers Bureau can bring authors to your live event. For more information or to book an event contact the Simon & Schuster Speakers Bureau at 1-866-248-3049 or visit our website at www.simonspeakers.com.

Designed by Esther Paradelo
Cover design by John Vairo Jr.

Manufactured in the United States of America

10 9 8 7 6 5 4 3 2 1

ISBN: 978-1-4767-4748-4

To Paula, my editor, and Jenny, my agent.
Thanks for believing in my story!

And to the fabulous Stacia Kane—you rock!

And a special thanks to L.A. Banks for
your enthusiasm and encouragement.

This wouldn't have happened without any of you.

She comes like the hush and beauty of the night,
And sees too deep for laughter;
Her touch is a vibration and a light
From worlds before and after.

—Edwin Markham, "Poetry"

Prologue

Kira sat on a rough-hewn bench with faded tapestry cushions, her back against the gray stone wall of the hall. Thick glass windows were set into the corridor walls every few feet in a vain attempt to brighten the cold, desolate passageway. She didn't know what this place was; she'd stopped caring and paying attention once she'd realized her parents were sending her away. She'd tried to stop caring about that too, but it was harder.

She knew they were on an island as they'd had to reach it by boat. They had then climbed a steep hill dotted with rocks and windswept grass to reach what looked like a sprawling sun-bleached castle perched atop a cliff set against a sky the same robin's egg blue as the water. Now, as she sat alone in the shadowy hallway, the sun and the sky and the sea seemed to have disappeared. The "castle" felt more like a prison than a palace.

She huddled in the oversized navy blue all-weather coat that had become her protection from the world ever since she'd hit puberty a few months before. Across the hall from her bench, a heavy wooden door separated her from the adults deciding her future—but not from their words.

"We can't do this anymore!" Her adoptive father.

Loud, but his deep voice shaking with anger . . . or fear. "She put our daughter in the hospital. Gilly's still in a coma!"

Kira flinched, then focused intently on her hands, encased in thick garden gloves with cuffs secured to the ends of her shirt sleeves by duct tape. The tape had been her idea, and her father hadn't disagreed. Her jaw still hurt from when he'd hit her, the one and only time he'd ever touched her. She'd deserved it, though, because of Gilly.

Gilly, who was afraid of thunderstorms at nine years old. Gilly, who'd been taught for the last five years not to touch her strange older sister but had come into Kira's bedroom anyway because she was more afraid of lightning than the way Kira's hands sometimes sparked blue.

Lying in bed, semicomatose after retching half the night, twelve-year-old Kira had been exhausted from reliving every painful step of how her dinner had gotten to her plate. Eating had become a nightmare. The only food she could keep down were fruits and vegetables she picked herself, everything else came with confusing flashes of emotion and life from every individual who had handled it, processed it, packaged it, stocked it, sold it . . . Meat was unthinkable.

But all the gardens in their community had been depleted as winter approached and Kira had been so desperately hungry she'd tried to eat, despite the consequences.

Kira had been too sick that stormy night to realize her sister was there, had crept into bed with her to escape her fear of thunder and lightning. Kira hadn't known she'd shifted and touched Gilly. Hadn't realized even when she'd dreamed she was Gilly, thinking of how her older sister must be a magical fairy princess and would someday take them both back to fairyland. Only her mother's screams had shocked her out of sleep, her father's hand knocking her out of bed and to the floor when she'd bolted upright. Only when she saw Gilly's limp form cradled in her mother's arms did she realize that something, everything, had gone totally and finally wrong.

"We've done everything we can do," her father continued, his voice thickening. "But she . . . she refuses to listen to us, and her . . . problem . . . just keeps growing. Bethany's at her wit's end."

Kira had tried. Tried to do what they wanted, tried to make them happy so they would keep her. For four years she'd kept expecting them to change their minds, these people who had rescued her from the orphanage. She'd always thought of Gilly as her sister, from the very beginning, but it was only this year she'd really begun to consider them all family. Only this year had she finally begun to believe that she belonged.

Then she'd gotten her period and her life had gone to hell. Twelve years old and her life was over.

It had started to hurt to wear clothes if she didn't wash them herself, to have anyone else come into her room and touch her things, to eat processed food that so many had a hand in creating. No part of her skin could touch anything or anyone else without crazy images filling her head and tiring her.

It was worse with her hands, especially when they started to glow. Her parents had bought her gloves, of course—all sorts of gloves—pretending she was starting a new fashion trend but really to protect themselves from Kira's touch—a touch that was, at first, like an uncomfortably heavy static charge but had progressed in the weeks following her menarche to being more like a high-voltage electric shock, a shock that somehow *drained* the recipient. Everything had become so hard that staying in her room had been the safest thing.

"We can't help her," her father's words came through the door. "We certainly don't dare touch her anymore. Not after what she did to Gilly!"

Kira slapped her hands over her ears, trying to escape the sound of his crying but unable to escape her own thoughts. She'd almost killed her sister. Why didn't he just say it like he'd said it that night, tell whoever he was talking to that she was a freak, a monster, and that she couldn't be around normal people? That they were afraid of her and what she might do next? She knew what they thought of her, had seen it all when her father had hit her.

Make it stop. Please, someone, make it stop!

Kira jumped to her feet, needing to get away, somewhere, anywhere. She took a step, just one, before the door opened. She turned, raising an arm to shield her eyes as brilliance flooded the hallway.

"Kira Solomon." The light resolved itself into a bronze-skinned woman with long dark brown hair and golden eyes. The floor-length gold dress and the ornate smoky topaz necklace she wore made her look like a princess. "I am Balm. Welcome to Santa Costa, the home of Gilead. Your new home."

Home. As if. She peered into the office, but there

was no sign of her father. Former father. Already gone, probably overjoyed that he'd gotten rid of her. "So he's just throwing me away? Just like that?"

The woman regarded her. "He could have thrown you over the side of the ferry, or worse still, handed you over to the authorities even though what happened was a horrible accident. Instead, your father brought you here. Why do you think that is?"

The answer was easy. "'Cause I'm a freak and this is a prison for freaks?"

Balm laughed. "We're all freaks here, but this is hardly a prison. Of course, you may think differently before we're done."

She stepped back, gesturing at the brightly lit doorway. "If you want to continue to sulk and feel sorry for yourself, then stay there. But if you want a warm bath, hot food that won't make you sick, and the chance to control your gifts and their effects, then you can come with me. Choose now."

Kira chose. Without another word, she followed the strange woman into her office, leaving her old life behind forever.

Chapter 1

The dagger reeked of ancient magic.

Kira Solomon stared down at it, trying not to salivate with longing. The blade itself, shining spotless and deadly, swept proudly from the ornate hilt. Swirls and symbols stood out in sharp relief on the gold-banded handle that gleamed like old ivory. Even shielded by her gloves, her palms itched with the urge to lift it, to hold it in her hands, to test its weight and sharpness.

The things she could do with such a blade.

"Well?"

Kira blinked, then looked up at her client and mentor, Bernie Comstock. The professor turned art dealer stood on the other side of her worktable, eyes shining in his sharp, dark face. He didn't seem affected by the weapon's energy, which Kira supposed was just as well. Being insensitive to magic made the art dealer good at his job. Detecting magic made Kira good at hers.

"I thought I was done with being tested, Bernie."

"This isn't a test, Kira," Comstock hastened to assure her. "I trust you completely."

She gestured to the blade, nestled in a custom-fitted gray foam core inside an aluminum travel case. "What is this, then?"

"I'm hoping you'll tell me."

"Old man." She suppressed a sigh mixed with exasperation and wry amusement. Even though she'd more than proven herself over the years, he still liked to slip a ringer in every now and again. The mentor in him would never die. As if she needed testing to stay sharp. If she wasn't sharp, she'd be dead.

"Fine," she said at last, deciding to go along with whatever game he was playing. "The markings on the handle are worn, but look to be Egyptian." She hadn't attempted to scan the blade with her extrasense yet, but she could feel magic radiating from it. The weapon called to her with a gentle but insistent call. She wondered what would happen when she took off her gloves and touched the dagger with her bare hands.

"The blade itself appears to be bronze, the hilt carved ivory with inset gold," she murmured, reaching out to drag the task lamp closer before bending over the silvery case again. "Obviously not ceremonial, since the blade is not gold and the wear on the handle suggests considerable use. It's in the style of daggers from the Middle Kingdom, meaning, if this is authentic, that the blade is roughly four thousand years old."

Thrusting her hands into her lab coat's pockets to keep from touching the handle, Kira looked at Comstock. "Considering the pristine condition of the blade, I'd say you have a very impressive fake."

"I thought so too, especially considering where I found it." Comstock's expression reminded her even more of a fox. "That is real ivory and the construction of the blade doesn't speak to modern manufacturing technology."

Kira's hands flexed with the need to lift the blade. She stepped back from the table instead. "This looks like something Wynne might make, except I doubt she'd be able to keep the creation of something so perfect a secret from me."

"Wynne Marlowe's one of the best metalworkers in the country and not just because she doesn't use modern technology when re-creating ancient weaponry, although that's certainly part of the reason," the art dealer acknowledged. "But this isn't her work."

"You know this because . . . ?" Wynne could certainly create a ritual weapon, Kira knew, especially if her husband Zoo channeled the magic into it. The boot daggers Wynne and Zoo had made for Kira proved that. She decided not to point the magical element out to her former mentor. It wasn't like he needed to know that Zoo was a real witch.

Comstock gave her a knowing glance. "Because, as you said, Wynne couldn't keep this a secret from you. I had a feeling that, once you'd seen it, you wouldn't let something like this out of your sight."

Kira knew he was right. The dagger was astounding as a replica. If it were the real thing . . .

Her gaze dropped to the blade again. She felt a little like Gollum looking at his "Precious." "You're not going to tell me how you came across this, are you?"

"And deny you the joy of discovering it for yourself when you touch it?" Comstock grinned, peeling years off his multiracial, sixty-ish face. "Besides, you know I'll share all my secrets with you only if you come to work for me."

"Come on, Bernie, you know I prefer being

freelance." Kira braced one hip against the edge of the worn oak surface, idly fingering the heavy Zuni silver necklace at her throat. "I like being able to set my own schedule."

"You'd still have autonomy," Comstock wheedled. "You'd also have fewer expenses and full access to my clients and their collections."

Kira hesitated, tempted as always. She worked well with Bernie. They'd clicked from the moment she'd stumbled into him at the Petrie Museum at University College in London during one of the few summers the Gilead Commission had allowed her a break from training to fight Shadow. She'd consequently transferred to the school to study under him and had then worked freelance for him when he retired from teaching, reduced his duties at the museum, and expanded his private antiquities business. At times she fantasized she'd even be happy working for him, surrounded by ancient artifacts and books, far away from people and things no human should ever know existed.

That happiness wouldn't last, though. One day Bernie would look at her and begin to wonder. She knew the questions would start—questions about her frequent absences, her penchant for dropping everything to run off to every corner of the globe, returning home bruised if not bloodied. Eventually he'd come to realize his former apprentice was using her job as an antiquities expert as a cover for a second, deadlier career.

Not having to answer to anyone best suited her second job, a job she preferred Comstock knew nothing about. It was one thing for Bernie to believe in magic and her ability to detect and defuse it; it was another for him to believe in demons and things that go bump in the night. Even if he could accept that much, he'd still never be convinced it was her sworn duty to eliminate the baddest of the bad: the Fallen and their Shadow Avatars. A duty she'd been trained for since she was twelve by the Gilead Commission. He wouldn't believe the Gilead Commission, the oldest and largest organization dedicated to fighting Shadow, was more advanced than the U.S. military machine and more effective than Homeland Security. He certainly wouldn't believe she'd grown up in the Commission's headquarters on the island of Santa Costa as the surrogate daughter of Balm, the ageless head of Gilead, or that her education had been more about learning to kill than learning to live.

Kira was a Shadowchaser, an elite fighter in Gilead's clandestine army. Humans with extrasensory skills and paramilitary training were used to police low-level half-breeds and humans experimenting in Chaos magic. Shadowchasers were sent in when upper echelon Shadow creatures attempted to disrupt the Universal Balance and tip the world into Shadow and Chaos, usually in ways that involved high body counts.

The fact she had yet to encounter a Shadow Avatar made her lucky, she supposed. From her time in Gilead she knew humans capable of being magically and physically honed into Shadowchasers were scarce and Balm worried about the relatively small number of Chasers worldwide. It gave Kira added pressure to be good, be ready, and be a survivor.

But someday, she liked to imagine, maybe there'd be an end to Chasing, an end to the constant danger.

Maybe there'd be a day when she could go to London and work with Bernie, finally go on one of the digs they'd talked about doing over the years. But, for now . . .

"I like being a renegade, Bernie," she said, giving him a brief smile. "If I worked for you or with you, there'd eventually come a day when one of us would piss the other off."

Comstock sighed as if he hadn't expected anything different. "You know I have to try at least once during my visits, Kira. You're like a daughter to me."

"I know." It was part of the reason she kept an ocean between them. She had enemies, dangerous enemies, and they didn't need to know how attached she was to the very human antiques dealer.

He looked about her cavernous room. "I must say, I'm glad to see you're finally starting to settle in. I can't believe you've been in one place two whole years—even if it does look like you just moved in. Atlanta agrees with you."

"I needed somewhere to put my stuff," she muttered, hunching her shoulders at the direct hit. She glanced at the organized clutter of her main floor. Boxes, notepads, and stacks of books littered the floor and lined the brick walls, piled around a haphazard mix of furniture and art that couldn't conceal the fact that her home had been a warehouse in its former life. Since she knew where everything was and never intended to have guests over to randomly touch anything and leave their imprints behind, she saw no reason to improve her current filing system. Besides, the main reason she'd picked this converted warehouse as her pied-à-terre was because it gave her ample room to display the array of weapons and other antiques she'd collected or confiscated from around the globe. It was also the only reasonably priced place she could find with a couple of underground storage areas she'd repurposed for her altar room and more dangerous collections.

"About the blade." Comstock gestured, drawing her attention to the heavy oak worktable again. "Could its excellent condition be indicative of magic?"

"Oh, there's definitely some sort of magic tied to it." The magical lure of the dagger was obvious to Kira and that, in and of itself, made her hesitate in touching it. If there was some sort of curse or impulse attached to the dagger, she didn't want to take hold of it with a defenseless Normal in the room. "It's extremely powerful to have lasted all these centuries, if it's authentic."

"Even if it's a replica, I'm interested in its history. It's already valuable, but once you authenticate it, its value will be off the charts."

She arched an eyebrow. "And if I say it's a fake?"

"Kira." He raised a hand as if to reach across the table and pat her gloved hand, then quickly lowered it. "Its value goes up just by having you touch it."

"Ah-ha. Now the truth comes out." She folded her arms across her chest, so she wouldn't be as tempted as he was to reach out and touch. It had been years since she'd voluntarily touched another human, gloved or not. "I think I'm going to have to up my fee."

"If you did, I'd happily pay every penny, as would anyone who knows what your word is worth. It just so happens that those who know are also the ones with the money." He settled back in his chair. "I think I've revealed enough secrets for today. How long do you think you'll need with the blade?"

"What, you're not going to ask to stay and watch?"

"After what happened the last time I tried to watch you work?" He visibly shuddered. "Thanks, but I've learned my lesson. I thought my eyebrows would never grow back."

"Be glad it was just your eyebrows, old man. It will probably take me longer than usual to scan the blade. There's a heck of a lot of magic surrounding it, so I want to be extra careful."

"You're always careful, even when bumbling old art dealers burst into the room."

"You rarely bumble, Bernie, and I've always suspected you weren't—"

The art dealer cut her off. "Kira . . . "

"Hmm?" She frowned at the odd note in his voice. "What's wrong?"

"I, well, I just wanted to say that I'm proud of you, Kira. Despite your circumstances, you've become a gifted and talented young woman. I feel a fatherly pride for all you've accomplished."

"Bernie." She didn't know what to say. Especially since the stories she'd told him of her past were just that, stories. Believable fictions that were nowhere close to the unbelievable truth.

He cleared his throat as he climbed to his feet. "Never mind the maudlin thoughts of an old man. Do you think you'll be able to get free for dinner? We really should catch up."

"Of course. Are you staying at the usual place?"

"Georgian Terrace, room six-forty."

"Got it." Kira straightened to her full height, topping Comstock's five-seven frame by a couple of inches. She smiled, unable to resist another dig. "Shall I pick you up?"

Comstock shuddered again. "Do you still have the death trap?"

"That death trap is a hundred-grand worth of prime street muscle." The Buell motorcycle was her baby and the money for its purchase and unique customization was well spent. Its speed and concealed weapons cache had saved her life on more than one occasion.

"I think I'll pass on the ride," Comstock said. "I did a little research and found a restaurant I'd like to try. It's on Peachtree, just a short walk from the hotel. I can meet you there instead."

"What's it called?"

"Dogwood. It actually has a grits bar!"

"A grits bar? Can't we just go to a Waffle House instead? There's almost one on every corner and they have all the grits you can stand."

He gave her a reproachful look. "I'm a gourmand, Kira. You know I don't eat anywhere that requires a tetanus shot or a hangover."

If he'd ever been out at three in the morning and exhausted from policing hybrids and Shadow Adepts, he'd appreciate the always-open chain and its kick-you-in-the-ass coffee. "All right. Dogwood it is."

After escorting the art dealer out, Kira returned to her worktable. The dagger lay as they'd left it, nestled in its specially fitted briefcase. She pondered taking it downstairs to her double-shielded office, then decided against it.

"Okay," she muttered, "time to see what you're made of."

Bracing her gloved hands on the worktable, she leaned over and focused her attention on the dagger. Exhaling slowly, she muted the input of her Normal senses, allowing her extrasense to dominate her mind. As always, she felt a slight resistance as the ordinary and extra-ordinary slid against each other, battling for dominance. Then her extrasense assumed control, reaching through Logic's Veil to touch the current of magic.

The dagger glowed in response, a sheen having little to do with the ivory and gold shaping its hilt. Oh yes, someone or something had imbued the dagger with a great deal of magic. What she didn't know was whether it was Shadow magic or not.

She frowned, allowing the Veil to thicken again. Shadow magic was always tricky to handle, based as it was on Chaos. She hadn't been surprised in a while. Then again, she hadn't come across a four-thousand-year-old magical knife before, either.

Concentrating, she thinned the Veil again, her extrasense cocooning the dagger. The ancient magic didn't react. Encouraging. Still, Kira took her time. The last thing she wanted was to be thrown across the room by a pissed-off blade.

She straightened, peeling off the thin surgical gloves. "Time to tell me your secrets."

Kira spread her hands above the dagger. It neither welcomed nor rejected her. She supposed this was a good thing. But it seemed to be waiting for her touch, somehow expecting it—and that, she supposed, was not a good thing.

"I'm not going to harm you," she said softly. "I just want to know more about you." It wouldn't hurt to talk to the blade, give it plenty of time to decide whether she was friendly or not. That whole throwing-one-across-the-room thing was definitely to be avoided, even if it took some extra time.

Until Kira touched the dagger, she wouldn't know if it would give up its secrets. She'd have to touch it to determine if the dagger's magic stemmed from its composition, a powerful spell, or a spirit inhabiting the blade. A spirit-bound weapon wasn't necessarily a bad thing, but when it was bad, it was very bad indeed.

After taking a moment to steady herself, she slipped her fingers beneath the blade, wrapping them around the ivory and gold handle. For a moment she felt only the smooth, cool surface of the hilt . . .

Then a rushing sound filled her head and the warehouse walls shimmered to translucency, then disappeared altogether. Turquoise spilled across the pipes and suspended lighting fixtures of her ceiling, a vivid sky brightened by the heat of the searing sun. Hot sand replaced the floor and old Persian rug under her battered worktable—except there was no table, nor were there books, chairs, artifacts . . . Rocky, sandy hills stretched away in the distance before her, but to one side were trees and green fields, the glint of what could only be water. A gleaming white pyramid cut into the sky.

Pyramid?

Disorientation swept over Kira as she felt herself being lifted, carried . . . No, not her. It was not Kira being held and lifted, it was the dagger, but she *was* the dagger and it was being taken on a gilded tray along a promenade of sweeping stone columns. Stately movement, tinkling instruments, the murmur of voices. A processional of some sort, moving from bright heat to a cooler interior. They moved along a grand corridor, every surface brilliantly decorated with colorful images of Egyptian gods, hieroglyphs, flora and fauna.

Finally they stopped. Silence filled the grand audience hall and yet she could feel a thrum of excitement, of anticipation, coming from the dagger. At last the reason for its existence had come. Someone worthy had come.

Moving again, the tray was offered up. A pair of golden brown hands cradled her. Disappointment. Not the one.

She balanced on a pair of hands, heard a voice—deep, masculine, melodious—saying words she did not understand but sounded formal to her ears. As she was lowered, Kira saw the uraeus first—a rearing golden cobra with its hood flared—then the *nemes,* the striped head cloth even those who knew nothing about ancient Egypt associated with pharaohs. Beneath the royal regalia, kohl-lined dark eyes and a broad but angular nose were set in a bronze face with full lips and a strong chin. Sun glinted off a broad gold and jeweled collar worn over a gleaming white linen tunic.

Another voice spoke; Kira sensed it asked a question. The pharaoh replied in what sounded like the negative, then stepped forward.

She was being offered to someone. A man, darker skinned than the pharaoh, prostrated himself on the woven mat that protected the god-king's feet from the stone floor of what Kira thought must be a palace, no . . .

a temple terrace. Light scars marred the dark satin of the man's broad, muscular back, scars—reminders of battles fought, not lashes given. Thick ropes of black hair covered his head and trailed across the mat.

This was the one.

The pharaoh spoke again and the dark-skinned warrior rose until he sat on his haunches with his arms lifted, palms raised upward. But he did not look directly at the living god. To do so was forbidden. Who could look upon the face of a god and survive?

The dagger shifted, passing from the pharaoh to the warrior's raised hands. The ruler spoke again, sounding pleased, then molded the warrior's fingers around the blade. For a moment the god-king's hands warmed the warrior's, together on the ivory hilt. The kneeling man pressed the flat of the blade to his lips, then touched his forehead to the stone again, speaking ceremonial words in a rich baritone that made Kira shiver.

Everything blurred, became dark . . .

Kira realized the dagger now dripped blood, as it was created to do. The acrid stench of something burning, something more than vegetation, filled her nostrils. Bodies littered the dusty ground, blood staining the dirt blackish red. She heard tears, screams, cries of pain. Above it all rose another sound, a darker tone, somehow more terrifying than the others. Laughter. The warrior laughed as he moved through the carnage; it was a cold laughter with an edge of madness to it. The blade swung in his fist, ringing like a clarion, thirsting for blood . . .

More images, more death, more blood. Not only in

Egypt, not only in Africa. Not only four thousand years ago. Chariots, cavalry, arrows, guns, bombs, armored vehicles, grenades . . . many weapons, many places, many times.

The rushing sound returned to Kira's brain, separating her awareness from the dagger. She opened her eyes with a gasp, finding herself sprawled on her oriental carpet, the dagger inches from her outstretched hand. She scrambled away from it, away from the emotion and sensation that threatened to drag her back through the Veil.

"Ma'at protect me," she whispered, drawing a shaky hand across her lips. By the Light, the dagger really was four thousand years old, and possessed of so much magic that it was almost sentient.

That knowledge wasn't the cause of the sudden cold in the pit of her stomach.

The dagger's owner, the dark warrior with the baritone voice, was still . . . somehow . . . alive.

And looking for his blade.

Chapter 2

C omstock was late.

Kira tapped the crystal face of her watch, considering. Bernie was known for several things: his love of all things antique, his penchant for local flavor, and his obsession with punctuality. She'd even given him enough teasers about the dagger over the phone to ensure that he'd arrive early, eager to hear more of her discoveries.

The dagger. Kira suppressed a shudder by reaching for her water glass and taking a slow, careful sip to steady her nerves. It had taken her several minutes before she could peel her ass off the floor, pull on her gloves, and put the damned blade back in its case. She'd added a few ready-made protective charms and safeties before locking it into an iron casket and hiding it in a safe behind a trompe l'oeil facade in her lead-lined basement office. Nothing wrong with a little paranoia. Experience had taught her more than once that it was better to be neurotic than dead.

Just as experience had taught her that Comstock was never late for anything. Ever.

Rising to her feet, Kira threw a couple of dollars onto the table, then left the restaurant. For a moment she considered going for her bike and the cache of weapons it concealed. She'd had to change its protections to park it in a public lot and she'd have to reactivate them to go hunting. Intuition told her that even those few minutes would be too much.

Tugging her vest straight, she turned north on Peachtree toward the Georgian Terrace two blocks away, struggling not to run. The temperature had fallen after the sun had set, chilling the October air. She'd dressed up for dinner, switching to a white silk blouse beneath a black leather vest, and black cargo pants with heeled leather boots instead of her usual Chaser's gear. Dressy enough to get into the upscale eatery without comment, comfortable enough for Shadowchasing, if necessary.

She hoped it wasn't necessary, that all the evening would bring was a relaxing dinner with a good friend.

She eased into a ground-eating stride, mentally cataloging her weapons. Knives in each boot, her Lightblade concealed under the pocket flap on her right thigh. Larger blade wedged under the vest against her spine, its hilt hidden by her thick braids. Small-caliber handgun in the holster at the small of her back, one general-issue protective charm concealed in the thick silver bracelet on her right wrist, and one ready-to-use assault spell behind the watch on her left. The heavy silver collar at her throat was a weapon of last resort—it took too many seconds to convert to a slinging blade for her liking. Sometimes mere seconds decided which way her fights would go.

She'd planned to return home after dinner to change into full Shadowchasing gear—could never have too many weapons or protections—for her nightly patrol around the city in order to avoid the brunt of Bernie's curiosity. She hoped she wouldn't need any of her more powerful equipment. She hoped Bernie had simply gotten caught up in some research about the blade and lost track of the time.

Across the street from Bernie's hotel, she skidded to a stop. The Georgian Terrace was Bernie's favorite place to stay in Atlanta not only because it was a century old and had hosted presidents and the *Gone With the Wind* premiere gala, but it was also directly across the street from the Fox Theatre with its Moorish and Egyptian decor. No performance was scheduled tonight, though the marquee still lit up the night. She didn't need the illumination to know something was wrong.

Although Normals would never notice, magic draped the hotel's white-marble-columned entrance, soaking into the grand French Renaissance architecture like a cloying fog. Kira immediately realized it was not the come-spend-your-money-here type of magic worked by a commerce witch for a human savvy enough to know such things existed. The stench was too strong to be Light-magic, too wild to be Adept. No, it carried the all-too-familiar rankness of Chaos.

Shadow-magic.

Kira pressed herself against the edge of the building being renovated across from the hotel, melting into the shadows beneath the scaffolding. Her gaze roamed over the Georgian's entrance and surroundings, the terrace restaurant open to Peachtree Street. People walked along, going about their business as usual; nothing seemed out of the ordinary. Time to push beyond.

Mindful of alerting any Shadow Adepts to her presence, Kira allowed a tendril of her extrasense to seep out, mentally pushing past the Normal, reaching around the Veil. A tingling sensation engulfed her as her regular five senses grappled for control, then acceded to her extrasense.

Chaos magic drenched the sidewalk leading from the hotel. To Kira, it looked like a pale phosphorescent mist that stained the air. Those with any trace of magical ability or extrasensory perception would recognize the wrongness of it. A couple of days of hard rain or a cleansing ritual would be needed to clear the area, but she'd have to worry about that later.

She crossed the street, following the trail past the hotel and theater. At Third Street it banked right, to the east. The wild magic seemed to concentrate at the entrance to an alley a few yards away, coalescing into a thin glowing curtain of power—all invisible to the mundane eye. Behind the curtain, the alley was a void, an absence of existence, unreachable by her extrasense.

Damn. Shadow magic leading from Bernie's hotel wasn't a good sign. The void in the alleyway was worse. Either something was hiding or something wanted something else to stay hidden for a while.

The complexity of the magical construct was unusual. It hinted at an Adept level, if not an Avatar. That knowledge mixed with the memory of her experience with the old blade, causing her stomach to churn with sudden worry.

There was only one reason for a Shadow Adept to be at Bernie's hotel: the ancient dagger. It emitted enough magical energy that anyone with a dash of extrasense could feel it and perhaps track it. She'd put enough protections around the dagger to ensure no one could sense it in her office and she'd showered with a salt scrub to rinse any magical residue off her body. No one could track it through her. But traces of energy would have lingered in Bernie's hotel room. If he'd handled the dagger—as he no doubt had—at least a small amount of magic would have clung to him. The more he'd touched it, the longer vestiges of the dagger's aura would remain.

Bernie was pure human, a Normal. He couldn't even sense Shadow magic, much less defend himself against it. He certainly wasn't a match for a four-thousand-year-old warrior who laughed while he killed.

With precise movements, Kira pulled off her gloves and tucked them into an inner pocket of her vest. Tension filled her as she flexed her fingers. Outside her home base, she only de-gloved to catalog artifacts or to take down Shadow creatures. Cataloging or killing, her hands knew their job well.

She reached into the false pocket on the right side of her cargo pants, drawing her Light-forged blade. Holding it flat against her thigh, Kira moved silently down the street, angling toward the mouth of the alley. The dead spot worried her, made her think it was a trap of some sort. Not that it mattered. As a Shadowchaser, she had to investigate any paranormal activity she encountered for the presence of Shadow magic. And, as Bernie's friend, she had to keep going anyway, even if it was an ambush.

Her left hand twitched with the urge to draw her gun, but she wouldn't pull it unless absolutely necessary. If she faced something more than human and capable of forging Chaos magic, the gun and its magically enhanced silver bullets would only slow it down. Besides, the gun had no silencer. The sound of gunshots would attract unwanted attention, and she didn't want any innocents getting in the line of fire.

Her Normal senses reasserted themselves. The alleyway lay shrouded in shadow and darkness, standard for this time of night. Ten feet in, however, the darkness was deeper, more complete: the curtain of Shadow magic as it manifested in the mundane world.

She wrenched her emotions and got her vision under control, shoving her awareness through the Veil again. Her blade reacted to the presence of Chaos magic, emitting a soft blue glow. Had it flared, she would have drawn her gun and assault spells, damn the attention.

Some of the tension left her shoulders when she sensed that whoever had erected the blank spot was already gone—meaning they weren't trying to conceal themselves, but something else. An attack spell?

A whispered word sent power surging through her blade. Balancing on the balls of her feet, Kira yanked the dagger up in a deadly arc, piercing the darkness, which parted like tissue paper, revealing the contents of the alley.

It took a moment for her brain to comprehend what her eyes saw. Kira had seen death in many forms. She'd seen ritual animal sacrifices and animals disembowel their prey as they tore into still-living flesh. This . . . this was worse, much worse. Evisceration of a human victim was horrifying, even for a Shadowchaser.

Her knees unhinged, dropping her to the pavement. She had to take a deep, ragged breath to keep her stomach from heaving in protest, to stop her mouth from screaming.

Bernie.

At least his eyes were closed, his expression peaceful despite the fact his throat—and more—had been ripped out. Who or what had done this to him?

She'd have to touch him to find out.

Her hand trembled as she unfisted it. Kira didn't want to touch him, not like this. Bernie had been like a father to her. So many times over the years she'd yearned to touch him, dreamed of putting her head on his shoulder, receiving a pat on the back or a hug after she'd confessed everything to him. That dream was now gone, and it seemed almost profane that her last chance to touch him, to feel his skin against hers, would be to find out who'd murdered him.

She'd forgotten about the blood pooled and drying about the body. So much blood, soaking into the scattered debris and cracked asphalt. As soon as she realized she could touch the blood instead of his cold pale skin, her left hand touched the pavement. Red-hued energy flared, racing up her body to her brain. Power steamrolled through her natural shields as the magic inherent in blood tripped her extrasense, flooding her with information. Images, thoughts, and emotions assaulted her, flying across her mind like arrows released by the hands of multiple expert archers.

Stepping onto the sidewalk. Excited. Kira has news. She'd never failed him, no matter how difficult or dangerous the artifact. He worries about her, though, worries about the cost each Shadow confrontation exacts from her. Perhaps it was time to tell her of his own involvement with the Gilead Commission. She'd be angry of course, but he has no doubt that she'd forgive him eventually.

A man walking his dog approaches. Who walks a dog, especially one so malformed and grotesque, in the business district at night?

The dog bumps into him, knocking him into the alley. It pins him to the ground. Not a dog. Not a dog, but something, oh God, something between a Doberman and a Komodo dragon. It strains against the iron chain leash, eyes glowing yellow. Dripping saliva sizzles as it drops onto his jacket and he realizes what it is.

Seeker demon.

A voice, soft and casual, asks for the blade. He can't see the second being's face, but knows to be afraid. Anyone who can control a seeker demon could easily rape his mind, control his body. Death is preferable. Using his tongue, keeping his mind blank, he loosens the cap on a back molar. Swift-acting poison, given to all handlers in case of capture, concealed in a capsule.

The man speaks again. The seeker demon's claws sink into his shoulder. Comstock bites down on the capsule, flooding his mouth with the poison. Death comes as an aneurysm. His last thought: forgive me.

The Veil dropped like the snap of a flag in a strong breeze.

"Bernie." Kira looked at the face of the man she would have called Father, struggling to overcome the grief that clawed at her heart.

He'd lied to her about who he was just as she'd

lied to him. Or, rather, thought she'd lied. He'd known all along she was a Shadowchaser. He'd been part of Gilead. He'd known about her other duties, had neatly filled the void Nico's death had left. He'd been her mentor and her friend, yes, but he'd also been her handler . . . and she'd never known.

Shadowchasers usually had handlers to act as intermediaries between them and Gilead. Kira thought she'd been an exception. By their very nature, Chasers weren't proficient in mundane details, focused as they were on battling Shadow in all its forms. They relied on their handlers to take mission orders from the Commission and to arrange the logistics of traveling from place to place easily and securely, acquiring weapons and information from Gilead's field offices, and filing and submitting the paperwork when the job was done. Shadowchasers traditionally didn't do well with bureaucratic busy-ness and Kira was no exception.

She'd already met and lost her first handler before going to London, fresh out of Chaser training. Nico's death had hollowed her out and she'd vowed not to take another handler, Gilead Commission's rules be damned. Bernie was so much the dashing younger Nico's opposite that she would have had a hard time accepting him as her handler even if he'd introduced himself as such.

Kira was a burr in Gilead's bureaucratic hide, but she'd thought she'd been managing on her own. Instead, Bernie—having worked as a curator in the Petrie Museum, a professor at University College, and proprietor of his own business, paperwork was second nature—had been quietly smoothing things for her. He'd probably been working behind the scenes, double-checking, filling out, correcting, saving her ass for— How long?

How long had he been her handler? From the moment she'd arrived in London? When she'd entered University? Had the first day they'd met—when she'd bumped into him while studying an exhibit at the Petrie—simply been a planned encounter set up by Balm so as not to arouse her suspicions? Balm obviously knew her well—Kira had never once suspected Bernie of being anything other than a cherished friend.

Kira thought he'd been her *out*. Her only escape. She'd dreamed of returning to London with him one day, learning the business she'd stumbled into all those years ago. She'd held on to that dream with a desperate hope, nurturing it on those cold nights when she wasn't entirely sure she'd defeated Shadow. It had been all that kept her going sometimes—and it had been a lie.

Slowly she climbed to her feet, then ripped the left sleeve from her blouse to wipe the blood from her trembling hands. There were times when dreams died just as hard, just as painfully, as people. She'd avenge Bernie's death. But she didn't think she'd ever forgive him.

Turning, she headed for the mouth of the alley and pulled her cell phone out of her pocket while she automatically scanned her surroundings. Nothing out of the ordinary, nothing at all. Shouldn't someone have noticed? A good man had died and the world kept on as if nothing had happened.

She hit the fourth entry on her speed dial, connecting to a Seattle exchange as she stalked up the street, back to the restaurant. It was answered on the first ring. "Travel Department. How may I help you?"

"You've got a bird down," she said without preamble, amazed at the steady monotone of her voice. She'd screamed the code into a phone in Venice six years ago, when she'd tried in vain to hold Nico's chest closed.

"Triangulating position. A team is being dispatched," the voice said as if losing a handler was an everyday occurrence for the Commission. It probably was, but not for Bernie.

Bernie.

"Remain nearby and prepare for pickup," the operator continued. "We'll need to debrief you."

"The hell I will," Kira snarled into the phone, glad to have a target, albeit a disembodied one. "You turn my friend into a handler without my knowledge and you expect me to wait to chase his killer? Fuck that noise."

"Solomon—"

She snapped her phone closed, then called her power. Her fingers flared blue, frying the phone's circuitry. For good measure she hurled the tiny device to the ground, slammed a boot heel on it, and was rewarded with a satisfying crunch.

After making short work of modifying her right sleeve to match her left, she strode back to the restaurant, found her bike, drew on her gloves, and climbed aboard the Buell. She probably had another five minutes before a Gilead Commission Recovery Team arrived. Gilead's technology rivaled that of any country's spy program, especially since they'd had a few millennia to develop it. They'd track her down soon enough, but she had no intention of making it easy for them. Time was short and she had Shadows to chase.

"Is she the one?"

The wraith, as translucent and shimmery as a half-seen cobweb, hovered a few feet off the ground further down Third Street from the alley. Trapped between here and there, it had no recognizable form but changed shape frequently as if being molded by a metaphysical breeze. "She is," the spirit finally replied. "But this one won't be easy."

"True," the man said. "But I could use a challenge for a change."

"What are you going to do?" the wraith asked.

"Follow her, study her. Find a weakness and exploit it."

"She's a Shadowchaser," the wraith pointed out. "They're not known for weakness."

"She's still human. All humans are weak."

"And if she's not?" The wraith solidified, its mercurial shape elongating before taking the appearance of an older black man.

"Doesn't matter. She has my blade. I will have it back."

Chapter 3

Kira pulled her bike to a stop in front of the one establishment in Atlanta where Gilead wouldn't dare follow her: the DMZ. The Goth club took its name from the military term "demilitarized zone"—an area between two belligerent powers where no fighting or other military activity was permitted—and it served pretty much the same purpose. Both sides of the Eternal Struggle could enter the DMZ freely as long as no weapons were drawn or confrontations occurred. Outside a hundred yards from the entrance, however, and you were fair game again.

With the tingle of DMZ's protective shielding buzzing along her arms, Kira eased her bike into a parked row of other motorcycles. As long as the shield held, nothing and no one—magical or human—could touch her bike.

The usual crowd milled around the steel and concrete industrial-looking entrance waiting their turn to enter, an eclectic mix of humans and half-breeds. Light and Shadow Adepts never had to queue up at the DMZ. If Avatars from either side ever showed themselves, they probably didn't use the front door—or any door, for that matter. Kira normally used a private entrance herself, but not tonight. Tonight she had a point to make.

One of the bouncers, a thick, tan-skinned man with nickel-sized holes in his ears, sniffed the air as she walked up. "You've got blood on you, Chaser," he informed her, saying her title the way some women called another "bitch" before they started pulling each other's hair.

Kira curled the fingers of her left hand around the bloodied sleeve in her cargo pocket. It had been hard enough to leave Bernie's scattered remains in the alley; she couldn't throw away his blood like trash.

She gave the bouncer a level stare, resisting the urge to wonder out loud if he had a dick. "So?"

"Fine." He shrugged and waved her in. As she walked past him, Kira wondered how his T-shirt stayed intact with so much muscle stretching the seams. "Check your weapons and stay out of the pit."

Right. Like she was that brand of stupid. Or suicidal. The DMZ's mosh pit tended toward the vicious, populated as it was by beings who enjoyed snacking on humans as well as throwing them around. No one, human or hybrid, entered the pit unless they signed a waiver releasing the DMZ from all claims.

She slipped past the bouncer, past the cashier who gave her a nod, and into the lobby of the DMZ. Restrooms flanked the double doors of the main-floor entrance. Scarred leather sofas crouched on a concrete floor near a smallish bar and the coat-check room, all presented in shades of gunmetal gray lit by black light. The only thing seemingly out of place was a large fish tank roughly six feet wide mounted in a side wall.

At least that was the Normal view.

Drawing on her extrasense, Kira watched the

yellow-white glow of the DMZ's protective aura shimmer into view. It ran in wide bars over every wall, corner, and door, far more reliable than any metal detector. She took another step into the lobby and the aura flashed an orange warning in response.

The coat-check girl pasted a wide smile on her pale, almost gray face. "Please check your weapons with me."

The perky voice grated on Kira's nerves, but she locked down her emotions. Demoz would have a field day if he knew how she felt and she had no intention of letting him feed off her. "No one touches my weapons."

The girl, half human, half something else, showed teeth this time. "You have a primed assault spell on you. That's not allowed on the floor. The larger gun is okay, but the small one and the Lightblade are against regulations. You know the rule: *You fire, you expire.* Even Chasers need to check their weapons."

"Really?" Kira checked the protective shielding, then took another step forward. "Have you just come out of incubation? You and those T-shirts are new."

Perkiness dimmed as the girl glanced down at the neat stack of black shirts, with "I Survived the Pit" emblazoned on them in putrid green. "I don't see what that has to do with—"

The phone beside her rang. The girl picked up the phone, listened, then gulped, her head bobbing rapidly. "Yes, sir. Of course, sir."

She replaced the receiver. "Apologies, Chaser Solomon," she said then, her voice almost humanly humble. "I didn't realize you would use the main entrance. Mr. D welcomes you to the DMZ and asks that you please remove the assault spell."

"Yeah." It was as close to charitable as Kira planned to get. Atlanta was her city—she was the only Shadowchaser in the Southeast U.S. If the girl could tell she was a Chaser, she had to know Kira was also *the* Chaser. She seriously doubted that any other Chasers who passed through town were five-foot-nine-inch black females with their hair in black and blue braids. It also made her wonder why Chasers were coming through her city long enough to use the DMZ without giving her at least a courtesy call. She'd have to look into that later.

Kira unstrapped her watch, removing the disc that contained the assault spell. The aura glowed a solid orange. She made a show of slowly stepping closer to the massive saltwater fish tank that dominated the left wall. An eel swam up from one dark corner and stared at her.

"Hi, Morey. Take care of this for me, will ya?" She tossed the disc inside. It fizzed like an antacid tablet as the salt water disrupted the magic. It flared as the eel zapped it before gulping it down.

"Thanks, Morey. If you feel up to leaving the tank, come take a turn with me out on the dance floor. It'll be fun." Fun in a shocking-everyone-within-two-feet sort of way.

Morey just grinned at her before sinking back to the bottom of the tank. He obviously preferred the simple life of his eel form to his walking, talking one. At that moment Kira couldn't blame him.

She turned back to the coat-check girl. If the new girl thought her most dangerous weapon was the assault charm, Kira wasn't about to educate her. Of course, Demoz knew that Chasers didn't hand over their Lightblades, not even in death. "Are we good?"

When the girl nodded, Kira headed for the main entrance to the floor. The doors were thick reinforced steel, spelled to muffle the sounds beyond. Above the door—written in flowing silver script—hung the words: THE CHOICE IS YOURS.

Kira paused as her control momentarily wavered. Sometimes the choice was die or die screaming.

She placed her gloved hands against the doors, feeling the vibrations pulsing through from the other side. There were days when she wondered what sort of hits she'd get if she dared touch anything in the DMZ without her gloves on. But you didn't have to touch a stove to know it could burn you.

A bass beat slammed into her as she pushed the doors open, startling her heart into an attempt to match the frenetic beat. Bare bulbs hung along the T-shaped corridor, becoming brighter to the left and darker to the right.

Just because she was feeling ornery, Kira swung to the right, the Shadow side. She pushed open another door and the music hit her full blast.

The DMZ flowed like a high-tech miniature Roman Colosseum on the inside, three levels ringing a pit that encircled a raised stage. Inviolate, an industrial Goth band, performed in sonic frenzy on the raised stage at the center of the DMZ. A seething mass of Normals and Not-Normals moshed in the pit surrounding and below the stage.

The Normals would be lucky if all they got were broken bones from their foray into the pit. Since they had to sign a waiver before going in, Kira wouldn't do anything about it. Free will and all. At least they'd get a T-shirt if they made it out alive.

The Light entrance, appropriately bright, was directly opposite where she stood. She noted several Light Adepts—magic workers who preferred to work on the Light side of the balance—and messengers. Almost all the full humans and quite a few hybrids congregated in the center, the club's clientele mimicking the Universal Balance. Some people just preferred not to mix, and some people liked the middle ground.

She needed information, and staying on the Light side wouldn't do it. She peeled off her gloves as Inviolate broke into "Flatline," a driving, frenetic song of insanity that she often hummed when she went out Chasing.

"You lost, little girl?"

Kira turned as a pair of half-demons came up to her. "Not even close, boys."

"Funny." The tall one gave her a measured look, then smiled, revealing an extra-wide row of very pointed teeth. "You look lost to me."

The short one laughed. "Nice one, Lonnie."

Kira realized they had no clue she was a Chaser. Or maybe Lonnie was so hyped up on something that he didn't care. Or, most likely, he was just stupid.

They were beginning to draw attention. Good. Kira held her hand aloft. "Look at my hand."

The man looked at her hand, then back at her. "So?"

"Not with human sight," she said patiently. Maybe he was too stupid to live. "*Really* look at my hand."

With a blink, she brought her extrasense forward, felt it when others did the same. Even if she couldn't tell they'd recognized her power in any other manner, she'd have known by the way those in the circle dropped back.

Lonnie's mouth dropped open as he stepped back, staring at her hand. Everyone with some sort of inherent magic could see the pale blue glow that surrounded her hand, the tendrils of magic that wisped from her fingers. Light magic had infused her body since her birth, or so she'd been told. It had only gotten stronger the longer she lived, though it was now concentrated primarily in her hands.

"Lonnie." She made sure she had his attention before speaking again. "I didn't come here looking for trouble." *Liar.* "Don't start none, won't be none. But if you bring it, I'll end it."

The circle edged further away. Lonnie unzipped a wide grin, showing more teeth than the average human could. "Hey, ain't nothing but a thang," he said, lifting his hands in a harmless gesture. "I ain't starting nothing."

Kira pulled her glove back over her hand. The tension on the floor eased considerably. Instantly two bodyguards built like defensive linemen on steroids sandwiched her in. "Come with us, please."

Without a word, Kira followed the first guard as he cut a wide swath through the crowd. Murmurs rose as they passed, some worried, most curious. She'd needed to do something to shake the crowd up; it was the only way she'd get Demoz to cooperate. Her standoff with Lonnie had probably done little more than whet

Demoz's unusual appetite, but she didn't have time for anything more to his personal preference. She wasn't in a mood to be low-key, not with every passing minute chilling the trail of Bernie's killer. If anyone in this crowd knew who killed Bernie, Demoz would find out.

The guards led her behind the bar and up a flight of stairs. Another guard blocked the head of the stairs. He was so identical to the two escorting her that Kira wondered if they'd hatched from the same clutch. The third man stepped back, allowing them to pass.

One smoked-glass wall—mirrored on the club side—of the large office overlooked the dance floor. The room was furnished in the same black leather and gunmetal as the lobby. A massive slab of clear quartz crystal, the largest specimen she'd ever seen, served as a table between the guest chairs. Demoz probably used it as a balancing mechanism between the Light and Shadow guests who entered his office, but she knew it could also serve as a magic amplifier for those with the ability to use it.

"Kira," Demoz rose to his feet as they entered. "You do know how to make an entrance."

"You know what they say, Demoz. If you're going to do it, do it in style."

"True, true." The big man regarded her, his skin black as tires and just as thick. If the Michelin Man had been dipped in tar—and dressed by Armani—Demoz would be his twin. The only traces of color on his plump body were the thin silver stripes in the fabric of his very expensive suit. He gestured her to a club chair facing the one-way mirror that overlooked the club's floor. "But showing so much skin—and removing your gloves? That could have been considered a provocative act."

She knew he didn't mean sexually provocative. Demoz didn't care about sex—at least she didn't think he did and she definitely had no plans to find out. The DMZ strictly enforced their neutrality, placing them in a delicate position straddling both sides of the Universal Balance.

Kira's provocation was, technically, pulling a weapon. It violated the house rules, regardless of who pulled the weapon or why. Given that her touch could be deadly to some and hurtful to most, Kira had taken a chance going onto the main level with so much skin showing, even with her extrasense muted. She'd taken the chance anyway, betting that Demoz would be waiting and feeding.

Kira adjusted her remaining weapons, then eased into the chair. "Then I suppose I should thank you for coming to get me—although I know you must've gotten something out of it for yourself."

"You know it." Demoz smacked his lips then released a delighted, deep-throated laugh. "The fear you invoked was delicious. The adrenaline alone fed me quite well."

The psychic vampire turned to the glass, staring down at the crowd. "The fear tasted almost as good as the lust you cause when you dance. I suppose, however, that's like trying to compare filet mignon to prime rib."

"If you say so." Kira crossed her arms. He didn't really expect her to be flattered, did he? She wasn't a girly girl by any stretch, but comparing her to cuts of beef wouldn't win Demoz brownie points with her.

Most informants liked being paid in money. Not Demoz. No, he preferred being paid in emotional energy. But then, what psychic vampire didn't?

He turned his bulk away from the window. "The fear is, regrettably, fading now. It feels as if a few of them have moved to anger, however. I don't believe that hybrid appreciated you showing him up in front of his friends. He doesn't have your best interests at heart tonight."

"Why, Demoz, I didn't think you cared."

The vamp grinned. "You are exquisite, Kira Solomon. I would miss you were you gone. Of course the psychic onslaught unleashed at the moment of your demise would certainly feed me for months."

"Sorry to disappoint you, Demoz, but I plan on sticking around for a little while longer." Keeping her emotions on lockdown out of habit, she braced her elbows on the arms of the black leather chair, steepling her fingers. "Besides, I've already fed you tonight."

"Forgive me. How gauche to need your reminder." He waved his perfectly manicured hand. Immediately the inner door opened to admit a young woman dressed head to foot in a hooded dress the color of opals. In her arms rested a silver tray bearing several bottles, each emitting a pale blue light. Purified water of such high quality human bottlers couldn't come close to it. It always made Kira wonder exactly who else made it to Demoz's private office, for him to keep a stash of Light-ready snacks on hand.

Kira remained silent while the girl placed glasses on the low table. She looked to be in her early twenties, her features calling to mind Pacific Islander heritage.

When Kira caught her eye, the girl smiled briefly. Kira sat back, satisfied the girl wasn't a prisoner, though she did wonder how the girl was able to remain so Light-pure in the DMZ.

Kira knew that most of Demoz's wait staff weren't psychic grazers. Like most vampires, he didn't like competition, preferring to keep for himself the emotional smorgasbord his patrons represented.

The waitress left. Kira felt a tendril of power on the edge of her consciousness and swatted it away easily. "Demoz, really, stop trying to cop a feel."

Demoz threw back his head and laughed. "How can I resist you, Kira Solomon? You'd do better to demand a shark to stop swimming."

He took the seat opposite hers. "Tell me what's going on. It's not like you to be so blatant when you visit. You are obviously on a mission. What information are you looking for today?"

"You already know why I'm here," she said, keeping a tight lock on her mental shields. It was one thing to allow Demoz to feed off the emotional reaction she caused; it was quite another to let him feed off her directly. If she showed any sort of expressive display, he'd work the gap until it opened wide and the feelings flowed freely—like a blood vampire sending anticoagulants into a vein.

"I can do many things, Kira, but reading the thoughts behind your gorgeous brown eyes isn't one of them. Our usual meetings happen on Thursdays. What couldn't wait until then?"

"The same as always. Information."

Demoz raised an eyebrow, his steel-gray eyes

curious, guarded. "What information couldn't wait until our regular meeting?"

"Someone unleashed a seeker demon tonight. I want to know who."

"A seeker demon?"

"Yeah." Kira had noted the slight widening of his eyes before he'd spoken. Of course Demoz knew something. Demoz *always* knew something. She tried a test. "The Commission lost a handler tonight."

"How terrible for you," Demoz clucked, his sympathetic tone completely at odds with the assessing glint of his eyes. "I felt the moment of his passing. A tragedy. Was it someone you knew?"

"This is my territory," Kira continued, ignoring his question. "A seeker demon killed the handler, but none of the skanks around here are strong enough to manage a seeker demon, are they?"

"Of course not, which makes me wonder if your information is indeed correct."

"It's an unimpeachable source," Kira stated. "Who's strong enough to control a seeker demon, Demoz?"

"I don't know."

"Really?" She didn't bother to hide her sarcasm. "Are you telling me that when you felt the moment of his passing, you knew he was a male handler but you couldn't tell he was slain at the hands of a seeker demon? You're getting sloppy in your old age."

The vampire's eyes tightened. "I haven't reached old age yet."

"But you certainly want to, right?" It wasn't a threat, not really.

"Kira, you're the most pragmatic of the Chasers

I've known. I have little doubt that you'd dispatch me if my usefulness waned."

"Not without a reason." She cocked her head, studying the outwardly complacent vampire. "Is there a reason?"

"Hardly. I enjoy life too much to get on the wrong side of any of my clients."

Kira noted his hesitation. "But?"

"But." Demoz sighed. "Something's going on. I don't yet know what it is, but all signs point to a heavy hitter coming to town."

"An Avatar?"

Demoz actually looked over his shoulder, as if her saying the word would call the being out. Finally he nodded.

"Where?"

The vampire shook his head. "Don't know."

"What do the Fallen want? Why is one of them here in its Avatar host?"

"They're tracking something. No one will say what or who it is, but they've got grunts all over the place looking for information. All I do know is that your opposition's nervous and when they get nervous—"

"Bad shit happens." She suppressed a sigh. "The question is, how bad is bad?"

Demoz spread his hands. Maybe he didn't know what was going on. Maybe he feared telling her more. As much as he professed a fondness for her, Demoz wouldn't hesitate to throw her to the wolves if it protected his own thick skin. It was all about maintaining Balance.

Most Chasers wouldn't associate with someone

who was ostensibly the enemy and the Commission certainly frowned on it. Kira didn't care. Not all humans were good and not all hybrids and demons were evil. As long as you didn't trust him, Demoz was useful. And, she had to admit, endearing in a suck-your-heart-out sort of way.

"This handler, he was close to you, wasn't he?"

"Doesn't matter if he was close to me or not, Demoz. He was an innocent. I don't care how high I have to go, but I'll find the being responsible."

Demoz stared at her, in that still, nonliving way that all vampires had. "Are you sure you want to go down this path, Kira Solomon?" he asked at last, his voice soft. "You may not like what you find at the end of it."

"I'm sure I won't." She stood. "But I'm a Shadowchaser. Going down the dark path is my job."

"I would advise you to take care when you step outside, sweet Kira," Demoz said. "My protection doesn't extend beyond these walls."

"Neither does your neutrality," she reminded him. "Don't worry; I'll wait until I'm out of the parking lot before drawing blood."

Chapter 4

Kira kept her word, not that it mattered much. Lonnie and some of his friends caught her about half a block from the DMZ, their bikes circling hers. Her Buell could outrun their glorified mopeds easily, even though it was built like a tank and weighed nearly as much. But driving all over the city would do nothing but waste time and gas and make her cranky. They were asking for it and she would be happy to give it to them—but she really didn't have much time to play.

Going to see Demoz had been a gamble that didn't pay off as she'd hoped it would. Not only had she wound up with minimal information—that an Avatar was in town looking for something, information that might or might not be connected to Bernie and the dagger—the wager had cost her a couple of spells. Worse, it had cost her time. Every moment she didn't spend chasing Bernie's killer was another advantage for whoever had killed him. With nothing else to go on, she'd have to return to the alley and hope Gilead was done with the cleanup but had still left enough metaphysical evidence that she could pick up a trail. The sooner she got back to the scene of the crime, the more likely the chances she'd find some sort of lead.

The halflings tried to pen her in as she headed

toward Peachtree Street. *As if.* She'd learned a thing or two from some of the best stunt riders in the country and these idiots were totally amateur. Dropping her visor, Kira bent low over her handlebars, calling her power. Blue light flared from her bare hands, spilling onto the handgrips and down through the frame. It was the only warning she intended to give them. Not her fault if they ignored it.

They ignored it. One of Lonnie's buddies, grinning and whooping and looking eerily like a hyena, made a grab for the clutch when he got close enough. Her power flared. Hyena Boy's hand flew in one direction while he and his bike went careening in another.

One down, three to go.

At midnight, North Avenue, which ran east to west, was largely deserted. Smart cops gave the DMZ and its clientele a wide berth—it was just safer and saner that way. The closer they got to Peachtree Street, the more likely Normal police would be on patrol.

Kira could see the three remaining bikers in her mirrors, too stupid or too mad at her for embarrassing them in the club to go back for their fallen friend. With her extrasense guiding the bike, she dropped her left hand to tap a panel open and pulled out a modified Glock 19. Normal ammunition didn't down hybrids permanently and despite her irritation, she didn't want to feed her power to the bullets in order to kill them. Killing required too much paperwork. Being shot still hurt like a bitch, no matter what you were, and she didn't mind hurting them at all. "Possible wounding" didn't entail filling out a form and the hybrids would heal soon enough.

Movement in the right mirror caught her eye; Lonnie had decided to make his move. Kira's lips curled. "Time to end this."

She pulled the clutch in, then hit the front brake. Her body rocked forward as the back of the bike lifted. She felt the sweet spot—the balance point—as Lonnie and his buddy zoomed past her. Jamming her knees into the gas tank, she let the bike roll forward, balanced on its front wheel, and fired off two rounds left-handed. Both hybrids and their rides slid an impressive distance as she dropped the back tire to the pavement.

Three down, one to go.

She circled around to face the final biker. He'd stopped in the middle of the street, jaw hanging as he stared at the speed bumps his friends had become. She pushed up her visor. "You want some?"

His eyes ping-ponged between her and his fallen buddies. "Screw this!"

He burned rubber turning his bike around to head back toward the DMZ—and crashed into the grill of a huge black SUV with blackout windows that couldn't have been more conspicuous if its license plate read FEDS. Except it wasn't the FBI.

The SUV's passenger's and driver's doors opened simultaneously and two tall men in suits exited onto the street. The Gilead Commission's version of the Men in Black. They even wore sunglasses although it had to be after midnight and the streetlighting didn't exactly cause a glare. It made her wonder if there were souls specifically destined for bureaucracy or if it was payment for wrongdoing in a previous life.

They paid no attention to the biker, now attached

to the front of their vehicle, as they walked toward Kira.

She pulled back her extrasense as the suits stopped in front of her. "Took you long enough."

They ignored the barb, just as they always did. *Ah, the camaraderie of working for Gilead,* Kira thought. It must have been a little like the love between beat cops and detectives or the navy and marines. Yeah, right.

"Chaser Solomon," the nondescript blond said, "the section chief would like to see you."

The section chief, one Estrella Sanchez, wasn't exactly a card-carrying member of the Kira Fan Club. The feeling was mutual. "I'm working."

"It's not a request."

"Didn't think it was." Sanchez was the epitome of everything Kira disliked about Gilead in general and the East Coast division of Gilead America in particular: bureaucracy, paperwork, and a fanatical devotion to policies and procedures. Like Adepts and Avatars gave a damn. "Where does the Grand Poobah want to meet?"

The suits frowned. Kira rolled her eyes. Were there any bureaucratic goons who had a sense of humor, in any organization?

"The gardens at the Carter Center." They finally looked at their new hood ornament. "What about your . . . friends?"

She rolled closer, then pushed the halfling off the hood with one booted foot. He slid to the pavement with a groan. "Don't worry. They're down, not out. They'll be fine in a couple of minutes. Besides, it's not like we can send them back to Shadow for being stupid." She dropped her visor, then gestured them on.

Leaving Lonnie and his buddies curbside, she followed the SUV for a couple of blocks to Freedom Parkway and on to the Carter Center. The Presidential Library and Museum nestled in the thirty-seven-acre bowl of the Center's grounds flanked by the lanes of the parkway. Several buildings there could host a variety of events and weddings, but what impressed Kira the most were the gardens. More than once—when the concrete jungle was getting to her—she'd come out to the gardens, walked the stepping stones to the center of the koi pond, and talked to the fish. Sometimes they even answered.

A matching SUV waited in the main parking lot when they arrived, complete with its own set of matching suits. Kira knew Gilead had impressive skills; she'd seen plenty of the results firsthand. As far as she knew, Gilead hadn't perfected cloning—either magical or scientific—but seeing all the nearly identical agents might lead her to wonder if they had.

She allowed a tendril of extrasense to seep out as she switched off her bike and pulled off her helmet. The natural earth energy greeted her, a steady hum that still held remnants of what had transpired during the day. She could feel the cool force of the koi pond and the larger lake, the subtle power of the verdant growing things slowing into autumn. Beyond that she felt the bland oatmeal sameness of the Commission agents and a peppery spice that had to be Estrella Sanchez.

No Shadow Avatars or Chaos magic waiting. Good.

Kira drew back her extrasense, then set off, following the phosphorescent lamps illuminating the walkway. It wasn't that she didn't trust the section chief. She didn't, but she could count on one hand the number of people she trusted, and she'd just lost one. If Bernie, her surrogate father, could betray her, Kira certainly wasn't going to add Sanchez as a friend on her Facebook page.

The section chief waited for her near the lake in a pool of light from a tall wrought-iron lamp. Sanchez was dressed in tailored business trousers with pointed-toed high heels peeking beneath the hems. Maybe not typical attire for a post-midnight garden stroll, but perfectly suitable for the diminutive woman, considering, as Kira knew from experience, Sanchez had the attitude of a driven executive who considered *The Art of War* her personal bible.

"Chaser Solomon. My condolences on the loss of your handler."

Sanchez said the words politely enough, but they still grated and goaded. Kira bunched her shoulders as the sentiments found their mark, bringing back every brutal moment of loss and betrayal and anger. She bit her tongue against the urge to lash out at the easy target Sanchez presented, something the section chief no doubt wanted her to do. She wouldn't give Sanchez the satisfaction or the excuse. Giving free rein to her sorrow and rage would have to wait until she was alone.

Squaring her shoulders, Kira prepared to give the chief an official briefing. "Report. Bernard Comstock, age sixty-seven. Antiques dealer and part-time curator at the British Museum, Magical Artifacts Department. Time of death sometime after nineteen-hundred."

"And the cause?"

"Cause of death: self-inflicted poison, followed by evisceration by a seeker demon."

"A seeker?" A breeze filtered through the trees around them, almost a whispered warning. Even Sanchez shivered in her expensive clothes. "Are you sure about this?"

"I touched his blood, read the scene myself. I'm sure."

"A team recovered the body in an alley not far from his hotel," Sanchez said. "We also found the pieces of your mobile. How did you know to look for him there?"

Kira frowned. She expected censure, but not the insinuation. What the hell did Sanchez mean by that? Something was off.

She continued her debrief with a careful mix of words and as little emotion as she could manage. "Comstock and I were supposed to meet for dinner. He said he had something he wanted to show me. He was late. He's never late. I went looking for him and found the alley near the hotel blocked by Chaos magic. I used my Lightblade to open it and that's when I found him. I couldn't find traces of the seeker demon's trail, so decided to tap various sources for information. End report."

Sanchez remained silent for a moment. "Why would someone send a seeker demon after a handler posing as a curator?"

"He wasn't posing." Kira ground out the words. "Dr. Comstock was an expert in pre-Dynastic Egyptian civilizations for the Petrie Museum, a professor at University College London, outstanding in his field, much respected and well-liked. His job was his passion, his life. So you're asking the wrong question."

"Oh? And just what is the right question?"

"Who in Gilead thought it wise to turn a university professor and museum curator into a handler?"

Sanchez folded her arms across her chest. "Regardless of what questions you think should or shouldn't be asked, someone with the ability to control a seeker demon is running around town. Who is it?"

"I don't know."

"I sent a team to Comstock's hotel room, but they didn't find anything out of the ordinary. Did you recover anything at the scene?"

"No."

That didn't make the section chief happy. "What could Comstock have that would be of interest to someone capable of controlling a seeker?"

Kira mimicked the section chief, folding her arms across her chest. "Shouldn't Gilead know more about that than I do? I mean, no one even bothered to tell me that I had been assigned a handler after Nico's death. Obviously I'm not kept in the loop."

"So what exactly *do* you know, Solomon?"

"About this? Precious damned little." Her anger flared. "I was in the middle of looking for leads when someone decided to call a meeting."

"You were playing tag with a couple of hybrids in the middle of a major thoroughfare." Sanchez took a step forward. "This after going to a club with questionable clientele. Not exactly the actions of a competent Shadowchaser looking for leads or grieving a loss."

It was so tempting to wrap her hand around Sanchez's severe bun and yank the life out of her. Not kill her exactly, but put a hurting on her and find out exactly what the woman had against her. *Oh yeah,* Kira thought, *I could do that, could drop the section chief before the goon quartet even realized what had happened.*

A flash of blue caught her attention, reminding her she hadn't put her gloves back on. She took a mental step back. Gilead had taught her better than that. She was a Shadowchaser first, last, and always. Going off on Sanchez would make her feel better for all of a few minutes, maybe even an hour. But it wouldn't bring Bernie back. It wouldn't help her find his killer. That was the most important thing to her.

"You wanna know what I know? Fine, I'll tell you. Seeker demons are brought through the Veil for one thing only—to find something for the person who calls them over. They're mindless, nasty, acid-dripping creatures that go through anything and everything until they find their target. When they find it, they're freed from the spell that brought them over. Every Shadow Adept that's summoned a seeker demon has been mauled to death and eaten. If they were lucky."

She stepped closer. Sanchez took a healthy step back before recovering. Kira hid a smile. "I didn't detect a flameout, so I think it's safe to assume that the seeker demon is still out there. Given the fact that any Adept who's tried to control one ended up being its snack after it found what it wanted, I'd also have to say that whatever's controlling this seeker is a Shadow Avatar for one of the Fallen."

"Fallen? Are you sure about that?" Even under the pale lights around them, Kira could see that Sanchez had gotten a little ill at the news. She couldn't fault the other woman—it meant her job had just become that much harder.

"Pretty damned sure." One of the first lessons Kira had learned at Gilead was that every human myth had a basis in reality, and the term "demon" was given to a variety of otherworldly beings with distinctly nonhuman capabilities.

Some were on the side of Light; some served Shadow. A large population lived in between, intermingling with the Children of Man and spawning hybrid offspring that had given rise to enduring tales of vampires, werefolk, merpeople, and others.

The Fallen, though . . . they were the heavy hitters of Shadow, the sons and daughters of Chaos and Darkness. Eons before humanity was a gleam in the primordial ooze, an epic interdimensional battle had been fought that threatened the very fabric of the Universe. Some of those belonging to Shadow had attempted to escape by opening a rift in the Veil—but in passing through had lost their ability to take corporeal form. The only way they could hide from the Light and interact on this plane was to inhabit a host body—an Avatar—and human bodies were easy to inhabit.

"The alley reeked of Chaos magic," Kira said. "And the construct on the barrier was in a pattern I haven't seen before, like someone making lace out of barbed wire. Shadow Adepts are good, but I've never seen one use that combination of artistry and brute strength. I certainly haven't seen one strong enough to funnel Chaos magic into anything other than a weapon. Only one thing's got that kind of power and that's Fallen."

Sanchez smoothed a hand over her bun. "If we have one of the Fallen here, looking for something your handler had in his possession . . . "

The section chief thought so hard that Kira could almost smell the gears burning in her brain. Ambition warred with the need for self-preservation.

"Things are about to get real nasty, Chief. Why don't you let me take this one?" Not that she had any choice. Fallen were Shadowchaser quarry.

"You?"

Kira didn't know how a woman four inches shorter than she, even in heels, could look down at her, but Sanchez managed it. "If you think you and your Men in Black clones can handle a Fallen, go ahead. But you better make sure your affairs are in order, because you will die. Quickly, if you're blessed. You and I both know that a Shadowchaser's the only one with any chance of going up against one of the Fallen. It's what Gilead developed us for, isn't it?"

"Being angry with the Commission's decisions isn't going to help you find out who did this to Comstock or why," Sanchez retorted. "It certainly isn't going to bring him back."

Kira refused to rise to Sanchez's bait. She knew the woman wanted her to go off like a Roman candle, just so she could file a complaint with Gilead. Staying calm would stick in Sanchez's craw and give her nothing to fill out forms about. The thought of really spoiling the chief's day that way was the first pleasant thing to pass through Kira's brain in hours. Keeping herself out of bureaucratic hot water was an added bonus.

Kira settled her hands on her hips. "Rumor has it that a few Shadowchasers have passed through town, and yet none of them have stopped by to say hello. Are you trying to replace me? That almost hurts my feelings."

Sanchez pursed her lips. "It pays to have contingency plans, Solomon, especially where you're concerned."

"What's your deal? Not that I care; I'm just curious."

"Gilead indulges you to its own detriment. You are a loose cannon, an undisciplined child with too much power. First Nico, now Comstock—"

Kira fisted her hands against the unbidden welling of her power. "Don't ever say their names again. You don't have the right."

Sanchez didn't flinch. "You're twenty-five. You've had two handlers since you left Santa Costa and they've both died violently."

"No one told me that Comstock was my handler, did they? Not you, not Gilead, not Comstock himself. Given that we were a few thousand miles apart at any given time and have never spoken about the Commission, why in the world would I think of him as my handler?"

"The fact that your handler didn't confide in you is even more troubling. People are starting to wonder."

"Like I give a crap. People have been wondering about me since my parents dumped me on Gilead's doorstep. So what?"

"There have been some who've questioned your loyalty, wondering who you really serve."

"Are you kidding me?" Kira laughed. "Obviously *some people* have too much time on their hands and need to get a life."

Sanchez didn't like that one, if the twist to her lips was any indication. "I don't know who you think you are—"

"I know who I am! I'm a Shadowchaser, raised by Balm herself. That woman's work ethic and ideas of discipline make Roman legions look like Boy Scouts. Gilead has been my world for half my life. I have used my training and my extrasense to serve the Light to the best of my ability despite losing Nico, despite what you people did to Comstock. I've seen more and done more than you and most of you suits on the Commission and yet I still serve the Light. I'm going to find Bernie's killer and send him back to Shadow no matter what it takes, and when I'm done, I'll still be holding my Lightblade."

Her skin glowed a pale neon blue. "I live and breathe the Light, more than I can say for many on the Gilead Commission. And you want to question my loyalty?" She turned on her heel, needing to leave before she really gave them a reason to doubt her.

"Chaser Solomon—"

"If you had more than idle speculation, I'd be talking to a Commissioner or to Balm herself, not a section chief. Quit wasting my time and let me do my job. We both know I'm the only one who can go up against whatever's controlling a seeker demon."

"You probably don't want to know what I think, Chaser Solomon. Still, Gilead seems to think you should take the lead on this. You'll be given access to

Comstock's reports and activities for the last six months. You'll also have the support of the section office."

Translation: Sanchez would have her own teams, led by the Men in Black, no doubt, combing the streets looking for clues. Gilead had an amazing network of humans, hybrids, and Light Adepts at their disposal, all capable investigators when dealing with mundane matters and low-level magical police work. Letting them hit the streets to search out a Shadow Avatar and a seeker demon was only asking for trouble. If Sanchez wanted to risk her people, the results would be on her head, not Kira's.

"Fine. I'll contact Gilead for access. Now tell your suits to get out of my way. I have a job to do."

The clone brothers stepped aside, giving her a wide berth as she stalked back up the path to her bike. She was spoiling for a fight, which meant she really needed to be alone. Light help whatever or whomever tried to get in her way.

It didn't matter that she'd spent more than half her life in the Commission's main holding. She knew how they worked. No one on the Commission would lie, but they were experts at the miserly dissemination of information. And she still couldn't forgive them for Nico . . . and now Bernie. Serving the Light was one thing; working through Gilead to do it was another.

If there was one bright spot in this shitcan of a night, it was that Gilead didn't seem to know why Comstock had come to her. They didn't know about the blade. If they had, Sanchez would have demanded she surrender it, which wouldn't have happened and that would have made a bad situation even worse.

She knew how impressive their network of prescients and psychic spies—Oracles and sweepers—was. She'd seen it up close during her stay in Santa Costa. But they didn't seem to know about the dagger or the fact that she had it.

For now, she intended to keep it that way.

Chapter 5

More than two hours later a frustrated and angry Kira made her way home. The search for the Fallen and the seeker demon had proven futile. She hadn't found a trace of Chaos magic anywhere other than the area surrounding the hotel, as if her quarry had somehow stepped back through the Veil. The amount of skill and power it took to conceal a seeker demon's trail meant Kira would have to be extra careful.

She paused at the end of her street, testing the area with her extrasense. Quiet draped the community, except for the low hum of electricity. She caught a glimpse of a few of downtown Atlanta's skyscrapers through batches of trees and rooftops. The East Atlanta neighborhood had begun a reclamation project several years ago, turning some of the larger condemned warehouses into condos and apartments. Her own place had been a car repair and parts warehouse and boasted two roll-up bay doors on the front and a small loading dock on the back—plenty of room to maneuver artifacts of various shapes and sizes in and out.

She hadn't done much in the way of outward renovation to the concrete and safety glass structure in the two years since she'd paid a bargain price for the warehouse. Most of the modifications were invisible to the naked eye—unless she had an intruder. By the time they saw anything, it would be way too late.

For a moment she almost wished she hadn't put such strong protections on the blade. If she hadn't, the seeker demon would have been able to trace the dagger to her. It would have left Bernie alone because it would have known he wasn't the last to handle the ancient weapon. She would have confronted the seeker demon and its Avatar master—and her mentor would still be alive.

Or the seeker would have come for her after it had finished Bernie.

She knew there was no point in conjuring up alternate scenarios that resulted in Bernie avoiding death. He was dead, and there was nothing she could do to bring him back.

The orangey glow of a security light illuminated the metal garage door set in the concrete wall of the two-story building. Slowing, Kira maneuvered the bike into a very specific spot in front of the door, then pushed up her visor so the biometric scanner over the doorway could identify her. She mentally added a coded stroke of power to the Normal science that was the warehouse's first line of defense, an extra precaution against the possibility of someone trying to use her against her will to gain entry. It had taken her, Zoo, and Wynne a couple of months to calibrate the door so that it responded properly to her unique combination and moved up and down with exact timing. With so many magical artifacts in her possession and Shadow folks running around, she needed more than ADT guarding her home.

The wards around the warehouse flashed once as the rolling door deactivated, an all-clear signal. Throttling the bike forward, she entered the former repair bay just as the automatic door began its glide back down.

Kira killed the engine and pulled her helmet off with a sigh. She wanted a hot shower and four or five glasses of rum. Maybe that would be enough to numb the pain that still roiled through her. It sure as hell wasn't something aspirin could take care of.

She couldn't give in to the grief. Not yet. First she had to make sure her protections would hold. Despite her earlier reckless thought, she had no intention of revealing the dagger's presence. She'd have to tighten the controls and defenses to make sure the dagger didn't emit anything that would bring the seeker demon and its master to her door . . . or catch Gilead's attention.

The mundane alarm had its own encrypted server; the only nonmagical communication it had was to Wynne and Zoo. Atop that, Zoo had placed several aversion and protection spells to deflect the casually curious and the majority of hybrids. Which left her own Light-reinforced wards to handle the heavy hitters.

Kira got off the bike, placed her helmet on the metal and sheetrock racking along the back wall that held assorted bike parts, and crossed to the control panel beside the large beige-painted metal door in the concrete block wall that divided garage space from living area. She splayed her hands on either side. Closing her eyes, she tried to push *beyond,* only to be stopped by a red-orange molten emotional bedrock of her own grief and anger.

She realized that just because she didn't want to feel the emotions didn't mean they weren't still there, waiting to pounce at the wrong moment. Kira couldn't afford to be crippled by emotion. There were more important things than her anger, than her grief. Like revenge.

The lavalike layer of rage and anguish pulsed. Kira pulled back, refusing to allow the inferno to erupt and consume her. This was much larger than revenge, she reminded herself. This was about justice.

"You don't win today," she whispered to her angry core. "I still control me."

She worked with the molten mass like a glassblower shaping a vase, using its own nature to mold it as she wanted—into extra protections. The added security to her shields would put a nasty burn on anyone who tried to breach them now. Not that she cared. No one breaking in would be after her teapot collection.

Finally she finished, easing back through the layers of technology and magic and emotion until her normal senses emerged. She rolled her head on her shoulders with a sigh. *Do the things that need doing, Kira. You can do the rest after you find this guy.*

As she moved through the side door into her not-quite living room, the red indicator light on her VOIP phone on the mission-style end table in the sitting area caught her attention. Since she'd trashed her mobile, only two people could be calling: Wynne or Balm. Wynne wouldn't appreciate a callback at close to four A.M. and Kira wasn't ready to talk to Balm. Not now. Not when the emotion was still too raw.

Her relationship with the head of the Gilead

Commission gave a whole new meaning to "complicated." Balm had saved her when her burgeoning extrasense had forced her adoptive parents to abandon her and threatened to drive Kira insane. Kira hadn't made it easy for Balm, but she'd been half-starved, half-mad, and half-broken by guilt and the burden of her strange powers. As with Normal adolescents, anger had become a defense and she'd channeled it into her training. Being able to go to any public place—a restaurant or theater, or even shop for food, clothing, necessities—without being bombarded with the thoughts and emotions of those who'd touched the things she wanted was all due to her training at Gilead.

The training allowed her as much of a life as she could have. Being "gifted" with the extrasense of psychometry gave her the ability to receive the thoughts, history, and emotions of others through touching them or their objects. The gift also cursed her: the smallest patch of exposed skin became a receptor and her psychometric power also siphoned off the life force of anyone she touched—no matter how slightly or accidentally. Unable to control her abilities, Kira could never have functioned in society at all without the instruction she'd received from Gilead.

That offset some of the other things Gilead had done—like making her into a Shadow killing machine, refusing to save Nico, hiding the truth about Comstock . . .

Kira ignored the blinking red message light and wound her way through stacks of books, equipment, and artifacts. Her steps faltered as she passed the worktable she and Comstock had leaned over so many hours before. His loss hit her again, sharply, the void of his absence filled with what-ifs as she continued through the room and past the freight elevator at the back to the stairs.

If she had known what he really was to her, if they'd just been honest with each other, she might have taken him down the spiral staircase to the lower level. She might have shown him some of the rarer objects she kept in her office or her most private space behind the replica mural from the Valley of the Queens that depicted Queen Nefertari playing *senet.* Her hand strayed to her pocket, the bloodstained fabric still tucked safely inside. She took small comfort in the knowledge that a part of Bernie was with her now and she could do something to ensure he found peace.

The mural slid to the left after she sent a pulse of power through it. More than a few people would consider her extra precautions nothing more than paranoia, but after an imp had slid through a fracture in the millennia-old pottery that held him and nearly destroyed her former office, she'd learned to be careful. Most of the time her protections were designed to keep things from getting in. They also served to keep things from getting out.

She moved steadily past her collection of weaponry—both ancient and advanced—past ritual gear too dangerous to remain in the mundane world, past her second, smaller office and its triple-guarded vault that currently housed the Egyptian dagger.

A lifesize reproduction of the Weighing of the Heart ceremony emblazoned the far wall with bright color. Ancient Egyptians believed the heart, not a soul, measured the deeds of a person's life. After a harrowing journey through the underworld, the dead arrived in Osiris's palace and were taken to the Hall of Judgment. The mural showed Osiris sitting on a throne as the ruler of the afterlife, with the forty-two gods arranged around him. They bore witness as the dead person confessed all the things he hadn't done to show that he had been a good person in life and deserved to continue living after death. The jackal-headed god Anubis stood by the gilded standing scales of truth and justice, ready to weigh the deceased's heart against the feather of Ma'at. The god Thoth stood nearby to record the result. In the shadows waited Ammit, the Devouress of the Dead. If the heart was heavier than Ma'at's feather, Ammit—with the head of a crocodile, forequarters of a lion, and hindquarters of a hippopotamus—would devour the heart, ensuring that the dead would die a complete death.

Kira stopped before the mural. Ma'at, her patroness, perched atop the scales to ensure their balance. Ma'at, with the curved white ostrich feather adorning her headdress, holding the scepter of rule in one hand and the ankh, the symbol of eternal life, in the other, the goddess who personified that which is right: Order, Truth—the things Kira desired most in life.

Closing her eyes, Kira centered her being, clearing her mind, preparing herself to go before the goddess.

On a soundless rush of air, the heavy panel pushed outward, then slid to the right, revealing her most private room. She called her extrasense, concentrating until it gathered in her right hand. Stepping inside the climate-controled space, she touched her hand to a spirit lantern waiting on a simple wooden pedestal beside the entrance. The pale blue light reflected and magnified against the concave mirror, spreading throughout the small chamber and slowly revealing its contents.

A large black silk cushion lay in the center of the tiled floor. Before it stood an acacia table, not quite three feet high, ornately carved with hieroglyphs. Three objects sat atop it: a sistrum, a golden statuette of winged Ma'at, and a gilded mirror. Beyond the table were more objects precious to her, artifacts of ancient Egypt given to her as gifts, for safekeeping, for services rendered.

She closed her eyes for a moment, letting the peace of the chamber settle into her pores. Her nights chasing Shadows always ended here, giving her a chance to purge her mind and soul in order to find solace in sleep. Most times it even worked.

Keeping her mind carefully clear, Kira approached the table, bowed low, then sat cross-legged on the pillow. The mirror gleamed at her even in the pale light. The surface was as still and dark as a pit, though highly reflective. It was, for all intents and purposes, an ordinary mirror. Once her extrasense touched it, it became much more: an instrument that allowed her to communicate with her patroness and perform a modified version of the Weighing of the Heart.

For the ancient Egyptians, the heart was the source of intellect and the center of personality, moral awareness, emotions, and memory. It was the heart that revealed a person's true character.

Every battle with Shadow, every brush with Chaos,

left a minute trace, a shadow in Kira's soul. It had been a gradual accumulation. She wouldn't have noticed if it hadn't been for a casual remark made by Bernie a handful of years ago—or perhaps, she now realized, not casual at all—about an unusual flash of yellow in the brown of her eyes. She'd known what it meant: she'd been tainted by Shadow. Never too much, never unchangeably. She always made her way back to the Light. Still ,the changes were enough to make her worry, and she didn't like to worry. Finding Balance helped.

Tonight wasn't about weighing her soul. She already knew it was heavy.

Resting her fingertips on the mirror's edge, she exhaled from deep in her belly. Her extrasense welled up, charging the mirror with a violet swirl of energy. The color faded but the energy remained; the Veil opened. She pulled the torn bloody fabric from her pocket and placed it on the silky black surface, fighting against falling through the Veil again. Successive touches usually didn't have the same intensity, but a murder—particularly this type of murder—could linger.

Her fingers shook as she smoothed out the pale cloth with its rusty brown spots. She shouldn't have left Bernie. She should have stayed beside him until the Gilead team arrived. She should have tried to read more from him. She should have done so many things.

"Ma'at, vessel of justice, please look favorably upon the soul of Bernard Comstock. Help him complete his journey and find his way to the Light."

She raised her chin, her eyes on the dark ceiling. "Ma'at, guide me. Allow me to serve Your will, to bring justice to the one who needs it."

Her eyes closed as she held her prayers in her heart, waiting. She never doubted her patron deity; enforcing order and justice were her life, and she lived the principles of Ma'at every day. Soon enough, she felt a brush of warmth, the answering touch of the goddess.

She opened her eyes in time to see the strip of cloth sinking into the slick surface of her mirror. A moment of grief and regret gripped her—she had to breathe it out slowly before it took root. It wouldn't have done to keep the cloth as some morbid memento. Comstock wouldn't have wanted her to remember him that way. Better to let the Universe take it.

The mirror's surface rippled, then stilled to an inky smoothness. A touch of her fingertip, and etheric scales would rise from the surface of the mirror, ready to weigh her soul. Instead, she drew back her extrasense, returning the mirror to normal. The ritual would have to wait for another night.

Her entire body felt heavy as she resealed the chamber, then made her way to her bedroom on the uppermost level. Sleep, by the Light. A shower and sleep. She had to hope that sunrise would bring the leads she needed to bring justice to Bernie.

Chapter 6

The warrior pulled the Dodge Charger over to the curb a hundred yards down the street from Kira's warehouse. The spires of downtown Atlanta rose up from the west, touched by the first fingers of dawn's light. He stared at the concrete and metal edifice that housed his prize. It must have been an auto-repair or tire store in its former life, he guessed, noting the roll-up garage doors. He couldn't tell if the second story was original or added on, but he could tell the bars covering the windows on the main door were sturdy, an effort to deter common thieves.

Good thing he was neither thief nor common.

"The dagger's there, or at least it was," he said to Nansee. The wraith was back to his usual guise of a white-haired elderly black man. "I can sense it, though barely. I suppose she's protecting it somehow."

"She's proving to be a very capable Shadowchaser, better than many you've met. She can certainly hold her own in a fight."

"The Commission interrupted her before things got interesting."

He had to admit, if only to himself, that he'd enjoyed watching her take out the hybrids. She had a lot of power packed into that lithe frame of hers, power he wouldn't mind facing. "Does that mean you're afraid to take her on, old man?"

A grunt. "Fear and self-preservation are two different things."

"If anyone would know, you'd be the one. Can you get inside?"

The old man faded from view. The warrior tapped out an ancient rhythm on the steering wheel as he waited, restless. Patience was something he'd learned the hard way. It had taken years, decades even.

After a minute or two Nansee coalesced beside him. He shivered like a dog shaking water from its coat. "It's well-protected. Multiple layers of encryption technology, metaphysical barriers, and good old-fashioned locks."

"Since when has technology stopped you, Traveler of Webs?"

"Since it is augmented by Light shields, the Chaser's own aura, and a couple of curses that could take out a demigod, I'll consider myself stopped. I like the way I've arranged my parts."

Damn. It wasn't unexpected, but it still angered him. To be so close to the dagger yet unable to reclaim it was frustrating. His own fault for dying and losing it in the first place.

He had to get it back. It had been out of his possession, his control, for far too long. Now a ranking member of the Fallen had its sights set on the dagger. The only comfort he could take was that if Nansee couldn't get in, neither could the Shadow Avatar.

"Fine. I'll think up some way to approach her and get my blade back. Take some time to find out more about her and what she does when she's not racing hybrids down public roads. I've waited this long. What's one more day?"

Kira woke up to the sound of someone knocking on her door. She opened her eyes to late-morning sunlight. *Damn it, I'll be behind schedule the rest of the day.*

"Wynne, that had better be you with a couple of large cups of coffee," she muttered, throwing back the bedcovers and kicking to her feet. The Light help anyone else who dared beat on her door like that.

She palmed her Lightblade from habit before heading out of the room. She pounded down the stairs, vowing to thank her visitor before ripping them a new one. Throwing open the locks, she yanked open the door—

And found herself on a sun-drenched hillside. The ocean sparkled a brilliant sapphire below, reflecting the clear sky above. A pavilion sat a hundred yards from the cliff's edge, its gauzy white curtains dancing in the sea air. An elaborate table for two had been set inside and someone waited for her there.

"Balm. I'm trying to sleep, you know."

The head of the Gilead Commission looked as if she'd just booked first-class passage on the *Titanic*—one of the many rumors about her past. Others were that she was a handmaiden of Cleopatra, a Maltese princess, illegitimate daughter of Alexander the Great, or Scheherazade herself. Balm was her name and title.

One of the ways she'd gotten a teenage Kira to study was by daring her to discover Balm's real identity.

After all these years, she still didn't have a clue. No one knew who or what Balm was, only that she had tremendous power and that there had always been a Balm in Gilead.

"Sleep. As if I haven't lost many a night's sleep worrying about you." Balm lifted a sapphire and gilt etched saucer with one gloved hand, a matching bone china cup chased with gold perched atop it. "Have some tea, dear. It's your favorite."

Kira's yoga pants and tank top had been changed into a formal Gibson Girl dress of Wedgwood blue. She didn't bother to touch her hair to see if the braids had been replaced with something more suitable for the scene. Instead, she suppressed a sigh as she took a seat and accepted the tea. It was Balm's dream after all and she could only be rude to Balm up to a point. Besides, Kira knew the head of Gilead could make a damn good cup of tea whether in dreamtime or awake.

She looked around the pavilion, trying to place its familiarity. She knew they were in the dream version of Santa Costa, but she'd never seen a pavilion like this on the island. Maybe she'd seen it in a painting or something. "You sure went to a lot of trouble."

"Why wouldn't I for my wayward daughter? Since you didn't return my call, I decided to walk your dreams to make sure you were all right."

Kira set her jaw. Balm's chiding tone made her feel guilty and furious and twelve years old at the same time. She lifted her teacup. "Whether I'm all right or not depends on how you define it."

Balm's chocolate eyes softened. "I'm so sorry about Mr. Comstock. I know how important he was to you."

The teacup rattled. Kira set it down, the lace of her gloves stretching as she curled her hands into fists. "Are you going to make me ask the questions?"

Balm sighed. "Comstock has been your handler almost from the moment you met him at the Petrie Museum. And if you must know, he volunteered."

"Volunteered?" Kira sat back in the woven plantation chair, absorbing the news. "How? How did he even know I'm a Shadowchaser? How did he find out about Gilead?"

"Gilead began a London search for a new handler after you decided to transfer to University. Comstock was at the top of the list of candidates we secretly vetted. We approached him after seeing how well you two got on together. Once he understood Gilead's mission and your role, he jumped at the chance to be your handler."

The bitter taste of betrayal clotted on her tongue. She forced herself to choke it down, then spoke. "So you watch me, then get my friends to report on me. Am I a Chaser or a suspect?"

Balm glared at her from beneath the wide brim of her hat. "I worried about you. Why would I not want to know what's going on with my own daughter?"

"Daughter? I don't need the subtle reminder that you took me in when no one else would. All that does is remind me of how you mentally deconstructed me and remade me into a walking, talking Shadowchaser Barbie."

"What I wanted was for you to be my successor," Balm said calmly, her chin held high. "Unfortunately, you were full of too much rage, especially for one so young. Since your temperament wasn't suited to the training necessary to become head of the Gilead Commission, I reluctantly went with my second choice for you."

"Funny, I didn't see a lot of reluctance back then."

"Your rage and your powers needed to be channeled somehow. Usually just being here on Santa Costa helps people. Walking the beaches, tending the gardens, even taking tea on this cliff has soothed many a soul. But not yours. Only discipline did that. You are the youngest person ever to undergo that sort of intensive training. Don't try to deny that you didn't enjoy it like a fish enjoys water."

Kira shifted in her chair. "Yeah, well, it's not like I would have made a good Oracle."

"No, I don't think the Seers Hall would have appreciated the disruption." Balm refreshed her tea. "So, as much as it pained me to put you through it, I'm glad I did. It's what any mother should do for her child."

"Yeah, you always doled out the tough love, didn't you, Mother? Like Venice, the night Nico died. Nice of you to show up then. Not."

"I was in Santa Costa, thinking that you'd listened when I asked you to remain in Budapest." She tugged on the froth of lace that edged her cuffs. "You defied me, Kira, the only person who's ever dared ignore a request from the Balm of Gilead. All I wanted was to protect you. I respected Nico, but he had a blind spot where you were concerned. He betrayed my trust and took advantage of you." Before Kira could object, Balm added, "Regardless of what you may think on the matter. His lapse in judgment cost him his life and scarred yours. For that, I don't think I can ever forgive him."

"Balm." It was hard to see the other woman's point of view, much less agree with it. Six years ago there was no way that she'd have followed Balm's order to not go scouting in Venice, a cover for the passionate weekend she and Nico had intended. Now she wondered if Balm had known the outcome and had tried to warn her.

Not that she would have listened. She'd been nineteen and sure of herself and her abilities and in love with her handler. Because of that, she'd gotten him killed. Fast forward a few years, and now Bernie, whom she loved as a father, could be added to the list of those who'd paid a heavy price for being close to her.

She reached for one of the little tea cakes for want of something to do with her hands. "I suppose you already have another handler on the way? I've got to say, though, that with my track record, I don't think anyone's beating down your door to work with me."

"Right now I believe another handler would do more harm than good. Given your penchant for thumbing your nose at authority, I think it's time you learned what it means to be in a position of authority yourself." Balm gave her a level look. "You have Mr. Comstock to thank for that, by the way. He seemed to think you were more than capable of working on your own."

"Considering that I thought I was working on my own, yeah, I understand why he would say that." *Good ol' Bernie*, she thought.

"I've asked Estrella Sanchez to turn over Mr. Comstock's personal effects to you. He will be cremated per his wishes and the remains delivered to you. He asked that you take him back to London. Will you do that for him?"

Kira gave a jerky nod. It took her a moment to find words. "There's something else I need to do first, but yeah. I'll take him back to London."

Balm reached out, wrapped a hand around Kira's hand, a gesture they could only make in these dream-walks. "I know I don't have to ask you to be careful, but please, for my sake, take care of yourself. Call on me if you need assistance. And stop antagonizing the section chief. The structure is in place for a reason. Sanchez can be of help to you, even with a seeker demon."

Kira wasn't so sure about that but decided to keep her opinions private. "I promise to take care of myself."

Balm gave her a look over the rim of her delicate teacup, as if she knew Kira's dodge. She probably did. "I have something for you," she said then. "A peace offering."

"What sort of peace offering?"

Balm nodded at something over Kira's shoulder. She turned around. A man stood at the edge of the cliff, nattily dressed in a beige suit and dark brown vest, a wide brimmed hat. He looked as if he'd been waiting for Howard Carter to get off the train in Cairo.

"Dammit, Balm," she choked out.

"Go on," the older woman urged gently. "You don't have a lot of time."

The chair almost fell over as she surged out of it. She took an impulsive step forward, then turned back to the woman who'd molded her into what she was. Balm looked as she always did, serenity personified, rich brown curls untarnished by gray and no visible marks of the passage of time, but Kira had learned early on that still waters ran deep.

The weight of leading the Gilead Commission, being responsible for hundreds of Shadowchasers and their handlers the world over—and the politics and bureaucracy that enabled it—couldn't have been an easy job on the best of days. Kira knew she'd done her fair share of complicating Balm's life, and she suddenly felt guilty about it. A little.

She reached out, wrapping her fingers around Balm's. The older woman looked up, surprise widening her eyes.

"Thank you, Balm." The words weren't easy, but they were important to say. Especially now. "I'll try to visit you more often, at least this way."

Balm squeezed her fingers, then let go. "That would please me."

Kira made her way up to the precipice, then stopped a few feet away. He looked like Bernie, but there was a smoothness to his expression, as if a great burden had been lifted. "Is it really you, Bernie?"

"Mostly." His smile sobered. "I'm sorry you had to find me that way."

She shuddered, her mind immediately flashing back to the alley. "Me too."

"I wish I could talk freely with you, Kira," Bernie said. "There's so much that I wish I could share, especially with what you now face."

Which meant even here, in this in-between place, she couldn't let down her guard. He apparently didn't want Gilead to know about the dagger. *Why?* "You accepted my extrasense so quickly and completely that I didn't think to question it. Now I understand why."

"I've known others with some sort of ability, but not as sharp or reliable as yours. I was amazed by your gift, Kira, and pleased to help you exercise it."

She asked the only question she dared, the only question she could. "Why didn't you tell me Gilead had made you my handler?"

Concern washed over his features. "They didn't *make* me do anything, Kira. I wasn't forced. When Balm approached me and asked me to watch over you, I didn't have to think twice. You were my student, a protégé, but I also felt as if you were the daughter I never had. Of course I'd protect you to the best of my ability. It was my choice to conceal that I was your handler, at least for a while."

"Why?"

His smile dimmed. "Selfishness, mostly. You trusted me, even looked up to me at times. Even though you didn't fully confide in me, I could see your anger and your loneliness because of Gilead and what happened in Venice. You would have shut me out if you'd known I was your handler. You'd have considered me one of them, and I didn't want that. I valued our friendship too much to let that happen."

Regrets and recriminations welled inside her. His reasons for not telling her he was her handler was the same reason she'd never told him about being a Shadowchaser. Before Wynne and Zoo, he'd been the only Normal in her life.

The anguish tightened as she thought about the

access she'd given to her friends. "Are Wynne and Zoo . . . ?"

"No. They are exactly what you think they are: dear friends who care for you very much. They have no connection to the Gilead Commission."

She closed her eyes, relief sweeping through her. She didn't know what she'd do if her friends were something else, something other than normal humans. "Thank you."

"Kira, you must listen to me." Bernie stepped closer to her, his expression sharpening with concern. "You must not hold on to—to material things. There are those who will help, if you let them. The last thing I want is for you to become a target."

She nodded to show she understood his code. This wasn't her dreamwalk, but she could still manipulate it enough to exchange the dress and corset for her more usual Shadowchasing gear. "I already am, Bernie. A seeker demon tracked you from England to the States. I think they can find me without trying very hard."

"I suppose you're right." He looked away briefly, his jaw working silently before he turned back to her. "I'm sorry, so sorry for keeping the truth from you—"

"Bernie." She held up her hands, an effort to ward off the emotional deluge. "Please, don't."

He gathered himself. "All right. On to more practical matters. You should know that I've left everything I own to you. My solicitor will probably contact you as soon as he realizes that I'm—no longer here. It's there—the London flat, the country cottage, my entire collection—when you're ready for it. I'd like for you to take my ashes back to England, but I also want you to know that you have a home there. Whenever you need it, it will be there for you."

She was conscious of Balm still sitting in the pavilion. Even in death, Bernie looked out for her, trying to give her a way out of Shadowchasing. Problem was, the time to walk away had been before she'd ever set foot in Gilead.

He coughed. "Well then. Now that there's no longer any danger of my eyebrows burning off, I'd like a hug from my surrogate daughter." He held out his arms. "Oblige an old man?"

She gave him a jerky nod then stepped into his embrace, holding tightly as she buried her face into his shoulder. He felt blessedly solid to her, and she wanted to hold him forever. With no knowledge of her birth parents and fuzzy memories of her adoptive caregivers, she'd always considered Bernie Comstock her father in all but blood. "You'd better save a place for me."

"Of course." He stepped back slightly, framing her face in his hands. "But you have to promise me that you'll live a long, happy life first. Don't think I won't drop in on you now and again to make sure."

"You'd better."

A kiss to her forehead, then he moved back completely. "Time for me to go. I have more adventures ahead, and so do you. Thank you for your prayers to Ma'at on my behalf."

Not yet. She stretched a hand toward him. "Bernie, wait."

"Think of me, but don't mourn for me. I've had a full and happy life and I can't regret one moment of it, especially the moments spent with you. Not a one." He slowly faded, his shape blending, then disappearing into the sunlight.

Kira awakened to the sound of her own crying, her pillow clutched to her chest, knowing it would never be enough.

Chapter 7

The Dagger of Kheferatum.

The longer Kira stared at the blade, the surer she became. Carefully coded searches through Gilead's online database had yielded little useful information. She hadn't dared to do a thorough online search outside of the Chasers network in case it triggered the notice of Gilead or the Fallen. Instead she'd plowed through her stacks of ancient books and ran a couple of query strings on her personal arcane server, and come back with the same result: the Dagger of Kheferatum.

Khefer, a bastardization of *Keper*, or the Egyptian-Greek hybrid *Xeper*, meaning "I have come into being." Symbolized by the scarab. Atum, also known as Temu, the primal creator god of gods.

No wonder the dagger was nearly sentient and coveted by mystics the way alchemists hungered for the philosopher's stone. It had been named and imbued with the power of creation. According to some of the ancient texts, the dagger was rumored to not only physically take life, but magically destroy it as well. One nick, one jab, and the blade would claim the soul. Did that mean that the dagger could transfer souls? Was that how it "created" life?

She looked down at her notes. She'd taken as much

care as possible cataloging the blade, using archival gloves and sterilized equipment to measure and weigh it before taking photos. Even through the gloves, she could feel the dagger's power. If the dagger could give and take life, she had even more reason to keep it locked away. Just keep it, period. Even through the display screen of her digital camera, the blade's beauty and pristine condition shone through. So ancient and so deadly, its very existence was a miracle that needed to be protected at all costs.

Of course, the best way to protect it would be to keep it with her, to carry it always. It called to her, whispering at her, coaxing her to wield it. *Only I can vanquish your enemies, only I can take the blood of the one who'd harmed you. Ma'at will bless you, make you the embodiment of justice. Together we will bring Order to Chaos—*

"No!"

She blinked, startled to discover she'd set the camera down and stripped off her gloves, her hand centimeters from grasping the blade. Quickly she jerked on her everyday gloves, slammed down the lid, fumbled the lock closed, then stepped back. Her body swayed toward the dagger and she stepped back again, acid churning in her stomach as she shook the sensation out of her hands.

She wanted the blade. Worse than that—she *craved* the dagger, wanted to hold it and feel its power with the intense gut-wrenching need of a junkie jonesing for another high. If just holding it for mere moments or being near it caused that sort of reaction, she couldn't trust herself to actually try to draw on its magic.

The dagger was one of the most dangerous artifacts she'd come across in a long time. No wonder one of the Fallen coveted it. Wielding that sort of power would do more than upset the Universal Balance: it could obliterate it.

Fighting for calm, she put the chest back into the wall safe, then drew her Lightblade. Feeling the weight of it in her hands chased back the pull of the ancient dagger. She'd earned her dagger after five hardscrabble years of training and then surviving a final exam that required every bit of mental, magical, and physical strength she possessed. At that time, limping into the Acceptance Hall, she'd only had eyes for the silver blade lying on a pale silk cloth and bathed in blue-white light.

Awe had filled her the first time she'd seen her blade. The top of the pommel bore radiating lines carved into the silver, to symbolize Light coming to the world to chase away Shadow. The grip was specially cured leather, dyed black and braided with silver wire, light piercing Dark. Silverwork continued in the guard, twin curves symbolizing the protecting embrace of order. The notched ricasso was engraved with Ma'at's feather on one side and an ankh on the other, personal totems she'd added after claiming the dagger. The blade itself swept another nine inches on a slight curve and was etched in a flowing pattern resembling sunlight rippling on water.

By the time a Shadowchaser completed training, Balm and the Gilead Commissioners had a good idea of what style of blade best suited the Chaser. Each weapon was as individual as the person who wielded it, and the blooding ritual in the Acceptance Hall bonded blade to owner. For Kira, the silver in her Lightblade enabled her to channel her power to the weapon, even to the point of extending its reach. It was truly an extension of her body, as much a part of her as her limbs. She doubted she'd be able to function without her dagger.

She exhaled fully, inhaled deeply, grounding herself before pushing through the Veil.

It took longer to ward the ancient dagger than it had the perimeter of the entire warehouse, simply because the dagger didn't like being contained, and it certainly didn't like her own blade. Using her Lightblade enabled her to carve protective sigils into the air surrounding the chest, the safe, the room itself. Only after the final sigil's glow had faded from the air into an invisible protective presence did she allow herself to relax.

The Dagger of Kheferatum would have to remain locked away until she could figure out what to do with it. Luckily she didn't need the original to lure the Fallen out into the open. Not when she knew an expert metalworker who'd love the challenge of re-creating an ancient magical weapon.

All I have to do is avoid my Gilead coworkers, an ancient warrior, a seeker demon, and a Shadow Avatar until the dagger is ready. All in a day's work for a Shadowchaser.

Pushing fatigue away, Kira transferred a few electronic files to a flash drive then shut down her laptop. She gathered her documentation, camera, and a few supplies into a backpack, checked her wards, then left, riding her bike into the Little Five Points area of Atlanta.

Considered an in-town community, the eclectic area—two and a half miles east of downtown proper and the other Five Points—was a magnet for artists, musicians, neohippies, and young professionals. The bohemian mix appealed to her, made her feel like she actually fit in some place.

She pulled her bike into the parking lot sandwiched between the Vortex Bar & Grill and Junkman's Daughter. The thought of massive amounts of Tater Tots piqued her appetite and almost had her opening the metal gate to the Vortex's large skull entrance, but she had business to take care of first.

Her thoughts swirled as she headed on foot past the restaurant into the heart of Little Five. Despite the dreamwalk and her late morning research, she felt as if she had more questions than answers. The Dagger of Kheferatum had plenty of power and its seductive lure was dangerous in and of itself, but that still didn't explain why one of the Fallen wanted it. Shadow Avatars and their kind had plenty of weapons in their destructive arsenal, some of which made atomic bombs look like hot air balloons. What was it about this particular dagger, Kira wondered, that had someone conjure a seeker demon, follow Bernie from London, and kill him to get it?

She turned the corner at Findley Plaza then made a beeline for Charms and Arms, Zoo and Wynne Marlowe's metaphysical gift shop. As she pushed open the door, she was immediately hit with a wall of energy from the multitude of crystals arrayed in front of the large picture window. Two customers were already in the shop, one in front by the crystals, the other at the jewelry counter being helped by Wynne's midday assistant.

Once one's senses got past the excitedly vibrating gems, the soft green of the walls combined with the scent of incense and the sound of a bubbling fountain wrapped visitors in a metaphysical blanket of peace and comfort. Open shelving held a plethora of books on magic, rituals, divination, and religion. One wall held a variety of natural and homeopathic products.

This was all for the fluffy-bunny neopagan clientele. More serious practitioners headed past the cases of jewelry and books on New Age and occult subjects to the back of the store. There, two rooms were set across from each other for divination sessions, flanking a doorway that led to another smaller showroom, where Wynne was likely to be. The area held more serious collections of athames and cups, scrying mirrors and gazing crystals, and upscale period-accurate weaponry Wynne made for Society for Creative Anachronism members.

With a nod to the salesclerk, Kira made her way to the back of the store. A shiver of awareness made her pause. Wynne wasn't alone.

As Kira pushed aside the beaded curtain, she caught sight of a lanky, silver-haired man curiously perusing the private collection. Wynne sat at a small table—her hair was fuchsia this week and plaited, then gathered into pigtails. Across from her sat a dark-skinned man in a white T-shirt with a cascade of braids falling past his shoulders.

Shit.

"Hey, Wynne, I'm sorry for interrupting." She

maintained what she hoped was an easy smile as she pulled her gloves off and then tucked them in her pocket. "Can I talk to you for a sec?"

"Sure." Wynne, noting her bare hands, immediately stood up. Braided Guy rose to his feet with her as if men still commonly did that these days.

The man with the braids was *him*. The warrior from her vision. The original owner of the blade, the man who'd gone on to kill and pillage and destroy thousands of lives. Standing, he was just a little taller than Kira, maybe five-ten, thin as a whip and just as dangerous. He must have seemed like a giant to the diminutive ancient Egyptians.

He reached behind him, wrapping long fingers around the dagger lying on the table. *Wrong move.* Kira called her power. The old man at the display counter straightened, his curious expression sharpening from mild to watchful. *Worst move.*

She pulled blade and gun, the Lightblade pointed at the old man's throat and the gun aimed squarely for the younger man's heart. Wynne moved slightly behind her and out of the line of fire.

"You can't kill me with that," the dark-skinned man said, his expression still easy as he held the dagger with an expert grip. "Regular bullets don't have an effect on me."

Wynne pulled out her own gun, thumbed off the safety, and chambered a round. "Then I guess it's a good thing we don't use regular bullets, huh?" She glanced back at Kira. "So who are these guys and why the hell are they in my shop asking me about magic daggers and rare athames?"

"I don't know what the old man is, but he's definitely not human. As for that one, he was human roughly four thousand years ago."

"Told you she was a smart one," the elderly looking gentleman said in a musical accent, speaking for the first time. A smile crinkled his open expression as he held his hands up. "Not like the other Shadowchasers we've met."

"Quiet, old man," the Nubian said, his voice dark but easy. He stared at Kira, his hand steady as he pointed the dagger at her. Thinking he was harmless would be like saying a cheetah was a tabby cat. She knew exactly how ruthless he could be. "Looks like we have a standoff."

"Standoff?" Kira rolled her eyes. "Age doesn't mean a thing around here. And whatever you and your grandfather can throw at us, trust me when I say we can throw it right back."

"Grandfather? To him?" The old man sounded affronted. "Hardly."

The Nubian's mouth tightened. "Perhaps we could talk through this? I don't think there's any need to disturb your customers with gunfire."

"You wanna talk? Go ahead then. Tell me why you killed Comstock."

Wynne gasped. "Comstock's dead?"

"I didn't kill the dealer," the warrior answered. "I know what did, which is why I need my blade back."

He didn't stink of seeker demon, but that didn't mean Kira believed him. Someone with enough power to control a seeker could probably mask the traces a seeker left on the psyche. She knew this guy, with his honed runner's build, couldn't have survived as long as he had by being stupid.

"I suppose you were the ones who tried to break into my house before dawn?" She let her amusement break through. "That must have hurt like a bitch."

"It did," the old man surprised her by saying. "I underestimated your talent. Something I will not do again. I like being here."

The Nubian's jaw tightened. "If you know how old I am, then you also know that I'm the true owner of that dagger. I must have it back."

Kira smiled. "And I must tell you no."

He frowned. "I need my dagger back. You will return it to me."

"And if I don't?"

He sighed. "I would prefer that we not get to that stage."

"You need to learn how to ask, not demand. Not that it matters anyway, because I'm still going to tell you no. You should have protected your possessions better if they're that precious to you."

He broke off a word that was obviously not a compliment. Kira bit back a smile. It was apparent the warrior was used to getting his way. *Long past time for him to learn that life doesn't always go your way and I have no problem being the hand of Ma'at in his lesson.*

"Shadowchaser . . ." The old man shifted.

"Uh-uh, old man." The air popped as her power flared along the Lightblade. "I don't know what you are, but I promise I can separate you from that shell without breaking a sweat."

The old man tried for charm, hands lifted in a

placating gesture. "Young lady, I have no doubt that you would indeed try. I, for one, have no interest in crossing you. I have no desire for this tale to end with my death. Not when it has become so entertaining."

"Flattery won't save your life, or distract my attention away from Mr. Braided Guy. *Dude.* Move again and I will shoot you."

The Nubian raised his hands, the tip of the dagger pointed at the floor. *Not that it meant anything to someone so skilled.* "I mean you no harm."

"I'm sure you don't. You'll have to forgive me for not taking your word for it, though."

"We need to talk. Seriously, and without weapons pointed at each other."

Kira looked to Wynne, who shrugged. She didn't see the harm in talking, especially if she could gather information to track down the seeker demon and its master. "Did you see the giant skull around the corner on the main road?"

He nodded. "It's hard to miss."

"That's the entrance to the Vortex restaurant. I'll meet you there on the deck at five o'clock."

Black eyes bored into her, his suspicion clear. "Do not think to trick me."

She gave him a wide smile. "Don't worry. I'm definitely coming after you."

Chapter 8

The old gentleman dipped his head at her, then strolled out grinning. He was a sharp contrast to the warrior, who took his time returning the dagger to the table, then stared at Kira as he backed his way out of the room. Kira crossed to the doorway, making sure both men left the shop before calling back her power and sheathing her blade and gun.

Wynne secured her own weapon, then crossed to the display table and picked up the athame. "Mind telling me why we just got into a Mexican standoff in my store?"

"That was the owner of an Egyptian dagger and his nonhuman sidekick," Kira explained, pulling her gloves free of her pocket and putting them back on. "The dagger's four thousand years old. So is he."

"He's mighty fine-looking for a mummy." Wynne scooted around the counter to return the blade to its place in the display case. "And he obviously wants his dagger back."

"He was never a mummy. And I don't give a rat's ass what he wants." She shouldered off her backpack, then placed it on the table. "Comstock gave his life to get that dagger to me, and I'm not turning it over anytime soon to anyone."

"Comstock's really dead?"

She gave a short nod, forced the words out. "Seeker demon, last night."

"Oh my God, Kira, I'm so sorry." Wynne sank into the chair. "Are you certain the mummy didn't do it? You should have let me shoot him!"

"It wasn't him. I don't think. The guy may be immortal, but I don't think he's got a lot of extrasense in him otherwise. Controlling a seeker demon is serious business. I don't know about the old man, if he really is an old man. He probably could have done it, especially since he tried to break in last night and lived to tell about it."

Wynne shoved her hands through her fuchsia hair. "Wait. This is going way too fast. Comstock was killed by a seeker demon because of an old knife and you just met a four-thousand-year-old guy who claims he owns it. Why the hell aren't you flipping out?"

"Can't afford to. It won't change what happened, what I have to do. What Bernie wants me to do. Turns out Bernie was also my handler."

"Are you kidding me? And no one told you this, all this time?" Wynne shot from her chair. Kira took a step back before her friend did something truly insane, like try to hug her. As fragile as her control was then, breaking it would leave them both worse for wear. "This is all Gilead's fault, isn't it? Damn the Commission and all the jerkwads in it, treating you like this!" Wynne began to pace, her hot pink ponytails swinging as she spun about in the narrow space between the display cases. "They'd better hope that I never meet one of them face-to-face!"

Despite Kira's mood, Wynne's hyper attitude kicked a smile out of her. Seeing her friend's outrage went a long way to making Kira believe Bernie's words—that Wynne and Zoo weren't affiliated with Gilead.

She relaxed slightly, shoving her hands into her pockets. Once Wynne got wound up, it was hard to get her to calm back down. Not that Kira minded. Since she couldn't afford to fall apart, having Wynne do it for her was the next best thing.

Wynne whirled to face Kira. "Whoever did this— you're going to hunt him down, aren't you?"

"You already know the answer to that."

"Bring in somebody else. I'm serious. You said seeker demon. *Seeker demon,* Kira. You can't go up against something like that. And you need to take a break, to take care of everything with Comstock . . ."

"Wynne." She waited until she was sure she could speak calmly. "Because it's a seeker demon, I have to be the one to stop it. It's going to find out soon enough that I have the dagger, so the crap's coming straight to my door whether I want it to or not. More than that, I owe Bernie. He didn't deserve to die like that."

Wynne just stared at her a moment, hazel eyes bright with care and concern. Then she nodded. "Fine. What do you need us to do?" She held up a hand before Kira could protest. "You know we're going to help you anyway. It'll be smoother if you go along with it from the jump."

Kira sighed, exasperation and affection spiraling through her. This was why she'd come to Charms and Arms, why she needed Wynne and Zoo. Their tactical support was only surpassed by the unconditional emotional support they offered.

She opened her backpack, extracted a flash drive and a sheaf of papers. "I'd like you to make a copy of the dagger. I made a drawing to scale, both sides. There's a couple of photos of it from multiple angles on my camera, and I've included all the stats on the drive."

Wynne let out a low whistle as she flipped through the printouts. "Aren't you just about the most beautiful thing I've ever seen? Bronze blade, ivory handle—I think I'm in love!"

"I did a little research before I came over," Kira explained as Wynne drooled over her specs. "And by little I mean several hours' worth. I think it's the Dagger of Kheferatum. Apparently it's been coveted by mystics and occultists for centuries, in hopes of mastering its power. I can testify that it's got a lot of power. So much power . . . "

Kira knew *she* could handle the ancient weapon. She had enough strength, enough skill. Enough will. Controlling it would be no problem. If she traded her Lightblade for the dagger, no Shadowlings, not even the Fallen themselves, would be able to stand against her . . .

"Kira!"

She blinked, surprised to find Wynne waving her hand in front of her face. "What?"

"Man, where did you go?"

"Just . . . planning. Did you ask me something?"

"Wow, that must be one helluva plan. This is what that guy was looking for?"

"Yeah."

"If he's what you say he is, there's no way I'm going to be able to fool him into thinking my replica is his blade. He's spent a gazillion years with it. He'll know. I'm good, but I'm not that good."

"He's not the one I'm trying to fool." She crossed to the open doorway, peered out. Everything in the shop seemed normal, on both levels. "He doesn't have that oily feel that a seeker demon leaves on its controllers. I just need your version to distract the demon's master long enough for me to take out the seeker and neutralize him."

Wynne got a worried look in her eyes again. "You know I'm going to do better than my best, but it would help if I could see it firsthand. You know, test the weight and balance, get a sense—"

"Uh-uh. Blade's too dangerous."

"Too dangerous. Like our soul-sucking scrying mirror dangerous?"

"Sucking out people's souls may be the least this blade can do." She crossed to the table and touched one of the photos. "I think its name is the clue. *Khefer* means to come into being. Atum is one of the primeval gods of Egypt. He is creation. Everything exists because he exists. On the flip side, he also *un-creates*. In the *Book of the Dead* he tells Osiris that he will annihilate creation, returning everything to nonexistence swallowed up by the primordial waters of Nun."

"Nice." Wynne twirled one of her bright pink ponytails. "So by naming this dagger Kheferatum, they're basically making it a tool of both creation and destruction."

Kira looked down at the papers, fighting off a shiver. "Basically. If I've interpreted everything right, anyway. The dagger is important because of its ability to give life as well as take it away."

"I'm sure I'm not going to like the answer, but here goes: why would a Shadow Avatar want it? Don't they already have stuff like this?"

"That's something I need to find out. It can't just be about the dagger's ability to make its owner virtually immortal, more powerful, that sort of thing. It might have something to do with the dagger being used as a weapon for the last four thousand years. Death is what it prefers."

"That's all?"

Kira shook her head ruefully. "No. It has a mind of its own and supposedly if it doesn't like its owner, it will kill him and go find another."

Wynne let out another low whistle. "Dang, that's harsh."

"Harsh ain't the word, girl, but I can't deny that Braided Guy lost his dagger somehow and it's found its way to me. I have to assume there's at least a little bit of truth in everything I've uncovered about the dagger so far. The dagger itself showed me enough death and bloodshed the first time I touched it that it might as well be alive. There's no way I'm letting Shadow get its hands on it."

"And you want me to try to replicate that?"

"I want Zoo to put a little bit of magic into it, too, but nobody could begin to duplicate the way this thing feels. No offense." She reached into the backpack again, pulled out a blade in a worn leather sheath wrapped in oilcloth. "Do you think you can use this as a base?"

Wynne unwrapped the sheath, then pulled the dagger free. "Holy crap, Kira! You want to use a real two-thousand-year-old dagger as a base for an imitation one?"

"Yeah." It was one of her favorite daggers—the blade was worn, a plain solid bronze weapon from the late Ptolemaic period and still a valuable artifact—but its sacrifice would be worth it. "It's the only other ivory-handled dagger I have that's close enough. I also brought some gold you can use to cover the bronze. Can you do it?"

"Of course I can do it. God made the world in seven days. Shouldn't be that hard for me to re-create a four-thousand-year-old half-alive dagger in . . . " Wynne looked up. "I guess you want this yesterday?"

"I hate to do you like that, but I also know that if anyone can do it, you can. You're that good. Even Comstock said so, when he brought the dagger to me." She dropped her gaze for a moment. "Anyway, just let me know when you get finished. I'm going to do my best to keep the real thing suppressed for as long as possible."

Wynne chewed on her bottom lip. "Is it going to be possible? That guy didn't seem like he wanted to take no for an answer."

"Then it's time he learned. I'll be more than happy to teach him."

"Just be careful, okay? You shouldn't be chasing after something like this alone."

More worry, more concern. While she appreciated it, it was beginning to needle her. "I won't be. Sanchez will have plenty of suits on the street policing the hybrids while I concentrate on the big bad. No matter what, I'm going to make sure that Bernie didn't die for nothing."

Chapter 9

What was that back there?"
"What?"

"Don't 'what' me, old man." Khefar stopped in the little open square. "We had the advantage. They wouldn't have dared shoot up that store. We could have gotten my blade back."

Nansee barked out a laugh. "My boy, I know you've been around for a while, but if you think you had the advantage over those two women, you obviously need to explore America more. Besides, she's one of your number."

Khefar jerked to a stop, shock racing through him. "What did you say?"

"You have another life to save, son of Nubia."

Finally. Khefar suddenly felt the need to sit down. It had been more than forty years since he'd been given a life to add to his tally. Forty years since the last one he'd tried to protect had been murdered. Forty years since he had been given a mission to keep a human from an untimely, unjust death.

"Which one? The one pointing the gun, or the one pointing the knife?"

"The Shadowchaser."

No, it couldn't be. "Are you sure?"

Nansee nodded.

"I'm supposed to keep a Shadowchaser alive, with a seeker demon coming after her sooner rather than later, and I don't even have my blade?" He cursed in frustration. "Why would I expect this to get easy?"

"You are two souls from done, warrior of the Two Lands," the wraith reminded him. "Will you give up now, so close to rejoining your family?"

"Enough, spider. You know I'll do what's required of me." After a millennium or three, he should have been immune to the trickster's barbs. But his family had always been his sore spot, his weakness, his reason. There was no way in Light or Shadow that he would quit now, even if it meant protecting a Shadowchaser with a death wish.

He clenched his hands. The Shadowchaser was a fighter and he surely hadn't expected to see her so calm and collected the day after the antiquity dealer's death. She had roiled with profound grief and hot rage after she'd found him. But he clearly remembered the way she had disobeyed her superiors—and her apparent lack of respect for authority. He'd seen how she entered a nightclub that obviously served Shadow and intentionally engaged the enemy even though she was outnumbered. She was on a fast track to oblivion. He knew the signs, having experienced them himself.

And I am supposed to keep her alive?

He'd do it. He knew he had no other choice. So many years, so many lives, and finally so close to being done. Four thousand years, sixty-four thousand souls. One more opportunity.

"I'll do what's required of me," he repeated, "but I have to wonder at your motives."

"My motives?" Nansee placed a hand over the spot his heart would be if he had actually possessed such an organ. "What makes you think I have motives?"

"Because you always do. You usually don't tell me if a life counts toward my total until after the save is done. Why tell me the Shadowchaser counts, if not for your own sadistic amusement?"

"You know me, Khefar, son of Jeru, son of Natek." The old man grinned, white teeth brilliant pearls in the mahogany of his face. "Yours is a story for the ages. Better than Herakles, than Marco Polo, even Gilgamesh. Nearly as eventful and exciting a story as my own."

"Still haven't learned a thing about modesty, I see." He looked back at the little gift shop, then resolutely turned his back. "Are you sure there aren't some Caribbean countries you need to visit for a while?"

Nansee beamed. "My boy, you know that I am both here and there. You're forgetting more than you're remembering in your old age." He leaned closer, silver hair glinting in the late afternoon sunlight. "Or is it that a certain Shadowchaser has the great warrior completely tossed off his game?"

"Don't even start with me, old man. I will do as the gods require of me. My gods, not you."

Nansee laughed. "Here you are, still clinging to the gods of Kemet despite all that you've seen and experienced."

"The gods of Kemet are what they are, what they have always been. My lady Isis is not fickle. Unlike some West African demigods I could name."

The old man raised his bushy white eyebrows but

held his tongue. Khefar was relieved that, for once, Nansee had no rejoinder. He really didn't want to hear anything the spider had to say. All he could think about was how close he was. After four millennia and sixty-four thousand lives, he was close to ending his torment and being free.

To earn his freedom and make his way to the Field of Reeds, he must keep only two more lives from facing final judgment before their appointed time. If he had to keep a fatally inclined Shadowchaser alive, he would do so. Whether she wanted his help or not.

Kira made her way back to the Vortex. Her mind roiled with plans, plots, and information. She had to give Wynne time to forge a replica of the Dagger of Kheferatum. That meant she had to find a way to dodge a seeker demon as well as the dagger's owner, and both were probably equally tenacious.

A four-thousand year-old Nubian warrior. She shook her head in amazement, questions burning through her. He was a walking, talking witness to history. The history, the stories he could share.

He'd be the perfect resource on a dig in Khartoum or Abu Simbel or Kerma. Had he been in Meroë when it was ruled by its line of powerful warrior queens? She'd done her dissertation for her masters in archaeology on the Kandakes of Meroë while at University College. How much better, she wondered, would she have done if she'd been able to interview him beforehand?

She stopped short. No. Braided Guy wanted to take the dagger from her. That made him an opponent, not a colleague. She'd have to set aside any questions concerning history and focus on those that would stop the Shadow Avatar.

She walked back up Moreland Avenue heading north to the giant skull entrance of the Vortex. Despite the menacing exterior, the bar boasted some of the best burgers around and kept her in Tater Tots. "Hey, Kira," the hostess greeted her. "You want up or down?"

"Hey, Shelby. Someone's supposed to be waiting for me. Medium height and build, braids."

"Oh, the gorgeous guy who looks like he has a board shoved up his butt?"

"Yeah, that's the one."

"I put him upstairs." The hostess grinned. "Don't think he was happy about that."

Kira grinned back. "I bet."

Shelby led her out to the metal staircase leading to the upstairs dining room, an area that had the feel of a covered glassed-in patio—if you could ignore the wall mural of two crossed wrenches between the teeth of a grinning helmeted skull and the two barely clothed devil ladies that sat on them.

The Nubian sat at one of the tables beneath the mural, facing the door. He looked up when they arrived, and Shel was right—Kira doubted the man had smiled since sometime in the ninth century.

"I'll let Bobby know you're here."

"Thanks, Shel."

The hostess left them. The Nubian stared at her curiously. "For a Shadowchaser, you have curious tastes in friends and food."

"I don't know about your eating habits, but I could

say the same thing about your friend. Where's your not-exactly-human sidekick?"

He grimaced. "Don't let him hear you call him a sidekick. He got distracted by the musicians on the plaza. Besides, he doesn't need to be here for this."

"And what, exactly, is this?"

"Negotiation." He leaned forward. "You have something that belongs to me, something very precious. I've been searching for it for a long time."

Bobby interrupted them. "Y'all ready to order?"

The warrior flipped through the menu, then laid it down. "I'll take the bison version of the steakhouse burger with onion rings."

Kira ordered a half-pound Blue 'Shroom burger with a side of Tater Tots and a ginger beer. "What's your name?" she asked after their waiter left.

"Excuse me?"

She stripped off her gloves, carefully bracing her elbows against the brushed metal tabletop. "You want to negotiate, fine. Negotiate all you want. But I think I have the right to know the name of the person making demands of me. I'm pretty sure even rudimentary social customs were around during your time."

His lips tightened. "My name is Kevin. Kevin Lambert."

She raised an eyebrow. "Are you seriously going to sit there expecting me to believe that your name is Kevin Lambert? I gotta tell ya, I find it hard to believe that 'Kevin' was a common name four thousand years ago."

He remained silent while their waiter brought their drinks, then left. Then he leaned forward. "My name is

Khefar, son of Jeru, son of Natek. And yes, I was born more than four millennia ago. Now that the introductions are over, may I have my dagger back?"

"I need you to answer some questions first."

A muscle in his right cheek ticked. "I want my blade back. I'll give you whatever you want."

"Really?"

"You have but to name your price."

"All right." She leaned forward. "Bring Bernie back."

Regret filled his features as he sat back. "I would if I could, Shadowchaser. The art dealer did not deserve to die in such a way."

"You admit to killing Bernie?" Blue flame engulfed her hands. She drew back, clutching her hands tight beneath her chin in an effort to conceal them, though most of the other diners had extrasense of some sort.

He remained unruffled. "I didn't kill the antiquities dealer."

"Were you there, in the alley"—despite her effort to subdue it, blue fire crackled along her fingers, causing her beer bottle to shudder—"watching while they killed him, and didn't try to stop it?"

"No. We arrived after you did. If I had been there earlier, I would have interceded."

Kira stared at him for a long moment. He returned her stare, his gaze unwavering. Finally she settled back in the chair, pushing the anger and her power away. She wanted to believe him. He was the rightful owner of the dagger, after all. Or at least he had been. The ancient dagger seemed to be looking for a new owner. She wondered what the Nubian had done to make the dagger seek someone else to wield it.

She started to ask him, but their food arrived. If Bobby had done his usual magic, her burger would be safe enough to eat, but she couldn't take any chances. She waved a hand over her plate, dissipating the aura around her food. The earlier power display had probably zapped the ginger beer, but she passed a hand over it anyway. Better safe than sprawled out on the floor.

The warrior paused, his hand hovering above his onion rings. "Why did you do that? Is something wrong with the food?"

"What? No." She'd had to "disarm" her food for so many years that it was second nature now. For the longest time she could only eat raw fruits and vegetables that she'd harvested herself on Santa Costa, before Balm taught her how to clean her food, to rid it of the brief but sharp impressions of those who had handled it before, with a burst of extrasense.

As her stomach plaintively reminded her, it had been eight hours since the coffee and granola bar that had been her breakfast as she had researched the dagger. "It's something I have to do so I can eat without flashing on the cook, the waitress, the dishwasher . . . even the damned cow."

"Flashing?"

"It's what I call what happens when I get psychic impressions from people and their possessions. I can usually tone down the hit from inanimate objects, but anything alive, well . . . "

He picked up an onion ring, then laid it back on the plate. "Pardon my curiosity, Shadowchaser. But given the . . . ambience of this place, I think you can understand my caution."

"I suppose so, but the food is fine. Don't worry. If you're worried about this place—which you shouldn't be—does that mean you're a Shadowchaser too?"

"No, I'm not." He took a bite of the onion ring.

Her burger suddenly wasn't as interesting. "So you work for Shadow? You're an Adept?"

"I work for myself, but I'm no friend of Shadow."

"Then what are you, besides really, really old? Are you immortal?"

"I'm not immortal in the sense that I am not subject to death. It's . . . complicated."

"I bet. I'd say after four thousand years or so you are close enough to immortal to call you that, whatever the complications may be."

The warrior gave her a brief nod of acknowledgment.

"So, what else?"

"I have a mission I must complete."

"What sort of mission?"

He shook his head. "I cannot tell you, but I need my dagger to do it."

"Hmph." The Nubian definitely had a one-track mind when it came to the dagger. She couldn't resist temptation any longer and popped a Tater Tot into her mouth. *Umm, carby goodness.* "So you followed me."

"From the restaurant last night."

"How did you know I was there? How did I even get on your radar in the first place?"

He chewed thoughtfully on his burger, as if gathering his thoughts or deciding how much information to share with her. "I can sense the trail my dagger leaves," he finally said. "I tracked Comstock to your office, but

I didn't feel the dagger on him when he left. I assumed he left it with you, so I didn't need to trail him any longer. You did a good job of removing evidence of your time with it, but just being close to it for a length of time is enough. I have carried that blade for millennia. I know it when I feel it."

"Makes sense." She looked down at her plate, oddly grateful he hadn't witnessed Bernie's death but uncomfortable with the thought that he'd witnessed her discovery and grief. "Do you know what killed him?"

"Seeker demon."

"Do you know who controls it?"

"Yes."

"Tell me."

"Of course."

She looked up, waited.

He smiled, a slash of pearl against mahogany. "As soon as you give my dagger back."

"I can't do that."

"The dagger belongs to me."

"I know. It was gifted to you by the god-king of the Two Lands, as reward for your prowess in battle."

The frown lightened to confusion. "How do you know this?"

"The dagger told me."

"The dagger told—" He leaned forward, his expression even more intense. "You touched it? It *communicated* with you?"

"I didn't say it spoke freely," she said, a little surprised by his reaction. "I had to coax it along a little. Why are you surprised?"

He shook his head in patent disbelief. "I'm surprised because you're still functioning. My blade can be . . . temperamental."

"I certainly wouldn't call it warm and cuddly. But once it began to spill its secrets, it didn't want to stop." He didn't have to know that she'd blacked out from information overload. He certainly didn't need to know of the dagger's attempts to seduce her into wielding it.

The warrior frowned, clearly unhappy with how chatty the dagger had been with her. She supposed she couldn't blame him. If what she had read was true, it probably meant the dagger wanted a new master. If so, then how could she possibly give the dagger back? Better to keep it so that she'd know it was in safe hands.

Something sparked in his eyes, as if he knew the path of her thoughts. "The Dagger of Kheferatum is extremely dangerous. Should it fall into the wrong hands, its destructive capabilities would be unstoppable."

"I don't intend to let it fall into the wrong hands," she retorted, mocking his melodramatic tone.

"Nor do you intend to return it to me."

"Bingo."

"Why?"

"Because I don't know you, despite what you and the dagger have told me. I sure as hell don't trust either you or that old man. He may look like Morgan Freeman, but I sure wouldn't cast him to play God. Any god. Bernie gave the dagger to me for safekeeping. I won't fail him."

His hand shot across the table, wrapped around her wrist. "Return my dagger to me, Kira Solomon."

Her extrasense instinctively activated in self-defense. The whole world seemed to freeze as she waited for his thoughts to bombard her, for his skin to ashen as his life force drained from his body. Neither happened.

Nothing happened.

Shock raced through her. "You're touching me."

"I wanted to get your attention."

"How are you touching me?"

He frowned even as he maintained his grip. "What are you talking about?"

Completely shaken, Kira tried to pull her wrist free of his grip. "Let me go."

He frowned as he released her. "I didn't hurt you."

"No, no you didn't. You just, you shouldn't be able to touch me like that. But you did. Oh, goddess, you did and I don't know what the hell that means."

It was hard to form coherent sentences. No one had ever been able to touch her like that, especially after she hit puberty. Guardians, humans, Shadow-lings—they all took a toll and paid a price when they touched her.

Only Nico had been able to touch her one weekend, one beautiful and terrible weekend before he died. Now suddenly here was this Nubian, this immortal warrior whom she might have to try to kill—and he could touch her with impunity?

She needed air.

Gulping, she surged to her feet, the chair screeching as she thrust it back. She fumbled in her pocket for a couple of bills, threw them on the table, and grabbed her gloves. "I-I've got to go."

"We're not done talking."

"We are *so* done talking. Don't touch me," she added when he rose, making another grab for her. "Stay away from me, just stay away."

She sprinted for the door, knowing he was going to follow her.

Chapter 10

He could touch her. The damned Nubian could actually touch her.

Shaken to the core, Kira scuttled down the staircase to the parking lot. She jumped aboard her bike just as Khefar reached the bottom of the stairs shouting, "What the hell is going on?"

Her fingers fumbled with the helmet strap. She was shaking, as if *this* was the one event to turn her life upside down. "I'm sorry; I have to go."

He said something else, but she'd already kicked her bike to life. She had to get home, had to get somewhere she could take a moment and think. Think about the fact that a four-thousand-year-old warrior was the only person on the planet who could touch her without being reduced to a gibbering mess.

Tires squealed as she pulled out of the parking lot and headed south on Moreland to DeKalb Avenue, her mind still reeling. She didn't get any impressions from his touch either—not his thoughts, his emotions, his past, his energy. She'd learned more from touching the knife than from touching him. What was it supposed to mean? Why was he the only person who could touch her? Was it the knife's doing, or something else? Was it some kind of trick to divert her attention away from

Bernie's killer? Would Balm know? Did Balm know already?

Why was this happening now?

A cold warning skittered down her spine when she was less than half a block from her house. Her training took over instinctively, kicking the chaotic thoughts out of her mind. She palmed her Lightblade a split second before the seeker demon slammed into her, knocking her off the bike.

Power erupted all around them, neon blue sparking against putrid yellow as she and the demon and her bike rolled and wrestled. Its teeth scraped loudly across the top of her helmet, leaving smears of acidic saliva behind.

Screeching turned to crunching as her bike stopped hard against a telephone pole. She ignored it, calling on all her rage and sorrow to power her magic. The seeker demon wouldn't stop its attack until Kira was dead or she had destroyed it. Here was a target she could take on, something she could attack, hurt, annihilate—unless it killed her. This was a fight to the finish. No stopping.

Screaming a curse, she shoved the heel of her left hand hard against its lower jaw, bringing up her blade to slash at its throat. Claws swung, knocking the blade from her hand.

Crap. At least we've stopped rolling on the pavement.

The seeker demon eluded her efforts to immobilize it, its superior strength pinning her to the asphalt instead. The sound of squealing brakes scraped through her ears, but she ignored it. She couldn't worry about who it might be or if anyone was witnessing something that shouldn't be witnessed. Kira was too busy trying to stay alive and kill the seeker to care.

Her extrasense glowed the steady sapphire sheen of a shield, protecting her from the seeker demon's attempts to scratch and bite. She had to reclaim her Lightblade and stop the seeker quickly before her strength ran out. Its master had to be somewhere nearby to control it, and that worried her far more than finishing off the demon.

Something barreled into the demon, knocking it off her. She rolled upright, then pulled off her helmet. Khefar. The Nubian drew in his legs, then pushed, jettisoning the seeker a good fifteen feet. He sprung upright in a graceful, fluid motion. Amazingly he held her Lightblade, its length still glowing purple-blue with her power.

How was that possible?

The seeker demon swung its head from the Nubian to her as if trying to decide which one to pursue. She drew her gun but Khefar took the choice away, charging the demon with her blade ready to strike.

Blurred motion, the scramble of claws, the meaty thud of bodies colliding. "Don't let it bite or scratch you," she called, scanning the area for the Shadow Avatar that controlled the demon. Nothing vibrated through her extrasense. Either the controller wasn't around—unlikely—or he was powerful enough to control the seeker and conceal his presence—disconcerting.

"This would be easier if I had my own blade," he yelled back. "Yours is slow."

"Slow? I'll show you slow. Keep that damned thing busy." He shouldn't be able to use her Lightblade in the first place, but she shoved that thought aside. She limped to her bike, righting it with an effort. It wasn't ruined, but it would definitely take more than a paint job to put it back on the street.

Incensed anew, she opened the side panel to extract a sawed-off shotgun, jacked a couple of shells into it, then charged it with her extrasense. Khefar was still holding his own against the seeker demon in an impressive display of skill, but the seeker had speed, strength, and energy on its side. The Nubian wouldn't last much longer.

"Come on, come on, give me a shot," Kira muttered. She tracked them, but getting a clear shot of just the demon would be tricky. Then again, Khefar said he was more or less immortal. She had to hope he wasn't delusional, and that the bullet wouldn't hurt him.

She fired a round from her handgun, hitting the Nubian in the shoulder. He spun enough to give her an opening to use the shotgun. In less than a heartbeat she swung it up, charged it with her power, aimed, fired.

The heavy round hit the demon in the forehead. Taking off the top of its head wouldn't be enough to keep it down, she knew, stalking forward to pump the second round into its muzzle.

Still the beast writhed and snarled. Khefar dragged her blade, still burning with power, across the demon's throat, then shoved it into the left side of its chest for good measure. Its shriek cut the air, leaving Kira's ears ringing. The death throes quickly subsided until the only sounds left were Khefar's labored breathing and the sizzle of the demon's yellow blood burning into the concrete.

Khefar regained his feet, slinging his braids back over his shoulder, her blade still glowing in his hand. "Are you all right?"

"Don't worry about me—"

He turned on her. "Are you hurt?"

"Hey, easy there. My ankle's twisted and it's going to hurt like a bitch in the morning, but I'll live. You got it off of me before he could do any real damage. What about you?"

"You shot me."

"I had to get you out of the way of my kill shot," she explained, holstering her gun. The seeker demon sank in on itself with a crackling noise, then imploded. If they were lucky, the mental backlash from its demise would kill its master. If they were lucky.

"By shooting me?"

"No one told you to follow me or jump into the fight," she reminded him. "Besides, you said you were immortal and regular bullets don't hurt you."

"I said it was more complicated than that." He winced, then slumped against the building, pressing his hand against his rib cage. "Damn, he must have got me."

"Crap." She reached for him, then hesitated. Nothing might happen if he casually touched her, but what if touching his wound ignited some sort of extrasense chain reaction? With the seeker demon's poison worming its way into his bloodstream, her touch could just hasten it along.

"My house is close. Can you make it?"

He pushed his back along the wall, getting his feet solidly beneath him. "I can."

She had her doubts. Thankful that she'd worn the padded bike jacket, she quickly pulled out her gloves and jerked them on, then thrust her shoulder beneath his, helping him along a couple of feet. "So did you lie to me about the whole immortal thing?"

"No lies, just not the whole truth. Besides, being immortal doesn't make me Superman." He winced. "Bullets don't bounce off and they hurt. I'd rather be run down by a rhino than take on another seeker. Nansee."

The old man just materialized out of the darkness. Rather quickly too, Kira noted. "Where were you during the fight? Thanks—*not*—for having our backs. I for one really would have appreciated the help."

"He can't directly interfere," Khefar gasped, handing her Lightblade back. The power enveloping the blade immediately winked out. "It's against the rules."

Rules? "Well, can he help you into my house or is that against the rules too?"

The old man thrust his shoulder beneath Khefar's, all but lifting the warrior off his feet. "You will have to release or ease your wards enough to allow me entry."

That brought a cold dose of reality back. "This isn't some sort of trick to get me to lower my guard so you can get the dagger, is it? Even if I remove the wards, there are other protections in place."

"We're not your enemy, Kira," Nansee said. "Surely we've proven that by now?"

"I don't profess to know how one of the Fallen or their Avatars would think," she replied, wiping her Lightblade against her pants leg. The pants were ruined anyway, a little demon blood wouldn't make it worse.

"If it would serve your purpose or trick me into trusting you, then I believe you would do whatever it takes, even destroying one of your brethren. There's little love among the Fallen."

"True." The warrior caught her gaze, held it. "I am a servant of the Light, Kira, a warrior like yourself. It is a duty I have performed for the last four thousand years."

"I don't know of any Shadowchasers who are immortal, with or without complications, despite the array of beings serving the Light."

Khefar gave her a small smile. "And how many Chasers do you know?"

"Personally? A few. It's not like Gilead holds conventions."

"True." He grimaced. "I give you my word that I will not try any funny business while I'm bleeding to death."

"Right." She quickly hobbled over to her bike, got it moving. The front fender scraped against the tire, the seat all but hanging off. If it was just a regular bike, she'd have scrapped it and bought another. "Nansee, can you tell if the seeker's controller is anywhere nearby?"

"He is not."

"Well, that's something, at least." She led them a couple of doors down to her converted home, disarmed the alarm, then ushered them quickly through the roll-up door then, as the metal door rolled back down, opened the door to her living area. "You can put him on the couch in the living room," she told the old man as she propped her bike up, then went back to re-engage the alarm. "I've got some medical supplies in the pantry."

Nansee stopped just inside the doorway to the main room. "There are no windows that face east in this room."

"Is that a problem?"

"If you want to damn his soul, then no."

She wanted to ask, needed to ask, but forced the questions back. Khefar didn't look good at all. The questions could be saved for later. He needed to be saved now.

She grabbed her general purpose first aid kit, then led Nansee and Khefar to the elevator she seldom used except for moving artifacts or heavy objects. There was no way they could use the stairs to get to her loft bedroom while nearly carrying Khefar.

The space had originally been two offices and a bathroom before she'd turned it into a large bedroom with a walk-in closet and spa bathroom with separate shower and soaking tub. Her bedroom had a king-size low-profile bed and oversized windows that faced east. The only other furniture in the room was a mahogany nightstand beside the bed and a matching six-drawer chest with a statue of winged Ma'at atop it, unless you counted the punching bag and yoga balls.

"This will work well." The old man helped Khefar sit on the edge of the bed. Kira could easily see the rips in the white T-shirt, and knew they didn't bode well. A seeker demon's claws were just as dangerous as their jaws, the talons loaded with a virulent and fast-acting poison. A Normal would die in less than five minutes. Would be dead by now.

"You mind telling me why this works? What the importance of east is?"

"Kira." Khefar's voice had thinned with pain. "This might freak you out."

"I'm a Shadowchaser. I don't freak out." But that was before she had two not-quite-human men in her house, touching her stuff.

"Good." He managed to pull the remnants of his T-shirt over his head, then lay back, grimacing in pain. The bullet, still lodged inside him, had made a slightly ragged quarter-sized hole in his shoulder. Furrows were etched deep into his right side, along his rib cage. Blood welled up from them, dark and thick and tinged with yellow.

Kira knew what that meant—demon poison mixing with his blood—but still decided to go through the motions with the first aid kit. She forced brightness into her tone. "You might be good, but that wound's not."

She handed one of Zoo's extrastrength charms to Nansee. "It's a healing charm. It might help."

The old man silently pressed the charm against Khefar's chest just above the demon wound. Kira tried not to stare at the amount of his skin displayed. The charm wouldn't counteract the poison but it would make him feel better. "The seeker's poison got into your system. It's corrosive and burns through your red blood cells, destroying them."

"I know." His breathing roughened. "I'm going to die in the next minute or two. But don't worry. I'll awaken as soon as the morning sunlight hits my body."

"What?" She looked to Nansee, who nodded. "What the hell kind of screwed-up immortality has you dying like some sort of *Highlander* rip-off?"

"It's part of the rules. Told you it was complicated."

"Your rules suck, big-time."

Khefar started to laugh, but it faded to a groan. She concentrated on pulling supplies out of her enhanced emergency kit so she could avoid staring at the wide expanse of skin showing above his dark denims. So much skin, skin she could touch. Except now he was dying, and while he and Nansee were sure that he'd come back to life, she had her doubts.

"I will take care of this," Nansee said as he took the box from her, his voice and eyes kind. "You took a nasty tumble. Perhaps you should refresh yourself, get off that ankle."

"I'm all right." That was a lie. Two days, two people dying on her watch.

"Kira." Khefar opened his eyes with effort, and focused on her. "I know you have more questions. So do I. I promise we'll both have our answers when the morning comes."

She gave him a jerky nod. *Questions, yes, thousands of those. They'll have to wait until after he dies and, I hope, lives again.*

"I need to go clean my Lightblade."

Chapter 11

Kira grabbed a change of clothes from her dresser, then used the elevator to escape to the ground floor. Her ankle would have made her limp down the stairs and shown she did need more attention than she was admitting. Already her body was protesting the simple demands she made of it, but she couldn't stop. If she stopped moving, she'd start thinking and she wasn't ready for that.

She quickly cleaned up in the half bath on the main floor, changing into soft cotton pants and a T-shirt and wrapping her ankle in a flexible bandage. After dumping her ruined clothes in the kitchen garbage, she began gathering the supplies to clean and purify her Lightblade and sheath.

The mundane chore of finding cleaning supplies couldn't keep her mind from whirling. Why was this happening, and why hadn't the Universe given her a head's up about it? Balm's extrasense was prescience; Kira couldn't understand why the head of Gilead didn't warn her about Comstock, the seeker demon, or the not-really-immortal warrior dying upstairs. Was it possible that Balm didn't know?

That didn't make sense to Kira. Balm always knew. She knew everything. But what if she hadn't known about this? What in the Universe did it mean for the head of the Gilead Commission to not know?

The Universe was a vast and mysterious place, impossible for any one person to know and understand. People spent entire lifetimes trying to understand earth religions. Those who knew about the Universal Balance, how the cosmos was aligned between Order and Chaos, Light and Shadow, and how every god, every thing, came from that source, could spend several lifetimes studying and not begin to scratch the surface.

Kira certainly couldn't begin to understand those she ultimately served, the Guardians of Light. Just as she doubted that even those Fallen into Shadow knew the full depth of the source of Chaos.

Of course, it was impossible to predict random coincidences, but believing the past few days were just a burp of fate would take the sort of mental gymnastics she knew she wasn't capable of.

Her mentor and handler had just happened to come upon an ancient Egyptian dagger. Egyptian weaponry was one of Bernie and Kira's special areas of expertise. He knew the artifact to be magical and therefore brought it to America—where Kira had the facilities to deal with it—instead of asking her to travel to London, which would have been easier for him if it had been merely a priceless object. A seeker demon and one of the Fallen had followed the dagger's trail. That trail had also led the dagger's original owner—the only being she'd ever encountered who was unaffected by her touch—straight to Kira.

That was the part she didn't understand at all. As far as she could remember, she could tell things about people by simply touching them, their lives replaying across her mind's eye like a disjointed movie of the week. She could pick up similar, if fainter, traces of people's lives from objects they had touched. The talent had grown as she'd matured. When she'd reached puberty, her "gift" had turned into a curse that had sent her adoptive sister to the hospital and her to Gilead. How could she have known that her ability to read people caused her to drain their energy, especially since she'd never met another being with her gift? She hadn't been able to safely touch another human being—except once, with Nico, under very special circumstances—since.

Until the Nubian touched her.

She gripped the edge of the counter. Now the Nubian and his—what, guide?—were in her home, upstairs in her bedroom. Not even Wynne or Zoo had been on the upper level, and now she had a man dying in her bed because he needed to be awakened by the morning sun. Kira liked to be awakened by the morning sun too, but the sun brought her to life metaphorically, not literally.

Kira grabbed a cold gel pack from the freezer, took it and her cleaning materials into the living area and sat down on the sofa. She put everything but the blue pack on the coffee table. Propping her bandaged ankle up on a sofa pillow, she placed the cold-pack on it. Kira looked at her hands as she adjusted the icy compress: they were shaking—and not from the cold. Her bare hands hadn't been that close to another person's skin since Nico had died in her arms, died because he'd wanted to please her. Now the Nubian prepared to face Anubis because he'd tried to save her.

"Ma'at, goddess of justice and order, is there a lesson here? Something that I'm supposed to learn? I have to believe there is. I have to think something more is at work. I have to believe these deaths mean something."

She knew the deaths meant something. She just had to find out what that something was. Which meant she had to find the Avatar of the Fallen who'd controlled the seeker demon.

At least they'd taken the seeker demon off the street. That was the only good thing that had come from the last two days. The downside was that if the Fallen's Avatar hadn't been taken out when the seeker demon imploded, it could possibly conjure up another one.

Nansee came down the stairs just as she began to polish her blade with a combination of metal polish and extrasense. She looked up. "So it's done? He's gone?"

"Yes." He ambled over to the chair and slowly folded his lanky frame into it. "You managed to clean your Lightblade, then?"

She held it up, sighting along the blade. "I normally let it sit overnight on a clear quartz crystal cluster on my nightstand too, but my bedroom's now off limits, seeing as how it was unexpectedly transformed into a morgue."

"This cluster?" He extended his hands to her. The quartz cluster, about six inches long, lay on a handkerchief in his hands. It looked like the one on her nightstand but she knew he hadn't had anything in his hands when he'd come downstairs.

"How did you . . . ?" She shook her head. "I'll just say thanks and, please, put it on the table."

Nansee placed the cluster within her reach, then

eased back. "If it makes you feel better, think of Khefar as falling unconscious from his injuries and needing rest to recover."

"Sure, let's give that a shot." She'd either have to believe him or call Sanchez to help her dispose of the body. Either way, at sunrise she'd know for sure.

Nansee ran a hand over his thick white hair. "I know this is not what you intended. Believe me when I say it isn't what he intended either."

"No, he just wanted his blade back."

"Of course." He gestured toward her own weapon. "If you'd lost your Lightblade, would you not do anything within your power to reclaim it?"

She looked down at the blade, gleaming with her extrasense. She could clearly remember the day Balm had introduced her to it, how it had been a prize she'd had paid dearly to earn. Earn it she did, through days, weeks, and months of hard training and harder discipline, and that made it all the more precious.

"This." She jerked her head toward the stairs. "This has happened before?"

"Yes, the last time was about fifty years ago."

"And I guess he always comes back, right?"

"Do not worry, Chaser Solomon. This is a tale that has been told before. Although the details may change, the ending is always the same."

He glanced at the open cabinets above her stove. "I notice that you have quite a collection of teapots. Does that mean you might have some rooibos?"

"Of course. How rude of me. I always break out the chai myself while I'm waiting for someone to rise from the dead." She dialed back her extrasense, placed her blade on the coffee table, and started to rise from the sofa to make her way to the kitchen.

Nansee quickly rose from his chair. "No, please, allow me. You need to rest your ankle." He beamed down at her. "And you still have your humor. That is a good thing."

"Keep my humor but lose my sanity?" She used a small burst of power to charge the crystal before balancing her blade on the points, then settled back down, shifting a pillow behind her back. Nansee had already removed the kettle from the stove and was filling it with water from the tap. He set it back on the burner to boil. "Don't know if that's a fair trade-off or not."

"You're not losing your sanity, Chaser. These are strange circumstances, to be sure, but really, you'd be more comfortable if you could just change your definition of death as it concerns Khefar." He opened a cupboard door and located the canister of loose red tea without asking its location.

"Sure, I'll work on that. In the meantime, are you going to tell me what's going on?"

"I can tell you some, but the rest will have to come from him." Nansee found two mugs and set them on the counter.

"Those mysterious 'rules' of yours again?"

Nansee smiled. "One might say so."

"Okay, let's start with something basic then. Why did he jump into my fight with the seeker demon?"

"It's what he does."

"Why? My extrasense protects me. He doesn't have that."

"His blade protects him."

That stopped her cold. "But he didn't have his blade. That makes it doubly my fault that he died."

"Kira." Nansee leaned on the counter that divided the kitchen from the "living room." "May I call you Kira?" She nodded. "This is not your fault. This is who he is, what he does. This has been his way for scores of centuries."

"Why? Why is he doing this? Why is he still alive? Why does he come back to life every morning? Is he a solar vampire or something?"

"His story is not mine to tell, Chaser Solomon," the old man said. "What I can tell you is that the Dagger of Kheferatum is his, a gift that became a curse he's had to bear for four millennia."

She stared at him, watching as he plucked a kente-patterned teapot from her collection. It clicked in her head then, softly and completely. "Oh my gods."

He turned to her, a decided twinkle in his eyes. "Yes?"

"Nansee. That's what he calls you. But that's not your name, is it? Not your whole name."

The kettle whistled. He lifted it from the stove, then poured a bit of steaming water into the teapot to warm it. "It is one of them. I've had many names over the centuries. A few of them have stuck."

"You're Anansi. *Kweku Ananse.* The spider god of the west."

He bowed low with a flourish. "A pleasure to make your acquaintance."

She had a real live demigod in her kitchen, making tea. She must have cracked or this was all a dream and she was still sleeping off the previous day's trauma.

"Funny, you don't seem like the trickster god of all the folktales."

"Times are different now," the old man said, his ever-present smile fading at the edges. He poured out the warming water, then spooned loose tea into her teapot. "Even gods have to grow up sometime. Besides, we are, at our essence, what people believe us to be."

"But I believe you're a god. Khefar *knows* you're a god." Bitterness flooded her, along with a healthy dose of anger. "So why didn't you save him? Why didn't you save Bernie?"

"Because all the higher forms of life are endowed with free will. And as such, some choices lead you to an inevitable conclusion, no matter how differently one may want the story to end. You, Kira, take risks every time you remove your gloves. Khefar knew that attacking the seeker demon without the Dagger of Kheferatum put him at a disadvantage. Your friend Bernie Comstock knew the dagger was dangerous, so dangerous that he decided to bring it to the one person in the world he trusted to safekeep it. Each of you knew the risks involved."

She clenched her fists, holding on to her power and her rage by the thinnest of grips. "But you could have stopped their deaths. You could have intervened. Any of you could have."

"Kira." For a moment the old man looked every bit of his supposed years. "Think about it. The Universe is about Balance. If a demigod who stands in Light had interceded on your behalf, what would Shadow have brought in to balance me?"

He was right. Of course he was right—he was a

demigod. Her body shook as her anger churned, needing a target, an outlet. Finally she just threw back her head and screamed, long, loud, and raw.

Silently he came around the counter and handed her his handkerchief, a tiny spider embroidered at the edge. The urge to laugh bubbled up, the remnants of releasing emotion. "Nice touch, that."

"Thank you."

She wiped at her eyes, wrestled herself back under control. "Well, since the Nubian isn't running down the stairs brandishing a towel bar he ripped off the bathroom wall, I can only conclude that scream wasn't loud enough to wake the dead."

"It was close. We'll have tea in just a moment more. Would you like toast with it, or do you have something else?"

He was being nice and it made her feel guilty. Gods were good at that, she supposed. "Just the tea will do. I don't think I could eat anything right now."

She tried to hand him back his handkerchief but he demurred. She thrust it into her back pocket, then blatantly changed the subject. "So, how did you, a West African demigod, get involved with a warrior from Kemet?"

"He fascinated me and since I collect stories, I wanted to acquire his. More than that, I like to think that I have kept him company all these centuries. No one should have to walk through this world alone." The demigod set the teapot and mugs on a tray and brought it into the living area. He set it on the coffee table.

"I'm sure he appreciates that." Her vision blurred over again, no doubt from the steam coming from the mugs as he poured the hot brew into each. Maybe no one should have to walk the world alone, but sometimes a person chose a solitary path because it was simply the safest way. Besides, in the end, facing final judgment, everyone was alone.

She wanted to go downstairs, sit before her altar, and commune with her goddess. It seemed a fitting tribute somehow, with a warrior of the Two Lands lying in state upstairs making his sacred journey through the underworld. *Ma'at, guide him safely.*

"Kira, have you ever been to a wake?"

She blinked rapidly. "No."

"Then let's have one, now. We can sit, drink tea, and I shall regale you with tales of wonder and awe . . . and bring you fresh ice packs."

A surprised laugh broke free, probably just as he intended. "You just want an excuse to share your tales with a captive audience."

"And here I thought I'd perfected the whole 'mysterious ways' persona." He smiled at her. "Drink your tea. I have a god's lifetime worth of history to choose from."

Chapter 12

Gold-white light pierced the darkness, the promise and potential of a new day. Next came the warmth, driving back the cold of death and night. Then came breath, the most precious of air. Light, warmth, breath—the triple gift of life.

Khefar dared to open his eyes completely. He lay sprawled on a large bed, his torso swathed in bandages. Blessed sunlight streamed through large windows, bathing the bed and giving the pale walls an airy feeling.

He turned his head, expecting to find the trickster grinning over him. Instead he found the Shadowchaser. She'd changed out of her layers of leather and into gray cotton pants and a white T-shirt. Curled up in a chair beside the bed, she looked so soft that he almost didn't recognize her.

She leaned forward as he stirred, the morning sun catching the tortoiseshell-brown flecks in her eyes. "You're awake."

"As promised, Isis be praised." He pushed himself upright. "Seeing you instead of Nansee is a most welcome change. Surely you didn't watch over me the entire time? And where is the old man?"

"Downstairs, preparing something he calls a proper resurrection feast." She shook her head. "And no, I didn't sit up here all night. Dealing with a dead man in my bed was a little much. Luckily I was entertained by a demigod who likes to be domestic."

"He revealed himself to you?"

"Once I thought about it, it was easy to make the connection. He decided to keep my mind occupied by plying me with tea and tales."

"That means he likes you." Which, thought the warrior, could be cause for worry. When Anansi took an interest in humans, especially women, things tended to go downhill fairly quickly.

"He didn't share any stories of you. Said they weren't his to tell." She stretched in the chair, bones cracking. "I'm curious about one thing—two, actually."

"Can I take the easy one first? I did just return from the dead, you know."

She didn't return his smile. Instead she seemed almost angry as she asked, "Why did you save me?"

"That's the easy question?"

"Just answer it."

"Why would you ask me that?"

"Because I need to know why." She rose . . . and he saw his blade grasped in her hand. "You didn't have your dagger and your immortality is, as I now understand, complicated. I had my blade and my extrasense, yet you decided to help me. Why?"

Danger thrummed through the air, heavy and potent. Her easy stance proved that she knew how to fight, both with a weapon and without—something he was already aware of, considering she'd come through a tussle with a seeker demon with nothing more than a twisted ankle.

"I didn't decide to save you, I just did. Fight, defend, protect. That's the warrior's way."

"The warrior's way is also to kill, destroy, pillage." She held up the dagger. His dagger. "Especially with a blade like this one."

"Blades such as that one are dangerous in their own right," he told her. "Even a good person could be turned by that dagger."

Skepticism shone plain in her expression. "Is that what happened to you? Were you turned by this dagger?"

"I was turned by my anger."

"Really?" Kira tossed her braids over her shoulder with a practiced gesture as she crossed to the bed. "Your blade showed me how it came to be in your possession, gifted by a High King of the Two Lands. Your blade also showed me how you destroyed an entire village, then kept on killing, century after century. Your blade also calls itself the Dagger of Kheferatum."

Khefar sighed. "My blade apparently talks too much."

In a blink, the tip of the blade pressed against his throat. He felt a slight sting, knew that she'd nicked him. Deliberately too, given how steady her arm was, how flat her eyes, the slight curve of her mouth. He had no doubt that if he so much as sneezed, he'd be dead. Again.

The dagger gleamed in the sunlight as she turned it slightly. "The magic in this blade is unprecedented," she whispered. "The power of Kheper combined with the might of Atum, bonded by centuries of bloodshed. No wonder mystics and alchemists and the power hungry have searched for it. I don't know if I could defuse its magic. I don't even know if I'd want to."

This isn't good. This was twice the warrior knew of that she'd handled the dagger. Twice that her extrasense had blended with its innate magic. Already he could see the glint in her eyes, the response to the dagger's call. It meant she had incredible strength, more strength than she probably knew. The dagger killed the weak.

"Now it's your turn to talk," she said, her voice as flat as her eyes. "Tell me what I want to know. How did you come to own this dagger?"

"I was a Medjay warrior, commanding a group of archers for the king. I saved his favorite son, and he rewarded me with the dagger you hold. While I was receiving my accolades, I got word that my village was attacked. The men left behind were overwhelmed and killed. I lost my wife, my children, my mother and sisters. None were left alive. Even the animals were killed. I vowed revenge, to deal what had been dealt to me. And that is what I did."

The blade at his throat moved back scant centimeters. "You found the men who raided your village?"

Four thousand years may have dulled the images in his mind, but his heart had never forgotten the pain, the anger, and the need for vengeance. "I found their villages, and I destroyed them. I made sure there would be nothing left. Nothing. And, when I was done, there was nothing. I destroyed their families and their homes, slaughtered their livestock, burned the fields, and then salted the soil so that nothing would ever grow again."

"That was more than avenging your family. That was annihilation. That is almost Shadow worthy."

"I am not of Shadow."

"So you tell me. So the spider tells me. But I don't know that, do I? I don't know what would happen were I to give you this dagger back."

She shifted the blade slightly. "Do you know how amused your dagger is to be on this side of you?" she asked casually. "It is thirsty and you have been stingy in letting it drink. It just wants blood; it doesn't care whose."

"And that is why I need it back," he said, forcing his tone to remain even. His muscles tensed with the need to leap up, to wrestle the blade from her. That would leave one or both of them dead. Words would have to work, and he had never been good with those. "It is a dangerous weapon and shouldn't be held lightly."

She snorted. "You think this is light? Tell me, Mr. Semi-Immortal, would you stay dead if you were killed by your own blade?"

He took a gamble, hoping to shock her enough to break the dagger's hold. "I didn't know Shadowchasers had a cruel streak. Where do you really stand on the Universal Balance, Kira Solomon?"

Surprise arced across her face. She drew back, her eyes sweeping from him to the dagger to her grip on its handle and back again.

"This wasn't my intent," she whispered, a tremor sweeping through her arm. "I wanted to give it back. Threatening you, holding the dagger to your throat—I didn't want to do this. But I can't seem to loosen my grip. Can you, can you take it from me?"

He brought his hands up, wrapped his fingers around hers. She gasped softly at the contact, but allowed him to ease her grip.

Finally, finally. The dagger was his again.

Her entire body shook like she'd just come in from the cold without a coat. He brought himself up to a sitting position and placed the dagger out of sight beneath his pillow. Her eyes followed the movement, her expression flush with hunger.

He squeezed her fingers and her gaze snapped back to his. The hunger remained. He could tell she craved both the dagger and his contact. Which did she want more?

"You reacted so bizarrely yesterday, when I grabbed your wrist. Why?"

"I told you that my extrasense allows me to read people and objects," she explained, staring intently at their hands. "I also use it to defuse magic and to protect myself from hybrids and Shadowlings. Unfortunately my power can also drain energy, so I haven't touched another human being for a long time. Most of the touching I do these days is cataloging artifacts or to kill or subdue those from Shadow."

What is that like for her, he wondered, *touching only to kill?* "I'm sorry. I know what it means to be in this world, yet apart from it."

Her fingers tightened on his. "But you don't know what this is like, what this means. How are you able to touch me?"

"I don't know."

"You don't know? What do you mean, you don't know? All my life I've been waiting for someone I can touch without putting them into a coma and—" she broke off, pulling out of his grasp and spinning away from him.

"Kira." He held a hand out to her when she turned around. She gawked at it like a wary animal, then slowly approached to slip her hands into his. He stroked over the back of her hand with his thumb, noting the tremor of her fingers. Though all he'd wanted in four thousand years was to reach the end of his penance, he hadn't been a monk. To never be able to touch another was incomprehensible to him.

"I don't know why you can touch me and not take my thoughts and my memories, or drain my energy. It could simply be because I've lived and died a thousand lifetimes. I am unique, as are you." He shifted his hand so his fingers slid between hers. "Does the how and why of this matter so much or is the important thing the fact that you can?"

"Yeah. Well." She glanced away, pulled her fingers from his, stepped back. "Anansi brought a change of clothes and some other things in for you. I put the bag in the bathroom through there." Kira pointed at the door to the bathroom. "When you're done, come downstairs. We'll eat and talk some more."

He stopped her before she made it to the stairs. "You asked me why I risked my life to save yours."

She paused, but didn't turn around. "So I did. And so you told me."

"No, not all of it. There is more. In taking my vengeance, I became a monster. Even after that, my pain didn't diminish. I became a mercenary, living only to fight, to inflict a measure of the pain I endured. I wanted the world to weep as my soul wept."

She turned slightly toward him, eyes and voice soft as she spoke. "To bleed as your loved ones bled."

"Yes. And had I continued on my destructive path, I might have become an Avatar to be filled by one of the Fallen. But the Light intervened."

"What happened?"

"I was killed. My soul rose from my body and I could see the carnage around me, carnage I had wrought. My soul cried then, for a completely different reason. It was then that I saw Her."

"Who?"

"Isis, Mother of All. She told me that the scales of my life were tilted in favor of Shadow, but it had been decided to give me a chance for redemption. All I had to do was save a life for every one that I had taken, either by my own hand or from directing armies, though I was not to know beforehand which lives counted to my tally. Only then would I be allowed to join my family in the Light."

"How many did you have to save?"

"Sixty-four thousand, eight hundred and thirty-one lives."

"And how many are left, after four thousand years?"

"Two."

The word hung in the air between them, crystalline.

Finally she nodded. "Thank you," she said quietly, not looking at him. "For saving me."

She left. He got out of bed, reaching beneath the pillow for his dagger. The glyphs gleamed in the sunlight. "You've given me a lot of trouble," he said to the dagger. "But you will remain my burden to bear a while longer. And so will the Shadowchaser."

Chapter 13

The spider god looked up as Kira returned. "Is our sleeping beauty awake?"

She nodded, wondering if he knew what had transpired upstairs, how tempted she'd been. By the blade and by the man. "As you said he would be. As he himself promised."

Her forward motion slid to a halt. Anansi had set three places at her coffee table, denoted by three of her Moroccan floor cushions. A strip of mudcloth contrasted the oak of the table and the pale color of her serviceable dinnerware, making both look better than they really were. Brightly patterned cloth napkins were tucked beside each setting, the silverware atop them gleaming like actual silver. Her sunflower teapot and a carafe of orange juice flanked a clear vase filled with bright red flowers.

Kira's stomach fluttered at the orderly domesticity of the scene. Her coffee table had often served as her dining table when it wasn't a bookshelf or worktable, simply because a formal dining table was an unnecessary piece of furniture for someone who never had guests.

That wasn't the strangest part of the tableau, however. That distinction belonged to the spider god.

Anansi stood at her cooktop wearing a bright red apron that read "Kiss the Cook" in white script, except that the last word had been crossed out and replaced by "Gods." Kira most decidedly did not own an apron like that—or any apron, for that matter.

Her stomach growled loudly, responding to the aromas of pancakes, sausages, and eggs. "Where in the world did all this food come from?"

"Your refrigerator."

"Impossible. My fridge is filled with energy drinks, a wilted head of lettuce, and cheese past its prime. I certainly didn't have eggs and sausages."

Anansi deftly flipped an egg over. "That's because you didn't believe you did. I believed you had the ingredients I needed and so you did."

She pressed the heel of her hand to her forehead, wishing she'd taken another dose of Zoo's healing herbs last night. She should have known bantering with a demigod would leave her with a headache. After a night listening to folktales and this morning's struggle to return Khefar's dagger, she was way off her game.

"Are you all right, Kira? I've brewed up a pot of coffee. Jamaica Blue Mountain, fresh from the roaster."

"How did you . . . never mind. I don't want to know. I'll just quietly stand here and freak out."

He glanced at her as he slid the over-easy egg onto a plate. "Why would you freak out on a good morning like this? The seeker demon's gone, Khefar has awakened, and breakfast is almost ready."

"Fighting a seeker demon doesn't freak me out. Having an ancient warrior rise from the dead in my bed doesn't freak me out. But having a demigod in my kitchen making breakfast . . . and that apron? Yeah, that strains my brain a bit."

"Why?"

"Why?" She blinked at him as he brought the plates over to the table. "You're a god."

"You've met them before. You talk to Ma'at quite often."

How does he know that? "Yeah, but she doesn't come to breakfast."

"Have you invited her?"

Her mouth opened and closed several times, but her brain refused to process speech. Finally she found a mouthful of words. "It doesn't work that way."

"Pity." He returned to the kitchen for maple syrup. There hadn't been any maple syrup in her house when she'd gone upstairs. "The old ones are sticklers for pomp and ceremony. Part of the reason why so many were lost in the sands of time—some quite literally. Much better to live on by changing with your worshippers, or finding new ways to survive. For instance, when I gave Al Gore the inspiration for the Internet . . ."

"Stop antagonizing her, old man. We've strained her hospitality as it is."

Khefar made his way into the living room. In his jeans and boots with his white T-shirt showing off every muscle, he hardly looked like a centuries-old Medjay warrior. At least, not until you noticed the dagger strapped to his left hip.

She focused on him. "I hope you're hungry. Our friendly neighborhood demigod cooked enough food for a small army."

"Good thing we're a small army."

They settled at her coffee table. She got about two bites into the best pancake she'd ever tasted when she recalled his words. "What do you mean, we're a small army?"

Khefar had already inhaled half his loaded plate and a glass of juice. Resurrection obviously made one hungry. "I've decided to help you stop whatever controlled the seeker demon, be it Adept, Avatar, or Fallen."

"Why? Adepts don't have the power necessary to manage seeker demons. If one was stupid enough to try, the backlash of the seeker's death took him out."

"Probably. Besides, you don't believe it was an Adept and neither do I."

She didn't. Not with the kind of control the seeker had been under. That didn't come from someone new to channeling Shadow. "What do you know about Shadowlings anyway? Sounds like you've been doing your own thing for the last four thousand years, not exactly standing with the Guardians of Light."

"Isis, like Ma'at, is aligned with the Light," he told her. At her questioning glance, he added, "I saw your statue of the Divine Truth in your bedroom. As I said before, my Lady Isis set me upon this course four millennia ago. In that time, I have known and forgotten much more than you can conceive of."

"I can conceive of a lot, show-off." She shrugged. "But please, feel free to share with the unenlightened what you do remember."

He gave her a sharp look, then poured more juice. "I know that the Fallen are the offspring of Chaos, present at the first battle between Light and Shadow with the balance of the Universe at stake. I know that when Shadow lost, its children ripped the very fabric of reality to get away, losing corporeal form in the process. When they Fell to this plane of existence, the only way they could take physical form was by taking over willing or corrupted humans as their Avatars. Lesser children of Shadow and Light also came through the Veil and, unable to return, blended and bred with the Children of Man. Humans and hybrids fall on both sides of the Universal Balance, but Shadow will always strive against Light. Fallen will always seek to regain what they have lost, even if it means ripping this reality apart. That's why Shadowchasers are needed and that's why you need my help."

She gave him a polite golf clap. "So you know your history, but you know little about me. What makes you think I need the help?"

He put his fork down. "It's not a question of whether I think you need the help. It's your risky behavior that I'm concerned with."

"Excuse me?"

"I spoke clearly enough."

"Maybe I just wanted to see if you'd dare say it again."

"Children, please," Anansi interrupted. "As entertaining as this conversation is, can you not wait until after breakfast? A demigod likes to know he's at least appreciated, if not worshipped."

"Fine." Kira stabbed a defenseless sausage with her fork, then ripped into it with a satisfying click of her teeth. *Risk. I'll show him a thing or two about risky behavior. Like insulting someone in her own home isn't risky?* "No offense, Nansee, but while I'm sure Mr.

Almost Immortal here has no problem hanging around with a demigod, I'm not looking to take on sidekicks." She forked a bite of pancake into her mouth.

"Sidekick?" Nansee spluttered. "Sidekick?"

"I'm not a sidekick," Khefar interjected smoothly. "Neither is he. I recognize your warrior spirit beneath the reckless demeanor—"

"Reckless demeanor?"

"And I believe that if we combine our forces and expertise, we'll eliminate this Shadowling sooner rather than later."

She tightened her grip on the fork.

The demigod noticed. "Kira."

She forced herself to relax at Nansee's gentle admonition. "It's not like it would do permanent damage if I stabbed him with it, Nansee. He'd only be dead for another twenty-four hours or so." She glared at Khefar. "Unless I bury him beneath Turner Field. You do stay dead if no sunlight hits you, right?"

Khefar frowned. "Why are you wanting to harm me? My offer makes perfect sense."

"So now I'm reckless and insensible?"

Anansi sighed. "Khefar, what Kira is trying to tell you—"

"Is that I can speak for myself, think for myself, and act for myself. I am a Shadowchaser."

"Who works," Khefar said as he swirled his last bite of pancake in the syrup on his plate, "with the support of a secretive international paramilitary organization with near unlimited resources, not to mention highly trained handlers assigned to each Shadowchaser." The forkful disappeared into his mouth.

"That's a mouthful of adjectives." Blood throbbed between her ears. "So a demigod can't antagonize me in my own house, but an octogenarian to the nth degree can?"

The Nubian's lips twisted. "Kira—"

"I don't know why you're in such a hurry to work with me anyway," Kira said. She put her fork down. Her mood had so soured that not even god-made pancakes and syrup could get her back to her sweet and happy place. Not that she knew where that was anymore. "People who work with me have a tendency to end up dead. So I'm not exactly into the whole partnership thing right now."

Was that regret flashing across his face? "I didn't handle this well."

"No, you didn't." She pushed to her feet. "Okay, let's go."

"Where are we going?"

"I'm going to the section chief's office of that 'secretive international paramilitary organization with near unlimited resources' to make a report and a requisition a new phone. You're going anywhere but there or here."

"Still no trust?" He didn't sound surprised.

"To be in my house while I'm not here, especially after the discussion we just had? No. I don't trust anyone for that and neither does my house. You got your dagger back and that's all you really wanted, isn't it? So come on, everybody out of the pool."

"I can drive you to the Commission's headquarters. It's the least I can do as apology for my rudeness."

She dragged to a stop. "Say what?"

"Your bike is damaged, remember? How else will you get to Gilead's offices?"

Damn. She hadn't thought of that. She didn't have time to make the necessary repairs either, even if she'd had the parts. Still, there was no way that she'd introduce Sanchez to the Nubian. Too many questions would follow, and she already had enough paperwork facing her over the seeker demon.

"Actually, I could use a ride. To the MARTA station."

His smile froze. "The what?"

"Our public transit. I can hop a train to downtown. The section offices are in Midtown. I'll get there without worrying about traffic or my carbon footprint."

"All right. I'll accompany you."

Now her smile froze. "No. Absolutely not."

"Why not?"

"How am I supposed to explain you to Gilead?" She pointed to Anansi. "How am I supposed to explain him?"

The demigod smiled beatifically as he bit into a bite of egg and sausage. "The Shadowchaser has a point."

"Of course she does. She always does." Khefar turned back to her. "Anansi will be fine left to his own devices, as most gods are. I will come with you on the MARTA, and see you to Gilead's doors."

"Why?"

"What do you mean, 'why?'"

"Why decide to help me and why accompany me to Gilead's offices? I'm not some wet-behind-the-ears Adept. I've been Chasing for a while now. I don't need a babysitter and yet you insist on playing bodyguard. Why?"

He looked away, and she wondered if he was going to lie to her. If he did, she'd be done with him and the spider god, even if it meant losing out on breakfasts like this.

Finally he looked up at her, his eyes clear with purpose. She realized then that she was still standing while he knelt on the cushion, and it suddenly felt familiar, as if she'd caught a glimpse of something much like this from her time with his dagger. It felt as if it was a scene one of them—or both of them—had played out before.

"Kira Solomon. You did not have to offer your hospitality after the fight with the seeker demon, yet you did. You did not have to return my dagger to me and yet you did. The Avatar who controlled the seeker demon is still out there and no doubt unhappy with the seeker's destruction. He will come for you and do everything in his power to destroy you. I would return the kindness you have shown me in the only way that I know how, by offering to help you and protect you until this threat passes."

By the gods, that was eloquent—and effective. Damn it! "All right, you win. This round anyway. Just stay off the Commission's radar, okay?"

He nodded, then turned to Anansi. "What will you do, old man?"

"A bit of traveling, as I usually do," he replied with a grin. "Perhaps I'll ride this MARTA myself. There are bound to be many interesting people there. I dare say I am one of the few demigods who is truly a people person."

She put her head in her hands. Any other time she

would have been fascinated by the presence of a demi-god walking around as Anansi did. She began to wonder if the old man just *thought* he was the spider god. But delusional psychosis wouldn't explain how he'd managed to conjure up so much food—or the apron or the flowers—and the Nubian vouched for him too. Either Nansee was the demigod he claimed to be or he was a crazy man with magical powers. Either way, the city was screwed.

"This happens all the time," Khefar assured her. "He'll be fine."

"I'm sure he will. It's the city I'm concerned with."

She had to trust them. No other options presented themselves and she certainly wasn't about to let either of her guests have free rein of her house when she was out and about working. Still, the idea of turning Anansi loose on the city made her teeth ache.

"I promise to be on my best behavior."

"That's exactly what I'm afraid of."

"I simply mean to explore this new town of yours." He gathered everything off the table, two, three, four hands grabbing. Kira decided to stop counting and not look as he made his way to her kitchen. "As much as I enjoy the islands, this city has such fascinating stories to share. Who knows? I might decide to stay here when all is told and done."

Khefar's hand shot out and wrapped around her wrist—the only indication she'd instinctively tried pulling her Lightblade. The Nubian leaned forward, a warning looming in his eyes. "Trickster god, remember?"

Oh yeah. She settled back, dropping her hand from her blade. She could handle whatever the Universe wanted to throw at her, even the overly curious demi-god loading her dishwasher. "Is he always like this?"

"Yes. I would say you get used to it, but you don't." He eased his hold, then stood. "We should get going before your goodwill is further eroded."

Chapter 14

"Nice ride," Kira commented, sliding into the leather bucket seat of the Charger. "Did a lot of custom work?"

"A little," Khefar admitted. "It came with the street performance package, but I called in a couple of favors to do it up right. It'll pass a cursory look by the police, but it's got serious horsepower attached to it."

"You know I have more questions for you, right?" Kira asked, trying to settle into the seat as he pulled away from the curb. She missed her bike, and even the open window and sunroof couldn't compare. "What have you been doing for the last dozen centuries?"

"Wandering the world," he said, hands sure on the wheel as he headed for the city proper. "I've been everywhere and seen everything. Experienced enough to know most humans are good people as long as they think they have all they need. It's when they realize that there's more—that they want more—that troubles begin."

"So the cause of mankind's ills is covetousness?"

"Exactly."

"I suppose I can see that. And it must be hard for you, to see pockets of your homeland devastated."

"Not all of Africa is devastated, Kira. There's good

to balance the bad. The same is true here and in Europe. There are good and bad people everywhere."

"Tell me about some of the people you've met. I studied ancient civilizations at university with a focus on the Intermediate Period of Egypt. I can't imagine how much better my papers would have been had I had you as a resource."

He turned north on Peachtree, following her directions to the Midtown section of Atlanta. "Your professors probably wouldn't have accepted or believed my version of history. Besides, I've forgotten more than I can remember. The first millennium passed in a blur. I spent some of my early immortal life in a cave, venturing out only to forage for food. I do not know how long I did this. Then I met Anansi, who told me that my task could not be completed if it was not begun. So I left my cave and went out into the world."

She couldn't stop a small sound of dismay. "Surely you kept a journal, artifacts, something! The amount of history you've witnessed—the Library of Alexandria, Cleopatra taking on Rome, the Kandakes of Meroë—surely there's something you can tell me!"

"I was Medjay, a soldier. Not a scribe. I had no need of reading or writing. Nubia didn't have a written language at that time. I don't think I needed to learn how to read or write until long after Rome came to power. Even then, sometimes you don't know history is happening until after it occurs. History is just ordinary people trying to live their lives and take care of their families and then something bad happens."

"But—"

"Do you remember what you had for supper two years ago on August twenty-seventh? Do you remember who you talked to, what they wore, what the area looked and felt and smelled like? Did you think that was an ordinary day, or something that should be recorded for posterity?"

"Okay, I see what you mean." She settled back into the seat. "Still, you're a living, breathing treasure trove of history."

"I am a man focused on saving people. I saved as many people as I could, from accidents, from burning dwellings, from hungry beasts, from drowning in floodwaters, from enemy troops. And so the centuries have passed."

"Do you remember the first life you saved for the Light?"

"What I mostly remember are the ones I failed to save, whether they would reduce my total or not," Khefar said, his eyes clouded over as he stared into the past. "I do not know if the lives I have saved have gone on to do things great or small. All I know is it is a burden that has been unending, like Atlas bearing the weight of the world on his shoulders." He raised his head. "I am not proud to say I am weary of this burden, but it is the truth. Yet I know I cannot and will not relinquish it."

"That I understand. I'm a Shadowchaser. No matter how I might wish otherwise, that's what I'll always be."

"What made you become a Chaser?"

"My adoptive parents dumped me on Gilead's doorstep after I accidentally put their daughter in a coma." She held up her gloved hands. "What else was I supposed to do? Massage therapy?"

"I don't suppose so." A smile curled his lips, then faded. "What happened to your birth parents?"

"I never knew them. No one could find any records. I don't even know what country I'm originally from. My adoptive parents raised me in British Columbia, then a brief stint in Greece before puberty hit and ruined my life. After that, all I knew was Gilead and Shadowchasing. Luckily for me, I took to Shadowchaser training like a crocodile to a zebra crossing. I'm good at my job. Sure, the hours suck and most of us die before we can take advantage of the retirement plan, but there are benefits. Besides, I like what I do. I like maintaining the Balance in this city."

Her hand dropped to the hilt of her blade. "You could even say it's a form of therapy. If I didn't have the Chase to relieve the pressure . . . well, I'd feel really bad for whatever city I'd call home. If they'd even let me out of Gilead, that is."

"Good thing you enjoy your calling, then."

She did enjoy it. More than that, she needed it. Needed the thrill of facing off with a skilled opponent, the thrill of the chase, the adrenaline rush of combat. The satisfaction of removing danger and pushing the Balance back to the Light. Of knowing that her presence made a difference in the world. If she didn't have this Chase, she'd probably turn Atlanta upside down until she found one.

She sighed. The perks that came with being a Shadowchaser—faster healing, speed, strength, using her extrasense as a weapon—would only last so long. Eventually her reflexes would slow, healing would be harder, fatigue would come sooner. As much as she dreamed of one day returning to the Petrie Museum or Comstock's antiques shop, she knew the odds were heavily against her living out her thirties. Any Shadowchaser who lasted longer than that probably wasn't doing their job.

"Is this it?" Khefar asked, breaking into her thoughts. He slowed the car. "Impressive lack of understatement."

Kira peered out the window. "That's Gilead East for you."

Midtown was a typical Atlanta mix of new and old buildings. The section offices took up most of the floors of the glass and steel midrise not far from the Arts Center complex. It housed some four hundred support and field personnel operating under the guise of a megacompany named Light International.

"Pull up about half a block down and I'll get out."

He eased over, then stopped. "Are you sure?"

"It's bureaucratic hell, but I'm sure I'll survive a couple of hours inside." She opened the car door. "You don't have to hang around."

He hesitated, clearly torn. He was being so . . . protective. It made her wonder if she was one of the last two souls he had to save before he could die and rejoin his family.

The honk of a car horn solved the dilemma for them. He thrust a card at her. "My cell number. Call me when you're done, and I'll come get you."

She took the card, thinking it strange that someone

who was around when the Twelfth Dynasty pyramids were being constructed had a cell phone. "Thanks."

"Be careful."

"Don't worry, cowboy," she said, hopping out. "I make it a habit never to trust anyone farther than I can throw them."

Chapter 15

Kira walked down the block to Gilead's headquarters, strengthening her mental shields as she went. Sanchez already knew she was coming to retrieve Bernie's effects. Still, she never liked entering the cold glass-and-steel edifice if she could help it. Too much bureaucracy, too many people—human and otherwise—just too much, period.

She felt the hum of the full body scanner as she pushed through the revolving doors. Part of the reason she hadn't wanted the Nubian to accompany her was because Gilead had all manner of sensors raking the lobby. Even if the revolving door didn't identify someone as friend or foe or Other before it completed its revolution, the other tracking devices would. She wasn't sure what they'd identify Khefar as nor what sort of reaction the dagger would set off, but she doubted he'd get very far.

Heads turned her way as she walked across the lobby. Her tan cargo pants and brown bomber jacket didn't fit in with the dark suits and black skirts of most of the people there, but then neither did the Lightblade strapped to her thigh. Most of the people walking across the marble expanse had handguns under their suit jackets. The man behind the welcome kiosk probably had something with a little more firepower.

He gave her a smile as she approached. "Welcome, Ms. Solomon. I've notified the chief of your arrival and called a car for you. The second elevator to the right."

"Thanks."

She turned, catching a few staffers averting their eyes as she headed for the elevator. It made her wonder what Sanchez had spread about her. Maybe the clone brothers had talked about her bike stunt with the hybrids. Maybe they just hadn't ever seen an actual Shadowchaser before. Maybe she really shouldn't give a damn what they thought.

She steeled herself on the ride up the elevator. It chafed her to know that Balm had spoken to the section chief about her. True, Gilead had to send directives concerning access to Bernie's files, but Kira doubted either Balm or Sanchez kept it to that. They'd probably been thick as thieves since she'd been assigned to the area. Why else would the section chief feel the need to criticize her at every turn?

The elevator slowed to a stop, then the doors slid open. A youngish suit took a step forward, got a good look at her, gulped, then immediately stepped back. The doors slid closed. Kira shook her head, disgusted. "Gods, people—we're on the same side!"

If people were afraid of her, she figured that was their problem, not hers. Shadowchasers were badass for a reason. The Special Response Teams handled run of the mill hybrids and Shadowling disturbances. Anything involving higher Shadow magic—Adepts or those practitioners strong enough to become Avatars, hosts of the Fallen—those cases were left to Shadowchasers. The specialized teams were consummate tactical professionals, but you didn't send mere humans up against someone who could make you turn on your teammates with just a whispered word.

The elevator slid open again, this time on the executive floor. She stepped out into another high-tech reception area, complete with circular desk and nattily dressed attendant. She was scanned again as she approached the gleaming chunk of metal. *Good thing I dissuaded Khefar and Anansi from tagging along.* She'd already considered the effect Khefar might have if he'd entered the building. Now just thinking about the response Anansi might receive strolling into the lobby almost made her break into a cold sweat.

"Welcome, Chaser Solomon. Section Chief Sanchez is waiting for you."

The attendant waved her toward the imposing dark double doors, which swung open as she approached. It wasn't quite akin to entering the lion's den, but it wasn't that far off from it either.

Sleek tinted glass and gleaming chrome dominated the section chief's office, along with a bank of monitors and a kick-ass view of Atlanta's skyline. It was an impressive display of power, if you were into that sort of thing. Kira personally preferred power that was a bit more organic.

The section chief rose and tugged on her smart navy blue jacket to straighten it to perfection. The severe bun of night before last had been somewhat relaxed into a tight ponytail. Obviously Sanchez felt comfortable here. The desk bore the usual accessories of an executive's office: monitor, multiline phone, high-end pen angled from a black onyx base all precisely placed. A digital picture frame was the only incongruous detail.

Kira gestured to the photo of a smiling girl, no more than seven, sitting on the steps of a cabin. "Is this your daughter?"

"My niece."

"She's beautiful."

"She's dead. Killed twelve years ago by a hybrid during summer camp."

"Gods, I'm sorry."

"Don't be." The section chief reached out a hand, fingers stroking the edge of the frame. "Every day her beautiful face reminds me of my purpose, my duty."

She smoothed a nonexistent wrinkle from her trousers. "I received your email that the seeker demon was eliminated last night. Good work."

"Thanks." It was far easier to be civil than not, and sending the preliminary report via email last night had kept her from focusing too much on the demigod or the dead Nubian. "Luckily it didn't do too much damage before I managed to send it back to Shadow."

Sanchez nodded, came around her desk. "Any ideas yet on what it was seeking?"

Kira shrugged, not ready to be completely buddy-buddy with the section chief despite what she'd just learned about her. "I figured it tagged Comstock for some reason, something he had, which is why it came to my door. The good news is, it picked the wrong door to come to. The bad news is, its controller is still out there. I'll make sure to file my complete report before I leave."

"What do you need Gilead to do to help you find the controller?"

Kira blinked in surprise. This was a completely different tack from the conversation two days ago. What the hell had Balm told her?

Sanchez smiled. "Comstock was one of us, Kira, and we always do for one of our own. He was a good man and I have no doubt that even if you weren't a Shadowchaser, you'd stop at nothing to find the person responsible."

"You're right. It's the least I owe him." Because she owed him, she'd dip into the bureaucracy that was Gilead. She didn't like the Commission's style, but that didn't mean that she was unfamiliar with it—or unable to work it to her benefit. Balm had taught her more than how to fight.

"Section Chief, my bike took some damage during the altercation with the seeker demon. I need to requisition temporary transport. I also need a new DataPhone."

"Of course." Sanchez pressed a button on her phone. "Get me Requisitions."

A beep, then, "Requisitions."

"I need an encrypted mobile DataPhone for Chaser Solomon, authorization Sanchez nine-one-four-alpha."

"Yes, ma'am. Right away, ma'am."

"Thank you. I also need one of our loaner vehicles prepped and standing by at the loading dock."

"They'll both be ready in half an hour."

"Good. Send the forms to my office."

"Understood, ma'am."

"Thank you." Sanchez smiled as she disconnected. "Being the section chief has its perks."

"I can see that. Thanks." It was becoming easier to

say. Voicing gratitude to Sanchez didn't exactly bother her; it was just an uncomfortable sensation, like an itch between the shoulder blades.

"The tech department can make any repairs to your motorcycle that you need."

Okay, that was too much. "Thank you, but that's not necessary."

"All right. Is there anything else you can think of?"

Since Sanchez was in such a giving mood . . . "I'd like Logistics to do a search on any fluctuations in known Shadow activity. I need the sweepers to report back on any unfamiliar power blips, no matter how minute. Something as powerful as an Avatar has to leave a trace."

Almost all of the people working in Logistics had at least low-level psychic ability of one type or another if not innate magic. They were tested as rigorously as applicants for the Central Intelligence Agency. If anyone outside of a Shadowchaser could find traces of an Avatar, the sweepers could.

"I'll assign a team to it immediately." Sanchez gestured to the door. "I have a copy of the forensics report for you, and the London office delivered Comstock's files. I had them placed in the conference room next door. We also have all of his electronic files and his personal effects recovered from his hotel room."

Kira followed Sanchez out into the hall. "Did they visit Comstock's flat, find anything useful there? What about the shop?"

"Unfortunately his solicitor denied us entry and since there weren't any Gilead markers of any type sensed in his home or the antiques shop, we had to comply. Apparently Comstock didn't take his work home with him, as least as far as being your handler is concerned."

A wave of admiration swept Kira. She knew the tech heads of Gilead wouldn't find any electronic markers, not with Comstock. Her mentor was too much of an antiques lover for that. If he kept any personal notes, they'd more than likely be in a hidebound journal and written in a dead language using quill and ink.

"The solicitor said that as Comstock's sole heir, you were welcome to review the contents of the flat once Comstock's assets are officially and legally transferred to you. You can probably expect a communication today or tomorrow."

"That's going to have to wait, then," Kira said, more than willing to postpone that task. "There's no way I'm leaving town while there's an Avatar still running loose."

Sanchez stopped outside another set of dark-paneled double doors. "It seems Comstock conveyed full knowledge of his duties and responsibilities to his solicitor, including the full nature of your relationship with him."

Ah, there was the old Sanchez. The one who continued to look for a way to cause her to bite her tongue. "The full nature of our relationship was that of mentor and student . . . and, as I only now know, Chaser and handler."

"Well in that case, perhaps there is one final bit of knowledge that your mentor can impart, something that will help in apprehending or eliminating the Avatar," Sanchez said as she swiped a card to unlock the door. "When you're done, just pick up the phone. I'll have everything transferred to the vehicle that will be waiting for you."

Sanchez left, leaving Kira alone with Bernie's possessions spread across the conference table. His suitcase and other items recovered from the hotel. A flash drive and several discs. A laptop. A pocketwatch. Three storage boxes, and one small, rectangular white cardboard box, completely nondescript except for the label identifying it as containing cremated remains.

Kira sank into a chair, knees suddenly weak. Bernie was really gone. It had been easy to set aside the dreamwalk as just a dream, to discount the Nubian, the demigod, and the seeker demon as quirks of her Shadowchaser life. Sitting here, seeing parts and pieces of her mentor's life so precisely arranged on the conference table, brought the loss home keenly.

Acutely aware of Gilead's monitoring capabilities, Kira took her time removing her gloves to use her extrasense. She had no idea what, if any, hits she'd get, but she certainly didn't want Sanchez recording her if she went sprawling. If it seemed like she'd received any sort of vision, no matter how fleeting, Sanchez would want to know about it, every detail. So, in Gilead's high-tech halls, she'd use her extrasense sparingly but with a liberal dose of pure deductive reasoning.

Kira allowed her normal vision to unfocus, concentrating her awareness on her hands. She powered on the laptop to start with the data files first, knowing they'd be more muted by the chill nature of technology. If she knew Sanchez, the section chief had already been through everything on the computer and the disks and no doubt had ordered a low-level psychic to review Bernie's personal effects. To do so would have gone against Balm's order and Kira would find traces of residual extrasense no matter how slight, but she knew Sanchez would take that risk. The section chief didn't appreciate being the last to know anything.

She hoped Bernie had left some sort of notation regarding when he had come into possession of the Dagger of Kheferatum, and how. The Nubian might tell her how he'd been separated from his blade. Then again, he might not. Not if the dagger had conspired to kill him so it could pass to someone else.

Kira wondered if Bernie had known about the dagger's true nature. He'd obviously known it wasn't a fake, but to travel across an ocean to personally put it into her hands? Bernie must have strongly felt it was better to give it to her himself and to keep knowledge of its whereabouts from Gilead. As an antiquities dealer, it would have been easy for him to catalog it as one of many magical artifacts in his possession.

There. A thrum along her extrasense, like a gently plucked guitar string. The power of bureaucracy was such that, even if Bernie had worked to conceal his reasoning for reaching out to her about the dagger, he couldn't conceal the travel request and projected expense form for his trip to America.

The original request had been made a month prior. Dimly she could feel Bernie's excitement as he'd completed the forms. Of course, as her handler, meeting with her was par for the course, but documentation still had to be completed. He'd left the reason for his travel deliberately vague, something he apparently had done every time he'd come to visit her.

The air shimmered before her eyes. The conference room faded, blended, re-emerged as a small paneled office. Comstock sat at an ornately carved Victorian desk, eyeglasses perched on the end of his nose as he peered at the computer screen.

He looked up, and it seemed as if he looked directly at her. "Hello, I've been waiting for you."

This wasn't like her normal visions. "Why?"

He smiled. "To help you, of course. The answers are there, if you know where to look. Since we're here, I'd say that you do."

"Bernie." How had he been able to do this? How had he known that he'd need to? Again she was all too aware of how little she actually knew about her mentor.

"I'm a composite of Bernie, your subconscious, and your magic, powered and manifested through your visions."

He tapped the monitor. "If you're in Gilead East's office, I would recommend that you not use your extrasense further, especially with my personal items." A grin: pure Bernie. "Not that I want to throw you across the room, but there's no need to let anyone who may be monitoring you know you've hit upon something, right?"

No, I don't think so, she thought. She didn't think anyone monitoring her could pick up on her visions, since even people in the room with her usually couldn't see them no matter how psychically skilled. They could pick up anything she said, though.

She looked at the monitor as he tapped it again.

He had a word processing program open. Four words in large block letters took up the entire screen: ENIG. KEPER. SAFE. NUBIA.

She had no idea what *Enig* meant, but she guessed that *Keper* referred to the dagger. *Safe* was rather obvious. *Nubia* must have meant the Nubian. The dagger was safe with the Nubian, but not with Enig. Was Enig the name of the Avatar?

"Nothing gives me more joy than to watch your brain work," Bernie told her. "You always were my best student."

Not only was Bernie helping her from beyond, he could also read her mind. She nodded silently, hoping he'd know that she understood.

His hands moved over the keyboard, deleting the letters onscreen. "I think that's enough for now. Any longer and they'll know you're having a vision of some sort."

She nodded again, knowing he was right. Bernie was doing his part to help. She'd do hers.

"I'll get to the bottom of this. I swear."

"I know you will, Kira. I know you won't rest until you find the Fallen responsible." His face grew solemn. "Which is why I hope you realize you don't have to do this alone. I told you before that there are those who can help you. Let them. Let him."

She froze, unsure which part of the construct was speaking now: Bernie, her subconscious, or her magic. Trust the Nubian? Sure, he had risked his life—and afterlife—taking on the seeker demon. The cynical part of her felt as if he'd interfered, not intervened. She would have finished the seeker if he hadn't butted in. It just would have taken longer.

Accepting Khefar's help was one thing. Having someone who could wield the Dagger of Kheferatum could only benefit her side. Trusting him was another. Trusting people meant letting them in, giving them a piece of yourself. All that did was leave you open for hurt. Kira had had a world of hurt in the last couple of days; she didn't really want to take on more.

I don't think I can do this.

Sadness filled Bernie's eyes. "You must try, Kira," he said as the room around him began to fade into darkness. "Danger is coming and you don't have a lot of time to prepare. Your life is at stake."

Slowly, so slowly, the darkness of the vision gave way to the flourescent lighting of the conference room, as if reluctant to let go. Kira blinked rapidly, then wiped at her eyes. *Yep, definitely can't do this.*

"Solomon?" Sanchez stood at the door, making Kira wonder if the section chief had been watching her the entire time on a video feed punched directly into her office. "Is everything all right?"

"Not really." She pulled on her gloves, then began gathering everything together. "Bernie's death, it—it's still too close and it's hard to push through the Veil here. I'll take everything home and conduct my review there."

Sanchez gave her an assessing gaze. "You'll keep me apprised of any information you uncover?"

Kira hesitated before picking up the box containing Bernie's ashes. "If I find anything pertinent to the investigation, I'll let you know."

"Very well." Sanchez stood aside. Two men in blue coveralls and gloves wheeled a cart into the room, then began stacking the files onto it. "Your new phone and vehicle are ready. I'll expect an email with your full report by the end of the day."

Kira nodded wordlessly, then headed for the door, clutching Bernie's ashes close. Even in death, her mentor made her think. She just wasn't sure she wanted to think the way he wanted her to.

Chapter 16

Khefar sat on the patio of a Greek restaurant with an unobstructed view of the Midtown building Kira had disappeared into. Just because he couldn't follow her didn't mean he couldn't do reconnaissance.

The Shadowchaser was, as they say, a piece of work. So much power packed onto her frame. So much anger and sadness. Frustration and impotence. He recognized it, recognized it all. He'd been much the same way four thousand years ago, after losing his family and village. There were times when he still felt that rage, the bleak misery, the inability to find the action that would make everything all right.

Anansi slid into the seat opposite his. "You really blew that, you know."

Khefar stifled a groan. "Thought you were out riding the rails?"

"How do you know I'm not?"

The waitress hurried up to him. "What can I do for you, Mr. Nansee?"

The demigod waggled his eyebrows. "So many things, my dear. Right now, I'll settle for lunch." He placed his order, a substantial amount given the feast he'd laid out at breakfast.

The waitress left, giggling. Anansi watched her

retreating form, whistled in admiration, then leaned toward Khefar again. "Now, let's get back to the task at hand."

"And that task is?"

"Trying to determine how you can stay in Kira's life long enough to save it. You need to change tactics, son of Nubia. That opening salvo over breakfast was disgracefully lacking in subtlety."

"I offered to assist her—"

"No, you didn't. You simply attempted to take over, convinced by your logic and reason that she'd instantly give in because you're right. Then, when she refused your counsel, you proceeded to point out her short-comings." Anansi sat back. "Not your finest hour, my friend. Since when did returning from the dead make you so grumpy?"

"I am not grumpy. I'm concerned with her safety. And I did apologize."

"Oh, I see. It was all part of some sort of psycho-logical maneuvering, was it? Have you forgotten when you served under Kandake Amanirenas?"

Khefar rubbed his forehead. "Yes and no."

"Did you learn nothing from dealing with power-ful women? Kira may not be a queen, but she has the spirit of the best warrior queens. How many people have you met who would take on a seeker demon with-out hesitation?"

"Not many. I know she can handle herself, Nansee. I'm sure she can handle just about any situation that the Universe throws at her and take care of it. But no one's taking care of her, and that's what concerns me."

The spider god looked at him for a long moment. It

was a look, part speculation, part discernment, that always made Khefar uncomfortable and served to remind him that Nansee was Anansi, and definitely not human.

"You did not ask me," said the demigod, "but if you did, I would say that offering friendship is the tack you need to take. She's a Shadowchaser and more than capable of facing down her enemies. What she is probably not capable of is making friends. Sound familiar?"

"Should it?"

Anansi snorted. "You have more in common with her than you think. She even has Ma'at as her patroness, you worshipper of Isis."

"I did not realize Kira was dedicated to Ma'at." Khefar had seen Ma'at's statue in Kira's bedroom but hadn't realized it represented anything other than her knowledge and love of ancient Egypt. "The Goddess of Truth speaks to her?"

Anansi solemnly nodded the affirmative, but his eyes twinkled. "It is understandable, great warrior. Between demanding your blade back, getting into a fight with a seeker, and coming back from the dead, you have been somewhat . . . distracted."

"All right, spider." Khefar slapped the tabletop lightly with his palm. "I will approach her in friendship. It's the least I can do for the return of my dagger."

"Good man, good man." The waitress brought Anansi's meal, three platters' worth. "You might want to go ahead and check out of the hotel, then. You can probably be back at her house by the time she leaves Gilead."

Khefar stared at the demigod. "I noticed you didn't include yourself. Do I even want to know your plans?"

Anansi grinned. "What human can dare to know

the ways of the gods?" He leaned to the side to get a better view of the retreating waitress. "I think I'm going to continue to savor the local flavor."

"Don't call me to bail you out of trouble, old man," Khefar said, standing. "In fact, if you do get into trouble, I think I'll call your father instead." He grinned. "Or I could call your wife."

The demigod paled slightly but perceptively. "You don't know how to reach her."

"Believe that if you want. I've read the stories too, you know. Have fun."

An hour later Khefar watched as Kira pulled up in front of her converted warehouse in one of those American sport utility vehicles that were supposed to blend in but instead stood out, especially in her emerging neighborhood.

He got out of the curb-parked Charger and followed her as she pulled into the garage, waiting until she killed the engine and opened the SUV's door. "You upgraded?"

"I hate this ugly thing," she said, getting out. "But I need transportation until I get my bike looked at."

"I would be happy to take you wherever you need to go."

"I don't need a chauffeur." She popped the hatch.

He decided to avoid what he realized was bound to be an argument he was sure to lose. "How did it go?"

"Better than I expected, probably because I suppressed my reckless demeanor." She reached into the cargo area and took out a small sealed cardboard box. "I've still got a bunch of stuff to go through."

"Do you need any help?"

She stopped, looked at him. He kept what he hoped was an open and friendly expression. Finally she shrugged. "Sure. If you could grab that storage box and bring it in, I'd appreciate it."

After she'd deactivated the protections to allow them through the door into the living area, he helped her carry everything in, following her through the living room area to a scarred and pitted wood table most people would have used as a dining surface.

"Anansi told me that you follow Ma'at."

Again she paused to stare at him. "I thought you knew that. You saw my statue."

"I saw it, but I didn't realize what it meant. What she meant to you."

"She called to me early, but I didn't realize it. I guess I was too angry then. Only when I began my training on Santa Costa did I understand it was Her voice that I heard. The more I learn about Her, the more I get to know Her, the more I became aware it was inevitable that I would stand against Chaos."

He nodded. "I think you're well-suited to each other."

"Thanks." She dipped her head. "I asked Her blessing while we waited for you to . . . you know."

"I appreciate that," he said. That she would do that for a stranger she wasn't sure she trusted touched him. "I tend to call that time sleeping without dreaming, but it's nice to have someone watching over me. Even nicer to have Ma'at's blessing. Isis is my patroness."

"Makes sense."

She headed back out to the garage. He followed.

"Of course," he said as she scanned the vehicle for anything she might have left, "the entire pantheon has had an impact on my life more or less, especially after I traveled north and became part of the pharaoh's army."

She closed the hatch on the SUV. "Now you want to be chatty?"

"I did promise to share stories. Besides, I want to make amends."

She settled her hands on her hips. "You want to stay here, don't you?"

He rubbed a hand over his braids, feeling sheepish. "If you don't mind, yes."

"Don't you have a hotel room or something?"

"Checked out."

"Why?"

"Because you're here."

"I don't need a babysitter."

"I'm not trying to be a babysitter."

She folded her arms across her chest. "What are you trying to do, then?"

"Keep you safe."

"And who's keeping you safe?"

He blinked in surprise. He had Anansi, but most of the time the demigod couldn't interfere. At least not when it came to direct conflicts. "Uh . . . "

"Uh-huh. You realize that if you answer, 'I can take care of myself,' you've lost your argument?"

"You got me." He walked to the open garage door, stopped, turned, and said, "I know you can take care of yourself and I'm sorry that I ever thought otherwise. I've seen for myself that you're more than capable of handling whatever comes your way."

"Well. Umm, yeah."

The warrior saw the compliment had clearly made her uncomfortable.

Taking out his car keys, Khefar pressed the button to unlock the Charger and exited the warehouse. Kira followed him onto the sidewalk and watched as he got into the car.

She moved closer as the garage door closed behind her. "What are you doing?"

"Getting comfortable." He eased the driver's seat into a reclining position.

"Are you really going to camp outside my door like that?"

"If I have to."

"It's broad daylight."

"The seat's comfortable enough."

"Liar." She narrowed her eyes at him. "I could just call the police."

He sighed. *Why did I think she'd make this easy?* "I'd rather you not."

"Yeah, I think I'm a little scared of what your version of resisting arrest looks like. But you can't stay out here. Come back around in the morning like a normal person."

"What if the Avatar pays you a visit? What if it conjures another seeker?"

"I gave you your dagger back, remember? If he conjures another seeker, it's coming after you, not me."

She was right. Another seeker would immediately go on the hunt for the dagger, since it had always been the target. Perhaps the better tactic to protect Kira was to draw the Avatar as far from her as possible.

He was about to turn the ignition on when she turned to the front door. "Come on."

He stared after her, wary. "You're inviting me in?"

"Call it my reckless demeanor." She unlocked the door, swung it open. "Come in before my rational self takes charge again."

Chapter 17

K hefar quickly popped the trunk open and got out of the car. He grabbed a duffel bag from the trunk and shouldered it. After locking the car, he followed Kira in. "Thanks."

"You want to thank me, you can pay me in information. Especially if we're going to be working together and all that. Have a seat." She gestured toward the sofa, then headed for the kitchen. "Want something to drink? There's water and energy drinks, and some of that juice Nansee had this morning."

"Water will be fine, thanks." The warrior dropped the duffel on the floor and sat down. "So you're okay with working with me?"

"Okay enough. I got an extrasense hit that the dagger's safe with you." She returned with two bottles of water and handed him one. "By the way, where is the old man?"

He accepted the bottle with a murmured thanks. "I'm not my sidekick's keeper. He comes and goes as he sees fit. He'll return when he's ready or should I really need him."

"Humph." She folded herself into the chair opposite him. "Must be nice, to have a demigod at your disposal as you complete your task."

Khefar laughed. "Anansi does as he wants, when he wants, as long as it doesn't upset Universal Law. My burden is my own and though he may tell me if the life I saved has placed me closer to seeing this eternity I've been condemned to end, he doesn't help me achieve my goals. Besides, why would you be jealous of one demigod tagging along with me when you work for an international team of metaphysical bounty hunters?"

She answered with a smile. "Your demigod is more entertaining than my bureaucrats."

"I'll give you that." He paused, then said, "What other hit did you get?"

"Excuse me?"

"You said you got a hit that the dagger's safe with me. As much as I appreciate the magical vote of confidence, I find it hard to believe that's the only information you gathered this afternoon."

She waved a hand toward the worktable on the other side of the room. "You saw all the stuff I brought back with me. I still have a lot of files to go through and I didn't want to touch Bernie's personal stuff while in the section chief's conference room. The only other thing I got while I was there was that the Avatar's name might be Enig. Doubt that's a real name, but it's all I've got so far."

"Enig. The name doesn't sound familiar to me, but I can probably dig up some information tomorrow."

"I'd appreciate that. We can divide and conquer some of this research, then regroup and come up with a game plan. We took out the seeker, so I hope we bought some time. My gut tells me the Avatar will probably be on the offensive again tomorrow, the day after at the latest."

"Twenty-four hours to find and eliminate one of the most powerful Shadow creatures walking the planet," Khefar said. "One who would probably stop at nothing to get the dagger." He took a sip of water. "I'm not a Shadowchaser, but I've come up against some of the second-tier halfings, the Adepts. Two of them cost me my dagger."

"How long ago was that?"

"Two months ago, in Germany."

"So somehow your dagger got from Germany to London in four weeks."

He turned to her. "How do you know it was four weeks?"

She set her water bottle on the table, still adorned with Nansee's mud cloth and vase of flowers. "As my handler, Bernie had to put in travel requisitions with Gilead a minimum of three weeks out. His records from the London office show he put in a travel req to come see me four weeks ago. Why would two Adepts want your dagger?"

"Why would an Avatar want my dagger?" He sank into the couch cushions. "The Dagger of Kheferatum. A pretentious name for a pretentious weapon."

"Is it sentient? The way it shared its history with me . . . it felt as if it was alive."

He rubbed his forehead. "It is. The dagger was already powerful when the king gifted me with it. You probably already know it was forged by priests of Atum and imbued with all the power of making and unmaking. My reward for risking my life for saving the prince's was to become the dagger's guardian. You know what happened after that."

"The destruction of your village." Her voice was soft, sympathetic. Neither of which, Khefar felt, he deserved.

"I fed the dagger's bloodlust, its need to unmake. In a way, I poisoned it. In my grief and madness I caused the dagger to become unbalanced. I've spent the last few centuries trying to wrestle it back to center."

"Have you ever thought about destroying it?"

He recoiled at the thought. The dagger sent a warning pulse too. "No, the dagger can't be destroyed, at least, not unless it's in very specific controlled circumstances. I don't know what those circumstances would be, because destroying the dagger honestly has never crossed my mind. I have to figure that any misstep in getting rid of it would result in the unmaking of creation."

"That's a lot of power," she said quietly. "And not only have all sorts of human and nonhuman people been looking for it for a millennia or so, now you've got Shadowlings after it too."

"It seems like it." He'd found and killed the two Adepts who had taken the dagger. He did not want to think about the dagger in the hands of an Adept and especially not in the hands of an Avatar.

She leaned forward as if she'd just thought of something. "Yesterday when we fought the seeker . . . "

"What about it?"

"When you took up my Lightblade, it still held my extrasense. You were able to use it as if you were me. You shouldn't be able to do that."

"Why?" He gave her a look out of the corner of his eye. "Did I violate some sort of Shadowchaser code?"

"Yes. No." She shook her head. "Look, Lightblades are bonded to the Shadowchasers who wield them. My blade is an extension of me, of my magic and my will. It's a protective measure so no one else can channel the blade's power. Anything of Shadow can't touch them—not without losing a limb or worse. At least, that's been my experience."

"I told you, I'm not of Shadow."

"I know that. So what are you, then?"

"I am a warrior, a master of weapons. Your blade knew that. It wanted to protect you from the seeker demon; it allowed me to use its power to save you."

"Wait. Are you saying that my blade talked to you the way your blade talked to me?"

"Your blade isn't as chatty." He looked down at his weapon, suddenly feeling tired. "Or as arbitrary."

"I think you're wrong."

"About what?"

"I don't think your blade is being arbitrary. I think it's challenging you."

"Challenging me? You might be right." He was beginning to wonder if he was still up to the challenge.

"Think about it." Earnestness lit her eyes. "Your blade is the very essence of Balance. Make and un-make. Creator and destroyer. Its nature is to be in balance. It's challenging you to get it back to center."

"You think so?" The hopefulness in his voice sounded unnatural to his ears. He couldn't recall the last time he'd felt something akin to hope. It had been too many years, too many lives ago.

She nodded. "Your blade could have called an Avatar to it when you were killed in Germany. . . . Man, it's so weird saying that! Anyway, it could have fallen to Shadow then, but where did it end up instead?"

"With an antiques dealer in London."

"With an antiques dealer in London who also happened to be a handler for the Gilead Commission. My handler. Do you think that was random?"

Khefar had seen his fair share of randomness over his lifetime. He'd also been around long enough to see patterns and purpose that most humans didn't. To him this seemed to have the hand of the gods in it.

"I think I need to go give thanks to the goddess."

She stared at him for a long moment, then stood. "Come with me."

He followed her to the table on which he'd earlier placed the box.

"This worktable is where Bernie first showed me your dagger and where your dagger talked to me," Kira said. She took a small white box off the table and clutched it close. "Bernie never made it to the lower level of my place while he was alive, so I'm taking him now. Will you get that other carton? Thanks."

Wordlessly, Khefar retrieved the storage box, then followed her down the spiral staircase to the lower level. They entered a large but cluttered office through a door she had to unlock. He could tell from the feel of it that the area was special. She might let visitors into the main level. In a pinch she probably even let someone use the bathroom on the uppermost level. He doubted that she ever allowed someone on this level.

"This is my main office. If you like, you can use this room."

He looked at the replica mural of Queen Nefertari at the back of the room. "You have a copy of a mural from the Valley of the Queens."

She smiled. "Would you believe me if I said it came with the place?"

The panel slid to the left when she pressed a hand to it. They entered a lighted hallway stocked with a wide variety of weapons, some of them of a type he'd actually used during his lifetime.

"You also have the Weighing of the Heart ritual painted on the wall back there."

"That's my altar room, sacred space. I think you'll understand why I don't let anyone else in there."

"Of course."

"This is my private office," she said, stepping into a smaller room. Overhead pot lights bathed the room in a muted glow, and a task light sat ready on the desk. He thought he'd seen plenty of books upstairs, but this room overflowed with volumes safely tucked behind glass doors. Khefar assumed that for these to be in a private underground office, the tomes had to be extremely rare or extremely dangerous. Probably a bit of both.

"My dagger remembers being in here," he said, dropping a hand to the hilt. One of the shelves of books actually weren't books at all, but a trompe l'oeil facade.

"I sealed it away for its protection and mine," she explained. "If you'd rather use this room instead of the outer office, that's fine. I have some incense in the desk drawer there."

"Thank you." He caught her free hand. "I mean that. You didn't have to bring me down here or offer me a place to pray. Thank you for trusting me with your space."

"You're welcome." She pulled away, wrapping her arms around the small box. "I'm going to go introduce Bernie to Ma'at. Why don't I just meet you upstairs when we're done?"

"All right. Thanks."

He lit a stick of incense, setting the burner on the floor in the center of the room. Kneeling, he cleared his mind completely, concentrating on his breath, his heartbeat, his soul, and gave thanks to his goddess.

"Hail, Mother of All, Luminous One who thrusts back the darkness, who illuminates every human creature with your rays, hail, Great One of many Names . . ."

After finishing his prayers, Khefar returned to the upper floor. Since Kira hadn't returned yet, he decided to make himself useful by heading upstairs to strip the sheets from her bed. His demon-poisoned wounds had seeped onto the linens. Other than the stains, he knew most people would be less than pleased to sleep with sheets someone had died on, even if he had also come back to life there.

He'd noticed a stacked laundry set tucked behind a pocket door in the master bathroom, but had no idea where clean sheets were and no inclination to go snooping. Instead, he put the linens into the washer, added detergent and bleach, and started the wash cycle, then retreated downstairs, hoping Kira would be back.

Kira looked up from a spread of the delivery

menus on the kitchen breakfast bar, staring up at the Nubian as he descended the stairs. She could clearly hear the rumble of her washing machine on the floor above. "You started my laundry?"

"I didn't take the sheets off the bed before we left," he explained. "I noticed the laundry alcove when I took a shower this morning, so I thought I'd— Hey, are you all right? Should I not have done that?"

"No, it's—it's all right." *Gods, with everything else going on, I'd forgotten he'd slept in my bed—correction, died and been resurrected in my bed.* She smoothed a hand over the quartz countertop, willing the cool surface to soothe her psyche. "I'm just, well, people in my house is new to me, especially in places I consider sacrosanct. Immortal men with domestic streaks will definitely take some getting used to."

"If it makes you feel any better, after four thousand years I'm still not good at any sort of cooking that doesn't involve meat over an open flame."

She laughed at that. "Then I suppose it's a good thing I have lots of takeout menus to choose from. Unless you're still full from Chef Nansee's resurrection feast?"

"No, I'm starving. What is there to choose from?"

They quickly chose a restaurant, then Kira called their orders in. She hung up the phone. "We've got about thirty minutes before the food gets here. So how about we spend it with you telling me everything you know about Shadowchasers?"

He took the chair she'd vacated earlier, stretching his legs out. She remained at the counter.

Khefar smiled. "I've just picked up a little bit here and there in my travels."

She laughed derisively. "Given some of the comments you've made, it doesn't seem to me that you've picked up 'just a little bit here and there.'"

"You're right. I've encountered a few Shadowchasers on my journey. You have been called many things over the centuries. I think the first person that I knew as something close to a Shadowchaser was called a Lightbringer and I met him some three thousand years ago."

"I guess Gilead has been in existence for three thousand years." Such longevity would go far in explaining why they seemed so set in their ways.

"Some form of Gilead has probably been around since humans had higher functioning capabilities," Khefar said. "Remember, your organization is based on maintaining the Universal Balance between Order and Chaos, Light and Shadow. That belief goes back to the dawn of humankind."

"So much for your passing knowledge about Shadowchasers," Kira noted.

"Like I said, I've been around for a while." He regarded her. "How long have you been with Gilead?"

"I bonded with my Lightblade when I was eighteen, so I've been a chaser just over seven years now." She hesitated. "I don't suppose on your travels you've ever met anyone with abilities like mine?"

He shook his head. "I'm sorry to say, but no. Are you looking for relatives?"

"Not really looking." She shrugged away an ancient hurt. "Never knew my birth parents and never found out anything about them either. I guess if you haven't met anyone with a gift of touch quite like mine, I must be one of a kind."

"We are each unique. Your skills have made you good at what you do."

"Yep, that's what I tell myself to get through." She finally edged around the counter, crossing to the coffee table to retrieve her bottle of water. "Where do you stay when you're not camping out on people's doorways?"

"I have a couple of places I like to stay. I have a small place in London, but the place in Cairo feels the most like home."

Cairo. Spitting distance from the Giza Plateau, and the Egyptian Museum in Cairo was home to the most extensive collection of ancient Egyptian artifacts on the planet. "I guess it makes you feel close to your family, your past."

"It does." He glanced down at his blade. "Cairo helps me remember."

"Remembering is important." It must have been hard for him, to have lived as long as he had, trying to remember a family he'd loved and lost so long ago. He didn't have family photos, videos, digital albums, or YouTube postings to help. All he had was his memory.

Kira was sure that part of the reason Anansi, the keeper of stories, accompanied Khefar was so that someone could remember when he couldn't. The spider god would keep the memories safe, as he had kept the stories of West Africa safe for centuries.

"You know what I think? I think a good way to remember is by telling stories. So how about when the pizza gets here, I'll pick a place and if you've been there, you'll tell me a story about your experiences there."

He stared at her with eyes darkened by memory.

"As long as you return the favor and tell me of your experiences in the places you've been."

She felt her smile freeze. Kira realized her effort to make him feel better—and she had to acknowledge his history fascinated her and she wanted to know more—had given him the opportunity to turn the tables on her. It would also limit her probing for more information.

All she had to do was avoid the dark blotches of her past. There were good stories in there; she just had to find them.

"You've got a deal."

Chapter 18

"A re you out of your mind?"

"Will you quit saying that, Wynne? It's getting a little old."

"But you're letting this guy stay with you. Staying in your house with you, Kira." Wynne shook her head. "How does someone who doesn't like people invading her space go from holding a gun to someone's head to inviting him in for a long-term sleepover?"

Kira looked over at Khefar, talking to Zoo at the shop's herb counter. Wynne's husband looked like he should have been behind the counter of a tattoo parlor, not a metaphysical store. He leaned over; his tattoo of a large owl clutching a gleaming crystal point stood out in brilliant color against the light olive of his shaved head. Both beefy arms were covered in tattoos, complicated patterns that only he knew the meaning of. He'd once told Kira the ink helped his magic and she saw no reason to disbelieve him. Having been the beneficiary of many of Zoo's spells, Kira knew the natural-born witch had great skill.

Despite his intimidating size and appearance and former duties as an Army sniper, Zoo had a warm soul, reflected in his soft green eyes. He was the kind of person who never met a stranger and he was a perfect foil for Wynne's frenetic personality. Knowing they had her back was a comfort, especially with Bernie gone.

The Nubian, at a seeming disadvantage of a couple of inches and thirty or so pounds, couldn't be mistaken for anything other than a fighter even in his long-sleeved black shirt and jeans. It was just the way he carried himself, the way he moved, with a leopard's grace and stealth. They'd shared a few stories last night, mostly positive stories of the lives he'd saved and the Shadows she'd chased.

It had been a natural thing to ask him to patrol with her, Khefar driving while she used her extrasense like radar, searching for any minute Shadow disturbances. There were precious few surges, not even Adepts raising power, making her wonder if the whole world waited for this one Fallen to reappear. Or, perhaps Gilead's suits were being some help with policing the paranormal populace, as Sanchez had promised.

Back at Kira's, Khefar had taken the sofa while she went upstairs to sleep in her own bed—after making it up with fresh sheets. All in all, not a bad way to end a day, though she had spent a good half hour trying to forget that the Nubian had died in her bed.

"A lot has happened in the last two days, Wynne. He helped me take down a seeker demon. And he really is the owner of the dagger. He's been a wealth of information that I desperately need. Besides, Comstock vouched for him from beyond."

"Which again has me questioning your sanity." Wynne's worried look hadn't lightened up.

"We stopped the seeker, not the Avatar. I need all

the help I can get on that score and he's got four thousand years of experience."

It was, Kira had to admit to herself, weird to have the Nubian in her house. Luckily he seemed to realize that and did his best to minimize his impact on her space. She'd been able to finish reviewing all of Comstock's items earlier that morning in her office without a bunch of interruptions. Though she had several new memories to hold close, no other clues about the Avatar had presented themselves.

Wynne leaned closer to her. "Are you sure you're okay? Comstock, a seeker demon, then this Nubian? And that old man is sorta strange."

Kira wasn't going to reveal Nansee's true identity. It was the demigod's business who he chose to reveal himself to. If she told Wynne the truth, her friend would probably see it as a reason to be even more concerned, not less.

"Come on, Wynne, it's a tactical arrangement, in place only until we can bring the Avatar down. Then life will go back to as close to normal as it can for me. Speaking of getting rid of the Avatar, how much longer do you think you'll need with that blade? Since I gave Khefar his dagger back, I'll really need to use yours as a decoy."

Wynne took one of the athames out of its display case to polish, even though it gleamed already. "One more day, two at the max. I want to make sure the magic is balanced inside it, so it's going to take some careful work with Zoo to put that down in the metal."

"We're going to have to make some sort of move," Kira said, trying to not let worry creep into her voice.

"It's been almost two full days and no hits on the Avatar at all."

"Do you think it left?"

Kira shook her head. "We wouldn't be that lucky. Not after he took the time to track the dagger from Europe. He's still here, still wanting the dagger. The fact that Gilead hasn't turned up anything yet bothers me too."

It more than bothered her. It was like the sword of Damocles hanging over her head, sure to fall at any moment.

Wynne sidled closer. "So, what's he like?"

"What do you mean, what's he like?"

"Oh come on. He's a guy; you're a girl. He's kinda easy on the eyes. And you said that you can touch him with no problem. You can say it's a tactical decision all you want, but you can't tell me you don't want the opportunity to get up close and personal with history."

"Gods, Wynne!" She had to force her voice down. *Trust Wynne to be completely inappropriate.* She had thought about getting up close and personal with Khefar—to pick his brain and corroborate her view of history, but that was far from Wynne's idea. "This isn't the time to be thinking about stuff like that!"

"There's never going to be a right time, Kira." The metalworker returned the athame to the display case, then looked up at Kira with earnest concern lighting her expression. "You have to make the time. I think even Comstock would want that for you."

She bristled. "Just had to go for the jugular, didn't you?"

Wynne didn't seem to care. "I'm your friend. I care

and I worry. You need to have some fun in the middle of all the Shadowchasing. You know, the whole Balance thing?" A mischievous glint lit her eyes, combining with the bright pink hair to give her a pixielike look. "Besides, if I can't verbally slap you upside the head, who can? You need to think about what I said. A girl's got needs. I'm betting a four-thousand-year-old hottie does too."

Khefar and Zoo chose that moment to join them. The Nubian held up a paper bag. "The witch has an impressive array of herbs and knows how to use them. I look forward to trying some of these out."

Wynne nudged Kira, then waggled her eyebrows. "Speaking of trying something out . . ."

Zoo grinned, clearly in on his wife's scheming. Khefar looked confused. "What?"

"Never mind. I need to drop a couple of specimens off at the Carlos Museum at Emory," Kira said. "You might like to check out their exhibits—it's the museum that returned the mummy of Ramesses I to Egypt and right now is working to expand its Nubian collection. I thought while we were there we could get a workout in at the faculty fitness center. The university allows me to use the facilities. You think you're up to sparring with me?"

Khefar smiled. "A sparring match sounds like an excellent idea."

Wynne nodded. "It's a great way to work off a little extra tension—"

Kira cut her off. "Let's get going while it's still early. I don't want to have to deal with traffic if we leave there too late."

Kira deliberately ignored Wynne's smug expression as they left. Getting a good hand-to-hand workout in with a warrior of Khefar's skill and incredible experience was something she welcomed, but she didn't want to think about the Nubian as anything other than a fellow fighter helping her eliminate a threat. She certainly didn't want to think about him in any sort of intimate way. She also knew that once the Avatar was taken care of, Khefar would be on his way to save his next soul and she'd be planning a trip to London with Bernie's ashes.

The drive from Little Five Points to the Emory campus was less than ten minutes, winding them through the tree-laden community of Druid Hills. Situated on a beautiful six-hundred-acre campus dominated by pink and gray Georgia marble, the university was known as much for its wide-ranging health care system as its research and education. The private university counted Salman Rushdie and His Holiness the XIV Dalai Lama among members of its faculty.

"It won't take me long to drop this off," Kira said as she turned off North Decatur Road toward the Fishburne parking deck. "The museum's just off the quad across the bridge. Then we can head to the faculty and staff fitness center in the Blomeyer. It's a pretty good distance down Clifton, so we may want to come back for the SUV after we leave the museum."

His expression soured. "Perhaps it will be better if I drop you at the museum's front door and wait with the truck since it won't take long."

She stopped the vehicle, turned to him. First he wanted to stick closer than her shadow, and now he didn't want to follow her into the museum? "You don't want to come in?"

"There's no point in me walking through relics of lives long gone," he said tightly. "Like viewing the remnants of a human zoo."

She blinked in surprise, then had to tamp down a sudden burst of anger. Given his history, she could understand his reluctance to view artifacts that might remind him of the life he used to have. That didn't explain the heat in his words, though.

"There's nothing wrong with museums or zoos. Archaeologists dig through the past in order to preserve it."

"If they wanted to preserve it, they should just leave it where they found it. Let the dead stay buried."

"But there's so much we can learn! For all that we know, there's so much more that we can only guess at. You yourself said that few people are aware of history as they live it. When archaeologists come along and discover these things, it's treasure to us. More than treasure, it's almost sacred. We get down on our hands and knees and scratch through decades and centuries of dirt and muck not because we want to put these things on display, but because we want to understand, because these things matter to us, these lives matter to us."

He sighed. "Look, I'm not trying to belittle your profession—"

"And I'm not trying to belittle your history. Most of which is lost to us, if you don't mind me saying so." She reached behind him for the silver transport case and pulled it into her lap. "Some of us think it's important to understand who we were and where we came from. To learn from the past in order to understand and face the future. Even those who have no clue what their past is."

"Kira—"

"I understand that it's hard for you. I just thought you might appreciate the museum's efforts at preserving your history. Just wait here; I'll be back in about fifteen minutes."

She got out of the SUV quickly, crossing the walk to the bridge that would take her to the Carlos. Embarrassment and a little hurt burned her cheeks. She thought she was doing a nice thing for him and he'd snapped at her instead. Last time she'd try to be nice to the Nubian.

Her step slowed as she crossed the bridge to South Kilgo Circle and the pale marble buildings that ran along the southeast side of the quadrangle green space. The Michael C. Carlos Museum sat between Carlos and Bowden Halls, with the Woodruff and Candler libraries forming the top of a T. Usually she loved the old trees and rolling hills, especially in afternoon sunlight, but Khefar's reaction bothered her more than she wanted to think.

She supposed she should be more understanding. His whole purpose for existing was to rejoin his family in the afterlife. Until then, he probably wanted no reminders of his former life. Seeing the Carlos's collection of Egyptian mummies and funerary objects as well as Nubian artifacts would only remind him of how far from his own world he really was. When he'd mentioned feeling at home in Cairo, she'd jumped to the wrong conclusion—ancient artifacts weren't a comfort to him.

Kira hadn't been back to Venice since Nico died. She'd told herself it was because her Shadowchaser duties kept her from returning. The truth was, it was too painful, even all these years later. Especially now, with the wound of Bernie's death still raw. No photos, no TV shows, no movies—anything that mentioned Venice had been excised from her life. If Venice was like that for her, what was seeing lifeless exhibits of preserved relics and remains like for Khefar?

She quickly dropped off the cleansed pre-Columbian artifacts with the assistant curator, then returned to the main floor. She thought about doing a quick run through the African and Egyptian sections to see if there was anything in the collection that might pique the Nubian's interest, then changed her mind. She didn't like being pushed; she was sure Khefar wouldn't like it either. Instead she headed for the door.

Something caught her eye, a flash of dark movement. She turned away from the entrance, making her way through the Greek and Roman sections and up the ramp that showed the path of the Nile. Veering right, into the Egyptian coffin room, she found Khefar staring at an ornate wooden sarcophagus from the Ptolemaic period. He'd dressed all in black today but the color suited him, just as he seemed to fit this place.

Kira stopped beside him, remaining silent for a moment. "I'm sorry for pushing you into something you didn't want to do."

He smiled at her. "Do you really think either one of

us can push the other into doing something the other doesn't want to do?"

"Good point." She relaxed, ridiculously pleased that the strained awkwardness between them had passed.

"You were right, Kira," he said then. "It's a nice collection. I'm glad I came in."

"Me too."

Khefar gestured around the room. "Is this where you work?"

"No. They already have a very established Egyptology department. I just do freelance stuff for the Carlos and other museums and private collectors, along with some independent research. Did you make it up to the top level where the Nubian and sub–Saharan Africa exhibits are?"

"I did." For a moment his lips thinned. When he turned back to her, his expression was carefully neutral. "You promised me a workout. You're not trying to get out of it, are you?"

She could have gotten whiplash from the abrupt change of topics. " 'Course not. I'm ready if you are."

They stepped back out into the afternoon sunlight. He started out down the quad back the way she'd originally come. As they reached the bridge, she asked, "Was that painful for you, seeing the exhibits?"

Khefar stopped, hands gripping the bridge railing. "Not as much as I thought it would be. It could be because my hindsight is extremely clouded and many of my memories have looped back onto each other and are no longer clear. Some, however, are as sharp as the day they happened."

Kira didn't have to ask which memories he meant. "Do you still remember them?"

He grimaced, staring over the side of the bridge to the creek below. "I've tried to remember their faces so I could have them painted and carry them with me always, but their images have been lost to me. Merire was my wife and she gave to me Henku, my firstborn, and Seneb, my youngest son, and Meri, my daughter and just as precious. Seneb was but three when they were taken from this life."

She didn't think about it. Kira just reached out, wrapping her gloved hand around his biceps, stopping him. He turned to her, surprise filling his eyes. She wondered if her expression mirrored his. She never impulsively touched anyone, but he needed the comfort and she felt driven to give it to him.

"Khefar. You have their names. Remember, as long as you can speak their names, they live."

He stared at her for a long, unfathomable moment. Then he lifted his free hand, covered hers. A brief squeeze, then he let go, digging into his front pocket to hand her the keys. "I parked this way."

She followed him to the SUV without a word, but the silence was a good one.

The Shadowchaser was an amazing piece of work.

Khefar changed into shorts and a T-shirt in the men's locker room, but his mind was focused more on Kira than on turning his shirt right side in. Kira had been so put off having him in her home even after they'd spent a night reconnoitering around the city, and yet she'd tried to comfort him. She'd touched him and offered reassurance and he was sure neither had been easy for her. It made the words, and the gesture, that much more precious. That simple act, those plain words, had beaten back the despair more than anything else could have.

Somehow, he'd return the favor. It had only been a couple of days since Comstock's brutal death. Kira held herself together by duty and determination; she hadn't even fully shared her grief with her friends at the store as far as he could tell. She was like a bow-string: taut, stretched almost to breaking, ready to let loose at any moment. He was an expert archer; he knew the strength, skill, and patience it took to master a powerful bow. Kira had already shown that she didn't appreciate his display of strength in at-tempting to help her. She was too mistrustful to yield to any skillful attempts to outmaneuver her. That left patience.

He sighed. Handling Kira would be much more difficult for him than trying to string Odysseus's bow had been for Penelope's suitors.

Kira was already waiting when he returned to the workout room. She'd exchanged her gloves for leather wrist guards and changed into formfitting navy yoga pants and a tank top that reminded him Kira was wholly, utterly female.

"Are you ready?" she asked, reaching up to secure her braids into a ponytail.

He smiled, pulling his T-shirt over his head and tossing it aside. "Definitely. What about you?"

Silence. He turned to see Kira staring at him as if she'd never seen him before. "What is it?"

"Nothing." She pulled her Lightblade free of its sheath. "Let's do this."

Khefar's dagger was instantly in his hand.

They circled each other. Khefar wondered if he would start out easy. He'd already seen her fight, toying with the hybrids on motorcycles and defending herself against the seeker demon. When she fought, she fought to win. He had no doubt that if he had truly been her enemy, she would have given her all to ensure he wouldn't walk away from the encounter.

Spotting an opening, Khefar struck first, to see if he could knock the blade from her hand. He didn't put nearly as much force behind the thrust as he would in a real fight. Kira blocked the thrust easily and sent it back to him, with more weight.

He parried. Khefar knew she'd give as good as she received, or even better. *Too bad we don't have shields to make the fight even more interesting,* he thought.

The parry caught her slightly off balance and she dropped to the padded floor and rolled. Kira gave the warrior a big toothy grin as she regained her stance. "You're not holding back. Now."

"Should I?"

"Only if you want to piss me off. Let's make it fun!"

More thuds, grunts, the metallic whine of metal against metal. She spewed curses after he dropped her the second time. "You're taking advantage of me, you bastard!"

"In what way?"

"All that damn skin showing—it's distracting!"

He gave her a hand up. "Like a seeker demon dripping acidic spit while trying to kill you isn't distracting?"

"You know what I mean. And it's not like I'm trying to kill you."

"All right then." He slid his blade back into its sheath, then tossed it atop his shirt. "Let's try hand-to-hand. That way, if you do decide you want to try to kill me, we can at least make it interesting."

"Just had to go issue a challenge, huh?" Kira sheathed her own dagger and set it aside, then swung her arms to further loosen her muscles, her grin almost childlike.

"So, what's your fighting style?" Khefar asked.

Kira stretched languidly. "Depends."

"On what?"

"On whether I'm bored or not." She smiled at him. "I like Brazilian Capoeira and jujitsu among other things. I also learned a modified Krav Maga while training to be a Shadowchaser. So I hope you took your vitamins today, old-timer."

"Who're you calling—oomph!"

Kira smashed her shoulder deep into his solar plexus, tackling him. They rolled, wrestled, and grappled until he managed to toss her off him. She scrambled to her feet just as he regained his.

A grin wreathed her face from ear to ear, her eyes were alight with joy. She moved in again, flowing easily from fighting style to fighting style, some he hadn't witnessed in a century or more. Gilead knew how to train their Shadowchasers.

After one particularly quick and brutal combination, they broke for a breather, the entire length of the room separating them. She laughed, a true laugh of unadorned delight that shook her entire frame. Khefar wasn't prepared for it—the laugh, the bright mood, his reaction to it. It made him careless. In a blur of motion Kira swooped in, sweeping his legs out from under him. Somehow she wound up atop him, left hand holding his shoulder down, her right forearm pressed into his throat. "I win!"

The warrior thought they both had won, but he wasn't going to tell her that. Her chest rose and fell with each exerted breath, taunting him to drop his gaze away from her face. Before he could say anything, her expression changed. She looked down at her hands, his bare chest. An unguarded expression of pure, naked longing crossed her face, then disappeared so quickly he'd have missed it had he blinked.

"You have so much skin showing," she whispered. She raised her hands, fingertips hovering above his chest. "I can touch you. If I touched you, touched all that beautiful skin, nothing would happen."

That wasn't true. Something very instinctive and very male would happen, and there was nothing he would be able to do about it.

"Shall we see?" Keeping his gaze locked to hers, Khefar threaded his fingers through hers. Slowly he moved their joined hands from his shoulder across to his throat and down his chest. She sucked in a breath, her eyes widening in reaction. He tried to remember the last time he'd caused a woman to make a sound like that. Nothing came to mind.

He pulled his hand away, stretching his arms out, allowing her to touch him as much as she wanted. It was such a simple thing, touching someone else. Something that people the world over took for granted. Even as he'd wandered the earth for millennia, he hadn't denied himself the basic human needs to comfort and be comforted. Such comfort could be bittersweet: if it deepened beyond a casual relationship, there would inevitably be pain. Humans aged. They died and were not reborn in this world. Only Khefar remained.

Yet Kira's powers denied her any opportunity at all to feed this basic human need. Even the brief embrace of congratulation, the supporting shoulder of friendship, the bonding trust of a handshake were denied her. A weaker person would have been driven mad.

Khefar knew Kira Solomon was not weak. But he wondered how—*if*—she remained truly sane.

Chapter 19

He felt . . . wonderful.

Kira shuddered as her fingertips slid over Khefar's exposed skin. Her hands burned, but not because of her power. No, a different sort of heat infused her, a heat she felt might consume her from within.

His skin was amazing, the finest dark mahogany, stretched tight over his muscles. A scattering of wiry hair tickled her fingertips, contrasting the silk of his skin, the hardness of his physique. The body of a warrior, lethal artistry. Such power and grace contained by muscle and bone and skin. She could feel his heart pounding beneath her fingertips, strong and sure and constant, not stuttering and struggling as she drained his essence.

Memories tangled with the present: the warm feel of a man's body thrumming with life beneath her. Sliding her hands across skin with greedy abandon, reveling in the sensations, the pure, basic drive to touch another living person, to be wrapped completely in another.

She wanted him to stop her. He'd have to be the one to stop this because she couldn't. Not with all that beautiful skin beneath her just waiting to be touched, to be explored and discovered. The padded floor of a workout room was neither the time nor the place to be thinking such thoughts, though she had no idea if there ever could be a right time and place.

Khefar swallowed thickly when she shifted backward to stroke lower across his chest. "Whatever you do, do not tell the spider how easily you pinned me. I'll never live it down."

Kira laughed. She knew what he was doing and appreciated it. Khefar was, she realized, a gentleman as well as a warrior. She rolled off of him and stood. "You knocked me on my back twice. I think you're still ahead."

She held out a hand to help him up. He locked his hand around her forearm as she pulled him to his feet. She dropped her gaze. She didn't know why, but being upright with him so close seemed more intimate than pinning him to the floor. "Thank you, for letting me do that."

"You're welcome." He held on when she started to move away. "When was the last time you touched someone, Kira?"

She felt her smile freeze. "Does pinning you to the floor or wrestling with a seeker demon count?"

"You know I'm not talking about dusting hybrids or Shadow Avatars," he said. "How long has it been since you touched another being—human or not—without the intent to subdue them?"

She broke free, then crossed to her gym bag, her movements jerky as she pulled the band from her hair. "Why?"

"How long?"

"Six years," she whispered, her voice flat with the

effort to repress her emotion. "Six years, four months, and sixteen days."

The significance of the tally wasn't lost on him. "A family member?"

She shook her head in denial, braids swinging free. "Nico was more than family. He was my teacher, my first handler. And for one weekend in Venice, he was my lover."

"Was?"

Pain, unmuted by time, welled within her. "He was killed by a Shadow Adept while all I could do was scream and try to hold his chest closed."

"Kira, I'm sorry—"

"No, if you want to know the story, I'll tell you." Her eyes briefly met his, then she looked past him. If she didn't look at him, she could tell the story. She needed to tell the story if only to remind herself why something like the time with Nico could never happen again. "I wasn't supposed to be in Venice. We disobeyed a direct order from the Balm of Gilead, but I was nineteen, continually headstrong, and in love with my handler. Nico said he'd found a way for my powers to be temporarily blocked, and I jumped at the chance. I didn't think about the costs, the ramifications, the consequences. All I cared about was that for once, for a little while, I could see what it was like to be normal."

She shoved her belongings into the bag, still not looking at him. "We had three days. Three amazing beautiful days in the most romantic city on the planet. And then one night we were attacked. I still don't know why they didn't kill me, why they chose to attack him instead. But they did, and I couldn't do anything to stop them."

She zipped the bag shut. "The awful thing is, I still can't, to this day, say that I would do anything differently. I wish Nico didn't have to give his life to teach me that lesson, but that's the only thing I know for sure I'd want different."

"What lesson do you think you were taught that day?"

"That some people aren't meant to have normal lives. Some people aren't meant to have what everyone else has or could have. Some of us are meant to be in this world, but not really and truly be a part of it. So I gave up those wishes and concentrated on others."

"What do you wish for now?"

She didn't hesitate. "To be good at my job, at both jobs. To protect those who don't even know they need protecting. To try to keep people who know me from being killed because of me." She pulled on her gloves. "And sometimes I wish I could stop wishing for more than that."

He looked stricken, as if he'd regretted pushing her for answers. She didn't want his pity. Yeah, maybe he understood what she was going through, but their paths weren't the same. He'd been alive for four millennia so he could repay his crimes, but that didn't compare to being unable to ever touch another human being, to know that your touch could hurt or kill. She was being punished, cruelly punished, and she hadn't committed any crimes. No one in the world would look at Kira's life and not think her cursed. What else could not being able to touch anyone, ever, be?

But she could touch him. She could touch him and neither one of them would hurt.

He stepped toward her. "Kira, why don't—"

She stepped back, something close to panic suddenly pounding in her chest. "I'm going to go take a shower. I'll, um, I'll meet you out front in about twenty minutes, okay?"

"Okay."

She ran. She wasn't sure exactly what she was running away from.

Instead of heading for the showers, Kira headed for the loaner SUV. She wasn't running away. Shadowchasers didn't run. No, she just needed a little space. Maybe, she thought as she stalked toward the parking lot, a drive would clear her head, ease the crazy pounding of her heart. Maybe it would keep her from wondering what the Nubian had been about to ask her.

Goddess, he'd felt nice. All that beautiful mahogany skin, so smooth and silky over his muscles and veins. How wonderful to feel the steady rhythm of his heart beneath her palm. And he'd been willing to let her touch him as much as she wanted. Which was a lot.

She still didn't understand why she could touch him. Was it because he was more than four thousand years old? Was it because he was sort of immortal?

Did it matter why? She could touch him. He would have let her keep touching him. Maybe even— She shook her head. She wasn't sure if she was ready for anything like that, whatever *that* was. It was enough to have a physical connection to someone, skin to skin contact, that didn't end with him slumping unconscious to the floor.

It wouldn't be so bad if she didn't know exactly what she was missing. Six years ago she'd been young and stupid and eager, blithely confident in her ability to control her world. Nico had given her everything she could have wanted—except forever.

Khefar had forever.

She shook her head. No, she reminded herself, Khefar had a mission. Save a life for every life he'd taken, then move on. With two lives to go, he wouldn't be around much longer. Then again, as a Shadowchaser, she had a short shelf life herself. Her line of work almost guaranteed she wouldn't be around long either.

Wynne's words echoed through her mind. She was a healthy twenty-five-year-old, nearly twenty-six. She did have needs, needs that she'd suppressed for more than six years. No matter how normal she wanted to be, she didn't want a traditional relationship even if she could have had it. Khefar seemed like the answer to prayers she didn't even know she'd petitioned for, at least for right now.

Her new Gilead-provided cell phone buzzed, a most welcome distraction. She stopped and dug it out from the side pocket of her gym bag. "Solomon here."

"Chaser Solomon, I have a message from Logistics."

Kira immediately tensed. The sweepers must have found something. *Finally.* "Tell me."

"We're showing elevated levels of Chaos energy near the Fulton County Airport. It seems to be fluctuating but it's not changing location."

"Good. Send me the details." She had a passing acquaintance with that area of Atlanta, west of the city proper. It was mainly an industrial area thick with tractor trailers and large warehouses interspersed with budget motels that became a ghost town after dark. Perfect place for an Avatar to set up shop and not be noticed.

"Transmitting." The operator paused. "The sweepers tell me there is a special response team on site. How do you wish to proceed?"

"What?" Kira kicked her pace up to a jog, her talk with Khefar all but forgotten. "Instruct the team to withdraw immediately. Under no circumstances are they to engage. I repeat: do not engage."

"Understood." The operator paused, then broke protocol with a whispered curse. "We've lost contact with the team. Standard procedure requires us to dispatch backup."

"I *am* your backup." What the hell was Sanchez thinking, sending a special response team to confront an Avatar? Even if the section chief had a Level Five Light Adept on call, they were no match for an Avatar fully charged with Shadow magic.

"I'm on my way." Kira broke into a run. "Do your best to re-establish contact and pull the team out. And do not under any circumstances think of sending anyone else."

She disconnected, then climbed into the SUV, and keyed it to life.

As she pulled out of the parking lot, the Shadowchaser calculated how much time driving from the Carlos to the west side of Atlanta would take, time the SRT probably didn't have.

Evening slid into night as she schemed and planned her way toward the highway. She almost circled back for the Nubian, then decided against it. With all they'd left up in the air . . . she had to focus, to prepare for what lay ahead. She didn't want emotions and confusion to distract her concentration. Kira had work to do. Work she'd always managed solo.

Even if she didn't work alone, she couldn't take Khefar with her on this mission. He was a target. Or rather, his blade was. Kira knew he'd be angry at her when he figured out she'd taken off without him and it would definitely erode the rapport they'd developed over the past two days—well, up until her messy confession anyway. While she admitted they probably could work well enough together to take down the Avatar, it wasn't worth the risk of losing the Dagger of Kheferatum to Shadow.

She whispered a prayer of thanks that Atlanta's notorious traffic had thinned enough for her to cruise above the speed limit. She checked the GPS as she took the off-ramp. She was roughly another mile away. No further calls from Gilead meant they still hadn't heard back from the special response team. Did they abort but were unable to radio in? Had they been captured? Taken out themselves? She had to hope that they'd extracted themselves but needed to maintain radio silence until they entered a safe zone. She didn't want anyone else to die. Not if she could help it.

Extinguishing the vehicle lights, she turned off the main road into a parking lot the Gilead-programmed GPS indicated, then killed the engine. There was no sign of the Gilead team or their vehicle. She dialed up her extrasense, allowing it to slowly spread outward. Nothing, nothing . . . *there.* Something from the southeast corner of the building, near the loading dock, a steady yellow glow.

She slipped out of the SUV, drew her Lightblade. Not a seeker demon. If it had been, she'd be fighting it already. It had to be the Avatar. He was inside, just past the loading dock, waiting for her.

Apprehension raised the hairs on the back of her neck. It was a trap, with the Avatar using himself as irresistible bait. Kira knew it and the Avatar probably knew she knew. The perfect lure and all he had to do was wait to see what she'd do next.

Leaving wasn't an option, especially since she didn't know if the Gilead team had safely retreated. The only person she'd dare call as backup was the one person who shouldn't come. Kira had no choice but to engage the enemy alone.

She advanced slowly, her blade and the Glock at the ready. Just because it was a trap didn't mean she had to rush headlong into it. Her goal was to get in and back out as close to unscathed as possible.

Something whizzed by her ear. Not a bullet; she knew those sounds. Georgia had some giant flying insects, but none that flew that quick—

Sharp stinging pain blossomed in her neck. Kira had only a moment to realize that it wasn't a mosquito, but a dart. *Stupid, stupid, to be so careless.* Her extrasense flared, responding to the presence of the potent toxin. She pulled the dart out of her neck, tried to focus on it in the deepening dark that invaded her. *Since when did Shadowlings use high-tech darts to neutralize people?*

Her heart pounded loud and slow, the bass beat

filling her ears. The Glock fell from her grip, the sound of it clattering to the asphalt echoing through her brain. Despite the paralysis sweeping through her, she still held on to her Lightblade, even though the sudden weight of it made it impossible to lift.

Indistinct figures separated from the building's shadows, resolving into several people in black uniforms. The special response team. "Guys." The word came out slurred and delayed. "Could use some help." Kira toppled over, her extrasense flickering and dimming. By the Light, what was happening to her?

Two of them held her while a third used a booted foot to kick her blade out of reach. "Target acquired."

Target? Gilead had tricked her? She rolled her head, trying to catch a glimpse of them. Each of them stared down at her, yellow flickering in their eyes. They'd been taken by Shadow, and in turn had taken her.

It was the last coherent thought she had.

She'd taken off without him.

Khefar stood in the parking lot, staring at the spot where the SUV had been. He couldn't blame Kira for leaving, for needing to clear her head, but still . . . He found it difficult to believe that their conversation had upset her to the point that she'd do something so abrupt. Kira knew how to set things aside to do what needed to be done.

He dug out his cell phone, dialed her number. No answer.

Unease settled between his shoulder blades. The Chaser knew she'd left him without a ride and darkness had fallen. No matter how upset she was at him, he was willing to bet she wouldn't deliberately leave anyone stranded without cause.

He dialed another number. "Anansi," he said aloud, "think you could show up here with the car?"

He didn't have to articulate the "where." Anansi was an expert at roads, wires, communications, the Internet. He'd be along soon enough.

Anansi arrived in less than five minutes. "Where's our beautiful Shadowchaser?"

"I don't know." Khefar took the wheel as the demigod slid over. "She took off and stranded me. Now she's not answering her phone."

"Really?" Anansi wiggled his bushy eyebrows. "Lovers' quarrel?"

He just glanced at Anansi as he headed for Charms and Arms. "You should know better than that. It was still daylight when she left. Even if she just wanted to cool off, she would have been back by now. And she's not answering her cell. Only one thing would make her go off like that."

"She found the Avatar."

He grit his teeth. When it came to Shadowchasing, Kira would think nothing of going off on her own, confident that her extrasense and her Lightblade would protect her.

"Can you sense her?"

Anansi's expression blanked as he focused on Kira. He frowned. "No."

Khefar's unease deepened, setting him on edge. The demigod should have been able to find Kira no matter where on the planet she was. If the spider god couldn't find her, did that mean that she was . . . ?

No, he refused to believe it. Kira was a Shadow-chaser. She was tough. She could survive.

"Let's get to Wynne and Zoo. I bet they have ways to track her."

He hoped he was right.

Chapter 20

Cold water shocked her back to awareness. She shook her drenched braids out of her eyes and discovered she was chained to a metal fence, half-sprawled on a concrete floor. Her blade and most of her clothing were missing.

People ringed her. At least, some of them used to be people. Some of them had never been anything other than what they were: hybrids and Shadowlings. They seemed thrilled to have her as a guest, if the leers and snarls were any indication.

A melodic masculine voice cut through the buzz. "Welcome, Kira Solomon, to my temporary home."

The Shadowlings parted and the voice's owner walked through the crowd toward her. He was, without a doubt, the most beautifully breathtaking man she'd ever seen: dark curly hair, silver eyes, knew how to wear a suit but she knew he'd look just as good—or better—in anything he wore . . . or didn't wear. She wondered if he'd been that beautiful when he was still human or if becoming an Avatar for one of the Fallen had given him the ethereal, gut-clenching gorgeousness.

"You may call me Enig, for now." He leaned over her. "I trust that you rested well?"

"You've tied me up, taken my clothes and my Lightblade," she reminded him, sounding extremely reasonable considering the circumstances. "Stop pretending that I'm anything other than a prisoner."

"Restraining you was a necessary precaution. I can't have you taking out my helpers, now can I?"

"Why not? I could use some more exercise."

"Surely you got enough exercise destroying my seeker demon? It took a lot of energy to raise the seeker and I'm a bit perturbed that you destroyed it so easily."

"Hope you got your deposit back."

He clapped once, the sound of booming thunder. "Such bravado. If all I wanted was amusement, I'd still choose you."

That didn't sound good. "Choose me for what?"

"I originally wanted the dagger," he said. "Since you returned it to the Nubian, I decided I'd have you instead. I'm beginning to think you are a much better weapon."

Her blood chilled, the fragile false confidence seeping away. "I'm no one's weapon."

"Really? I think the Gilead Commission and quite a few children of Shadow would disagree with you."

The air around them seemed to change, grow darker. Bile rose in her throat. She ground her teeth, wanting nothing more than to break free and reclaim her blade. She tried pushing through the Veil again, but it wouldn't give, as if someone had dropped an unyielding barrier between her and her extrasense. *Why couldn't she call her power?*

"What have you done to me?" Now her voice had an edge to it, not nearly enough of it fury. She needed fury, not fear. Fear could cripple. Fury had been a part of her life for far too long to be anything other than a tool, a weapon. *Where was her well of anger?* "Damn you, answer me!"

"It's a block, one you should already be familiar with. It's temporary for now, so that you'll listen instead of attack. I couldn't have you going all Super Shadow-chaser on me, now could I?"

"Oh, I don't know. I'd certainly like to try." What did he mean—a block she was familiar with?

He grabbed a length of the chain, then casually pulled her upright. Even through the drugs she could feel his power radiating outward, battering at her. Fear slithered down her back and she had to struggle against it, struggle not to let it show. She had a feeling that he'd more than work her fear to his advantage; he'd use it to control her.

"I am here to establish a new order to this world," he told her, his voice as beautiful as his expression. Only his eyes betrayed the ugliness inside. "The order that only pure Chaos can bring. You would do well to stand with me now, else you'll fall hard later."

"I'm not going to let you destroy this world."

"Destroy it?" He laughed. "Please. Do you know how long it would take to rebuild the infrastructure? No, I don't want to destroy this world. Just take it over and unite it, finally, under one flag. My flag."

"You're insane."

"I am a child of Chaos. I can't be insane. I'm just being true to my nature." He gave her another beautiful smile. "With a healthy dose of ambition thrown in."

She tried to call her extrasense again. Nothing.

"You know the other Fallen will not stand for this. Neither will the Shadowchasers. There are more who will stand against you than will stand with you. You're not going to win."

Again the amused smile. "I've been planning this for longer than you've been alive, Kira Solomon, working my way onward and upward through my brethren. I am the personification of the free market system at work, Darwin triumphant. I am the fittest and I alone will reign. My plans are coming to fruition. All I need now is the Dagger of Kheferatum."

He nodded and one of the hybrids came forward with a key. "I'm going to let you go."

That surprised her—and made her suspicious. "Why?"

"So you can kill the Nubian, retrieve the Dagger of Kheferatum, and bring it to me."

Absolutely not. It was obvious that he had already started to gather his army. Like hell she'd give him a weapon of mass destruction. "I know what the Dagger of Kheferatum is, what it's reputed to do. What makes you think I'd do something as stupid as give you the power to obliterate existence?"

"Because you're going to join with me," Enig said, as if stating the obvious. "Of your own free will, you will return and you will bring the dagger. In return I'll give you what you long for most."

"What I long for most?" She smiled grimly. "As if you know what that is."

"Don't I?" He stepped forward, one hand reaching up to caress the air about her head. She felt his touch even though he had not made contact with her flesh.

"There's one thing you want above all else. One thing you desire even more than being touched and touching without killing. I can give you that. I can give you whatever you want."

"You have no concept of what I want." She had to taunt him to cover a sudden, sickening wrench of fear.

"You want a key. And that key is information to unlock the mystery of who—or what—you are and where you come from. Who your parents are. Why you have this singular ability. I can give you that key, that truth, if you join with me."

Kira burst out laughing. "Good speech. Forgive me for not applauding, but I'm a little tied up at the moment."

Enig's smile widened, but the glint in his eyes warned her a second before the back of his hand connected with her right cheek. "You dare to reject my truth?"

It took a moment to blink back the pain and reply. "You'd gift me with lies. You know it. I know it. That's all your kind is capable of."

His eyes flashed like an amped-up traffic light: red-yellow-green. "You're mistaken, Kira Solomon. Lies are what humanity craves. It's always been truth that's been shunned and relegated to Shadow. Humans need the lies, the bright and pretty baubles, because truth isn't pretty."

He gripped her chin, perfectly manicured claws digging into her skin. "Truth isn't soft and cuddly and perfect. Truth is hard and sweaty and bloody. Truth is pain and bitterness and loneliness. Truth is ugly and that's why humanity rejects it. They only want the pretty with the least amount of effort possible."

"Like your version would be any better." She spat at him. Why the hell couldn't she call her power? "I don't want your lies or anything else from you!"

"Not yet. But you will. You belong to me, to Shadow, already. You just haven't realized it yet."

No. She didn't belong to Shadow. She'd never belong to Shadow. "I reject you. I reject your truth."

Enig smiled. "Resistance. So pretty, coming from you. That makes this all the more delicious."

He held out his free hand. One of his underlings slithered forward to hand him a long-needled syringe. Whatever it was wouldn't be good, even if the sludgy liquid inside didn't glow a sickly peachy-orange color when he brought it near her. "What the hell is that?"

"Something to make you more . . . malleable."

"You'd better hope it's something that makes me more dead. Because when I get free, I will kill you."

Laughter answered her. "Oh no, you don't get the easy way. You don't get the lies. Breaking your body is novice-demon stuff."

His hold tightened on her jaw. "I'm going to break your mind, piece by delicious piece, Kira Solomon. Then I'm going to break your spirit. Once you are broken you will come to me. You will come to me, on your hands and knees and begging, because no one else will have you. You will know my mercy because I will claim you as mine and make you welcome. And all in Shadow and Light will know that I am the master."

He shoved the needle deep into her neck, piercing her jugular vein. Pain stole her ability to scream. Her eyes bulged as fire raced to her heart, then exploded through her body. She could feel her power gathering intensity, her skin pulsing. The bonds holding her melted off her wrists, and her heart leaped in response. *Finally! She'd make them pay for what they'd done.*

Something was terribly wrong. Power flared, burning away layer upon layer of blocks and controls. Not just her hands, her entire body throbbed with light. *Ma'at protect me!*

Hands touched her, triggering her defenses. Power ripped from her, her vision going blue-white as the drug hit her brain like a bullet.

Then the screams began.

Chapter 21

Wynne was just locking up as Khefar shouldered his way into the shop. "Kira's missing. She's not answering her cell phone. Where is she?"

"That's what we've been trying to find out <u>since</u> her blade sent a <u>warning</u> about fifteen minutes ago that she's incapacitated."

Dread slid down his spine. "What do you mean, incapacitated?"

"Injured or captured. Either way, it means she's in deep shit and she needs our help." Wynne, already wearing one-piece Nomex coveralls, walked to the back of the shop and pulled on a white Tyvek jumpsuit over it—hazmat gear commonly called a "<u>bunny suit</u>."

"When Kira goes out on a solo Chase, we're usually on standby. She'll give us a two-hour window before we're to try to contact or track her down, but she didn't inform us to stand by and with the blade's warning . . . "

Wynne gestured over her shoulder. Her husband had a map spread atop the glass counter, four quartz clusters at each cardinal point, and a PDA in his hand. "Zoo's looking now, but even with his magical enhancement of the GPS it isn't turning up anything—and that always works." Wynne zipped up, then hooked on a tactical belt. "Or it did before now."

"Perhaps I can be of assistance?" Nansee joined the male witch.

Khefar turned back to Wynne. "She's in trouble. I can feel it."

"I know. We've got locator spells on her Lightblade and her bike, but the bike's still at the house. We thought you were with her." Wynne didn't bother to disguise the slight hint of accusation in her voice.

"I was. We went to the museum and then to the faculty gym on the campus, just as planned. We sparred and she told me she was going to take a shower, then meet me outside, but she never showed up. I went to the parking lot and the SUV was gone. She's disappeared. Do you think Gilead called her about the Avatar?"

"It's the only thing I can think of that would make her cut and run like that." Wynne waited a moment, as if waiting for Khefar to volunteer more information about why Kira might have taken off without him. He remained silent. Wynne could intuit something had happened between the two of them all she wanted, but it was obvious that as far as Khefar was concerned, whatever happened between him and Kira would remain between him and Kira.

"I'm going to find her," Khefar said. He reined in his impatience with an effort. If Kira was in danger, he had to save her. If he couldn't save her, he'd be that much further from his goal. And, the Nubian realized, even if she weren't now part of his mission, he would still be committed to saving her because she was . . . Kira.

"You're going to need our help," Wynne said

calmly. "And we're going to need yours. Kira will recognize us, I think, but even in protective gear, we could be vulnerable."

"What? Why?"

Zoo looked up from the map. "If she's off the chain, that makes her a threat to everyone and everything," he explained. "Anything organic of hers that touches us would knock us out cold—and that's if we're lucky. We've developed ways—gloves, clothing, magic—to protect ourselves that we've used in emergencies before, but we've never confronted a situation like this. You can touch her. We might be able to bring her in, but we may need you to restrain her."

"We've found her," Nansee said calmly. "She just appeared out of nowhere a few miles west of here. She's on the move, but it's erratic."

Both Zoo and Wynne grabbed black gear bags, headed for a corridor that led to the rear door of the shop. "Everyone out to the van."

"Nansee?" Khefar's tone was short.

"If you let me drive, I can get us there faster," the old man offered. "Streets are just concrete webs to me."

"Nansee. *Anansi.* Figures you're not normal." Wynne shook her head. "Fine, I'll take point. Zoo?"

"Gotcha, babe." They stepped out into the alley behind the shop. The large man closed the door, then pressed his hand against the doorjamb. Khefar felt a surge of power and the shop locked up tight.

The van looked like a salvage-yard rescue incapable of moving faster than a person could walk. Graffiti fought with rust for dominance. Khefar doubted there was anyone left alive who could guess its original color.

"My Charger is faster, and less likely to shake apart shifting into second."

Zoo grinned. "Considering that you've been wandering the world for all those centuries, you gotta know by now that looks are deceiving." He opened the back door.

control!

Khefar noticed the bank of computer equipment on the left side first. The right had a locker that doubled as a jump seat and room enough to hold six heavily armed men. "Impressive."

"We can do emergency medical too. I hope we won't need it." Wynne climbed in beside Nansee. "There are extra weapons in the jump seat."

"You have an amazing wife," Khefar told the witch as they climbed into the back.

"You have no idea." The large man swung the rear door closed. "We served together in the army. She's an excellent shot: Distinguished Rifleman and Pistol Shot badges." He touched a panel above the jump seat. It slid open to reveal an impressive array of handguns, shotguns, blades, and grenades.

Khefar watched as the other man armed himself with the quiet efficiency of someone with more than a little experience. "You've had to do this before?"

"We back Kira up when she asks us to and sometimes when she doesn't. Mostly we do strategic support. Our girl's used to doing things solo, prefers it even. Once we knew what she was doing and how useless those assholes at Gilead East are, we decided she needed us."

Zoo grinned. "Besides, Wynne and I like the challenge of gearing her up. My spellcraft's <u>much</u>

using women for power not [handwritten annotation]

better than before I met her. And Wynne's firepower is sweet."

He tossed Khefar a shotgun. "We're not planning on hand-to-hand here, so you don't need your blade. The mission's to get Kira and get the hell out."

"Understood." He began to load the shells Zoo handed him. He'd led plenty of men over the millennia, archers, cavalry, platoons and, for a brief stint had served with the Tuskegee Airmen. He could have taken over this operation, but he wouldn't. Zoo and Wynne seemed more than capable despite their very human frailties. This was obviously something they'd planned for.

But if a Shadow Avatar had hurt Kira, he'd toss the shotgun and draw his blade without a second thought. [handwritten // annotation]

Zoo turned toward Anansi. "Just a heads-up: some of our firepower is geared for Shadow. Now I'm gonna assume that you're not from Shadow, but if you've got any doubts about protecting yourself, you may not want to be nearby if we have to start shooting."

The old man nodded. "I am not of Shadow, witch. Trust me, my healthy dose of self-preservation is why I'm still here when so many of my brethren are not."

Anansi started the van.

"Oh, gods, it looks like a war zone."

Khefar peered through the windshield as Anansi brought the van to a crawl. He had to echo Wynne's sentiment. A cacophony of blue and red strobe lights bounced off the brick and concrete warehouses around them before they saw the first emergency vehicle. Overlying that, he could see the orange-red throb of a building fully enflamed.

"Wynne, we don't need to go in hot," Zoo said, pulling on a suit that matched hers. "Why don't you take point?"

"Got it."

"We're close," Zoo said, worry finally creeping into his voice. He checked the global positioning application on his PDA. "I don't think she's moving anymore."

"She isn't," the old man confirmed. His eyes glowed blue as he looked through the Veil, his hand raised as if to trace Kira's path. "The trail begins at that burning building, then crosses the railroad tracks. She's in the cemetery."

"Oakland?" Zoo's expression was grim. "We've got to get her out of there. There are ex-slaves and Confederate soldiers buried in there. If she's careening around in there out of control—"

"All right." Wynne checked her weapon. "There's probably at least one guard, I think he's in the Bell Tower building if he's not making rounds. We'll have to park at the main gate and take our chances."

"We also have Six Feet Under across the street," Zoo said, jerking his head in the direction of the bar they'd just driven by. "It still has a crowd on its deck."

"Anansi, can you block sight of the van and make sure no one sees us?" Khefar asked.

"Yes."

The demigod pulled the van to a stop at the intersection of MLK and Oakland, just across from the entrance to the cemetery. The curving brick and iron entrance with its three sweeping arches glowed softly under the streetlamps as they quickly exited the van.

The silence beyond the gate contrasted sharply with the sirens a few blocks away.

Zoo and Wynne donned night-vision goggles after they got out of the van, but Khefar refused his pair. His blade would give him all the warning he needed and his night vision was better than human. The spider god, of course, could see beyond the Veil of Reality. Darkness wouldn't be a hindrance.

"The gate's locked," he said. "Are we sure she's in there?"

"I'm sure," the demigod answered.

Khefar supposed Kira could have easily climbed over the iron side gates or even the red brick wall of the cemetery's outer perimeter, none of which were very high. How she could have done it without being spotted, he didn't know. If she'd been spotted, been forced to confront a very human security guard . . .

He used his blade to take care of the gate's lock. The dagger vibrated in his hand, reacting to the thousands of bodies interred just beyond. *There's nothing for you here.*

The blade vibrated again. Khefar frowned. His dagger cared for two things: death and dying. Not even a new burial would generate its bloodlust. But Shadowlings would. So would someone close to death.

"Do you sense Shadow inside?" Zoo asked Anansi, who stood gazing past the gate and into the cemetery.

"Not clearly."

Zoo paused. "What do you mean, not clearly?"

Anansi frowned. "There's Light, but there's Shadow too. The levels come and go. We need to hurry."

Khefar's gut lurched at Anansi's grim announcement.

He knew if the spider wanted to hurry, Kira had to be in bad shape.

They moved in through the gates and fanned out, Wynne at the front, then Zoo with Anansi and Khefar taking up the rear. The cemetery spread before them, acres and acres of rolling hills, monuments, and towering oak trees separated by paved roads and walkways, seeming too large to find one person. "Which way do we go?"

"Past that." Zoo pointed. "The statue of the dude sitting on his mausoleum."

It was an unusual marker to say the least, but Khefar didn't care. He had no idea what awaited them on the other side of the life-sized stone replica or if Kira had made it here on her own or been dragged by the Avatar. He wondered if some sort of Shadow-engineered trap was waiting for them.

Deeper into the cemetery, the ambient light changed. Now Khefar could make out a blue-green pulsing light coming from the other side of a tall monument.

"Kira." Wynne broke into a jog.

"Wynne!" Zoo grabbed her arm. "It could be a trap."

"I know. But if she's hurt, and her powers are messed up, in the cemetery—"

"I know, babe. I know." He raised his weapon. "Okay. I got your six."

Worry weighed heavily on Khefar as Wynne and Zoo went around the left side of the building and he and Anansi took the right. If her protective barriers really were torn away, Khefar couldn't help wondering what Kira's exposed extrasense felt among these tributes to the dead.

As they approached the Kontz family monument, he could see why Kira—after somehow dragging herself away from the burning warehouse—had chosen it: the columns were carved with lotus blossoms at the bottom with the winged sun disk of Ra stretched across the top. He could just make out an ornate crown-and-cross design carved into the ceiling of the monument's interior, flickering in the greenish light. The monument seemed like a doorway between worlds, or an escape route for a Shadowchaser more aligned to old gods than new.

He eased his way around the corner, then froze. His chest seized up tight. It was as bad as they had feared.

Kira sprawled at the foot of the granite column, wearing a ragged tank top and panties, nothing else. Her body writhed and jerked as sapphire and emerald arcs of power danced along her skin, illuminating her wounds.

Welts and bruises crisscrossed her arms and legs alongside a multitude of cuts. Blood stained her skin, dark splotches against her skin and underwear. Khefar realized with sick certainty that not all of the very human blood was hers.

"Oh, Kira."

Wynne pushed up her goggles as she started forward, but Zoo blocked her. "There's Shadow-magic in her."

"What? Kira's a Shadowchaser. She can't have Shadow-magic."

"The witch is right," Anansi said. "Her body is filled with Chaos. That's the green energy you see, the yellow of Shadow mixing with the blue of Light. She's trying to fight it."

Khefar turned to Anansi. "It looks like she's losing."

The spider god remained silent and that proved to Khefar how dire Kira's situation really was. "We've got to get her out of here."

"Right. Let's do this." Zoo and Wynne moved forward.

"Stay away from me!" The sound of her voice, raw and guttural, had them all sliding to a stop. Khefar halted, but his body tensed with the urge to act. He was exceedingly conscious of the two-story white building too close for comfort, even with Nansee shielding them. That's where the night guard was, unless he was out making his rounds—or Kira had already encountered him.

Khefar didn't want to think that Kira had disposed of the security patrol. If so, with her powers sparking out of control, the guard was already beyond their help.

Kira dragged herself to a crouch, hands raised, her entire body pulsing waves of violet and pea green. Even her eyes swirled with dual colors. "Monsters," she hissed. "Spawns of Shadow! You won't touch me again!"

"Kira, it's me, Zoo." The man stepped forward. "You remember your buddy Zoo, right? Wynne's here too. We're going to take you home, make sure you're okay—"

"I said, stay away!"

A bolt of turquoise light hit Zoo. The large man spun with the blast, then slumped to the ground.

"Zoo!" Wynne ran to her husband.

Kira ignored them, her head turning to focus on Khefar. "You." Her voice dropped several levels. "Give me the Dagger of Kheferatum!"

Khefar moved forward, instinctively drawing his blade. "Don't do it," Anansi urged. "That's not all Kira in there anymore."

"I know." He stepped cautiously. "Nansee, I'm going to need the spider."

The demigod nodded. Khefar held up his blade, allowing it to catch the limited light. Kira's glowing eyes followed its every movement. "You want the dagger? Come and get it, if you can!"

Her quick movements surprised him. She scrambled out of the monument, skittering like a crab. A blast hit him square on his collarbone, pain radiating outward as the hit of raw greenish power burned through leather to skin on the right side of his chest. "Now, Nansee!"

A string of etheric webbing flew over his left shoulder, hitting Kira just as she launched herself at him. She screamed, body flaring pollen-yellow and bowing off the ground as she tried to fight the bonds coiling around her body, immobilizing her. A sizzling sound slid through the air, punctuated with an acrid scent.

"Gods, they're burning her!"

Khefar fell to his knees, dagger flashing as he sliced through the bonds. She screamed and thrashed, fighting him, kicking and screaming and biting, power twisting and flaring as the webbing fell from her singed flesh. His dagger screamed as well, wanting to taste the blood, her blood. *Give me death, give me death!*

As if she heard it, Kira wrapped her fingers around the blade. "Yes," she hissed, pulling against his strength to guide the tip of the dagger towards her heart. "Kill it. Kill the Shadow."

"No!" Adrenaline surged through Khefar as he fought her, prying her fingers one by one from the blade, leaving both their hands bloody. Even as Kira scrambled up, trying to reach the blade, he lifted it high, then jammed it into the consecrated ground with all his strength. "Be silent!"

The dagger obeyed, its magic muzzled. Kira lunged for it again. Khefar threw his arms around her waist, dragged her back and down. "Kira, stop!"

She froze. "Kira," she stuttered. "My name is Kira. My name. Kira my name." Blinking through the dirt, sweat, and blood caking her face, she focused on him, fingers skimming his jaw. "You don't die. I can touch you and you don't die."

That sounded more like Kira's voice, Kira's thoughts. "No, I'm not going to die. Not today. You aren't either."

"Burns. Pain burns cold. It kills. But you touch and it sleeps."

She buried her face against his neck. "Don't let go," she whispered against his heart. "Please don't let go."

"I won't," he vowed, pulling her close. "I'll take care of you."

"Okay." Her head slumped backward. The power chasing along her skin dimmed, then winked out.

"Kira!" He touched fingers to her throat, heart banging with relief when he found her pulse, thready and erratic.

He looked up at Anansi. "Something's wrong with her. Seriously wrong."

"She's been poisoned," the demigod said quietly. "The Veil no longer shields her extrasense and Shadow is gaining a foothold, body and spirit."

"Will she be all right? Can you fix this?"

"The bruises, cracked ribs, and the dislocated hip are easy enough to repair. The combination of the drugs and the assault may have caused permanent damage to her mind."

Khefar's hand shook as he pulled his dagger from the ground, sheathed it. Clutching Kira close, he managed to climb to his feet. Wynne had helped her husband up. Both still had weapons at the ready, but Zoo leaned a little too heavily against his wife.

The warrior asked Wynne, "How is he?"

"I'm all right." Zoo replied himself, grimacing and clasping his right shoulder. "Hurts like a bitch, but I'll live. Would have been worse if the Kevlar hadn't slowed it down a little."

"I know what you mean," Wynne added. "My suit's ruined. Since when could she shoot light blasts like that?"

"Since never," her husband answered.

Wynne started back along the path toward the gate. "We can have a Q and A later. Now we've got to get the hell out of here and get these two back home before we get company."

"We've got to get Zoo to a hospital," Khefar insisted. "He needs that arm looked at and stitched up. Is there one nearby?"

Zoo shook his head. "It's just a scratch. Wynne can

fix me up, and I've got spells to take care of the rest. I'll survive. Besides, taking me to a hospital means too many questions none of us need to answer."

Khefar tucked Kira's head against his chest, then carefully got into the van. "Can either of you get into Kira's place?" he said when Nansee moved to shut the door. "I know she's got stuff there we can use."

"We have to go to our place," Wynne said, her voice unsteady. "I don't know how many protections she's got on hers and we don't have time to unlock each one. We already have a room that's safe for her. Emergency supplies too."

"Something like this has happened before?"

Wynne shook her head, her expression raw. "Nothing like *this* has ever happened before. She's been through some serious crap, but she's never not recognized us. She's never attacked us."

"All right." He could tell Wynne was close to losing her control. "Let's get out of here."

Chapter 22

I s that it?"

"Sure is." Nico held up the small vial of clear liquid.

Kira stared at it, fidgeting with excitement. Finally, after months of planning, they were in the most romantic hotel in Venice for a long weekend, though Balm and Gilead thought they were in Brussels. Disobeying the Balm of Gilead gave her an illicit thrill but paled in comparison to the thrill she experienced when looking into Nico's eyes.

Soon, very soon, they'd finally be together the way they both wanted. She had no idea what the liquid was or where Nico had gotten it, and she didn't care. All she cared about was that it would take away her curse and she and Nico could stop being Chaser and handler and instead become lovers.

"How long will we have?"

"Three days, I'm told." The laughter always present in his smoky topaz eyes sobered. "I will ask you for the last time: Are you sure you want to do this?"

Instead of answering, she snatched the vial from him, pulled the stopper, then tossed back the liquid. Tears blurred her vision as the concoction burned its way down her throat. It seemed to spread through every cell of her body, changing her. She'd had liquor before, but it hadn't scorched her insides like this.

Nico rubbed her back as she coughed and gagged her way through the burn. "How will we know it worked?" she asked when she could speak again.

He took the vial from her, placed it on the night-stand. "Let's find out."

He leaned over her as she eased back onto the pillows. Energy crackled between them, but not the blue of her power. Expectation and yearning caused her heart to slam inside her chest.

She was afraid and nervous and excited, but ready, oh so ready. From the moment she'd seen Nicolo Daryalos, she'd wanted him. Every female Chaser in training had wanted him and no one, not even Kira, had speculated that she would become his charge. She'd secretly gloated when he'd been assigned as her handler, bitterly disappointing the other trainees and forever cementing their dislike of her. Not that she cared. Nico belonged to her and always would as long as they both lived. Discovering the attraction wasn't simple teacher-student infatuation, but was in fact reciprocated, was the best moment of Kira's life.

Until now.

His fingers brushed her cheek. She stuttered out a sigh, curling into his touch. So warm. "What do you want to do, my love?"

She cupped his face in her hands, marveling at the feel of his skin against hers, the way his thick dark hair tickled the edges of her hands. "Everything."

He touched her, touched her as she had never been touched. She learned the differences between holding, petting, stroking, between caressing and fondling. She discovered the glory of lips and teeth and tongue and all the wonderful things the male form could do with the female. In the early morning hours, secure in her ability to please and be pleased, she learned how to make a man shiver and shake as he called out her name.

They stayed in their hotel room for two days, exploring each other fully, until Nico suggested dinner at one of the cafés near the Grand Canal. Kira didn't want to go out, but the idea of leaving behind her Lightblade and wandering the Piazza San Marco like the hundreds of other tourists and lovers had a certain appeal.

Gorgeous by day, the square was absolutely stunning by night, golden light bathing the historic buildings with an etheric beauty. Arm in arm, they crossed the Piazza, heading for the arcade. "Where are you taking me? I would have been happy to order in again."

"My dear, we cannot come to Venice and not walk the Piazza," Nico said, his grin infectious. "There's a late night restaurant near Teatro La Fenice with a most impressive collection of wines."

"We're not going to stay out too late, are we?" Kira asked. "If it's our last night together, I don't want to waste too much time on food."

Nico laughed. "If this is to be our last night together, my sweet, I need to keep up my strength. But not to worry, they have takeaway service."

All at once, hundreds of Venice's ubiquitous pigeons took to the air, swirling around them, separating them. Even without her extrasense, Kira could sense something was different, wrong. The pigeons should have been at roost, not filling the Piazza, flying away, not attacking. She instinctively reached for her Lightblade only to remember that she'd left it in the hotel room. "Nico!"

A muffled shout lost in the fluttering of thousands of wings. So many, so unnatural, something from a Hitchcock movie. Holding one arm up to keep the pigeons from clawing at her face, Kira reached out for her handler.

"Nico!"

He lay sprawled at the base of Saint Teodoro's granite column. His chest had been sliced open, blood staining the bricks beneath him.

"No!" Frantic, she searched the Piazza for help, but the square was strangely deserted. "Don't die, Nico, please don't die!"

She fumbled through his pockets for a phone, repeatedly keyed Gilead's emergency code. Screaming into the phone, calling for help, trying to hold Nico's chest closed, hold his life in. Blood carried power, reactivating her extrasense, flooding her senses with his thoughts and emotions. *The desire to possess, to take her away from Balm, away from Gilead. The abrupt transformation to need, then to love. Defying Balm, defying nature, even if it meant death, to give Kira what she needed, what every human should have . . .*

"Nico . . . "

"Ki-Kira." Air gurgled in his throat as he looked at her, the smile half-formed on his lips as he died.

Laughter. She raised her head, saw two men standing a few feet away, hands in their pockets. One reptilian, one heart-stoppingly beautiful, familiar. They laughed again, revealing pointed teeth. Shadowlings. The handsome one blew a kiss at her before both turned and strolled away.

No. Not this time. You won't escape this time. I've got my power back and I'm going to make you pay for what you did to Nico.

Power flooded her body. She drew her blade. It wasn't her Lightblade, but an older dagger, Egyptian. It didn't matter. It wanted to kill and at that moment, so did she.

She leaped at the Shadowlings, consumed with the urge to destroy. More Shadowlings flooded the square like a flock of birds coming home to roost. She screamed, blade flashing as she swung again and again. Yellow rain fell as she split Shadowlings apart. Yet no matter how many times she killed them, they kept coming back.

Venice disappeared. She stumbled through a nightmarish landscape pierced by bolts of two-colored lightning—yellow and blue. Fire careened around her, burning through her veins. It felt as if thousands of little teeth gnawed at her, ripping her apart from the inside out, blinding her with pain. Shadowlings and wraiths swirled around her like ghosts in a fog, taunting her, thwarting her attempts to break through.

She screamed again, fighting her way through with fists and feet and teeth, desperate to get away, get to safety. Balm called to her through the storm but she couldn't make it through. She felt as if she struggled through quicksand as tombstones toppled around her, being pulled further and further down into the abyss of Chaos and Shadow.

There was no use in fighting it. She was trapped. Every effort to claw her way free was met with failure. She might as well give up.

Kira!

The wind wailed her name. At least, she thought it was the wind. But what if it wasn't? What if it was someone she knew, someone trying to help?

Desperate, she flung her hand up, reaching for something, anything to pull herself to freedom. Something caught her hand. She looked up.

Khefar looked down at her, his face set in familiar implacable lines, his eyes burning. "Fight! If you want to escape this Chaos and live, you have got to fight!"

Reaching deep, she found the last reserves of her will and fought to pull free, Khefar's demands ringing in her ears. Her body and her will stretched past their limits, tearing, screaming; the Chaos holding her, reluctant to let go.

One last kick and she launched free, panicked and flying, fearful and falling. But Khefar was there, and he caught her.

It took a long time to swim up through the darkness, longer still to stop hearing the screams. Every time her grip slipped, every time she thought she'd plunge back into the depths, she'd be pulled back.

She opened her eyes, expecting to find Wynne beside her, Zoo ready to dose her with one of his herbal cocktails. Instead she found the Nubian, and he held her hand.

Wordlessly she stared down at his fingers, his bare brown fingers, threaded through her own. No leather, no plastic, no layers of armor. Just warm skin against warm skin, and a feeling she could only compare to inhaling wintergreen, cool and crisp.

"It seemed to comfort you," he said into the quiet. "I didn't mind."

It had more than comforted her. It had kept her anchored. "How long?"

"It's been a couple of days."

Two days? "Oh gods. I need a phone."

Wordlessly Khefar dug a mobile out of his back pocket. Her hands shook and her vision blurred as she attempted to tap in a number.

Khefar took the phone from her. "Tell me the number."

She did. He punched it in, then pressed the phone to her cheek. She whispered her thanks, clutching the phone close, too unnerved to wonder why she didn't receive any impressions from the device. Her heart pounded against her rib cage and she could almost hear her blood racing through her veins. *Don't let me be too late, please don't let me be too late.*

The phone didn't complete its first ring. "That had better be you, daughter."

"Balm." She tried again. "Mother. Just wanted to call to tell you I'm fine."

"You don't sound fine. You sound like you were pulled back from death."

She looked up at Khefar. "I was. But I'm back now. I'm sorry I didn't call earlier."

"That's because you couldn't call earlier." Balm's voice shook. She sounded angry, upset and relieved, revealing far more emotion than Kira had ever heard from her. "I called for you, but you didn't answer. For a full day you didn't answer."

Oh, no. "Are you on your way here?"

"I made it to New York a couple of hours ago. The plane is being refueled and then I'll be on my way. I'm bringing specialists with me, and we'll take you back to Santa Costa where you can be properly taken care of."

No, no, no. "Please go back home, Mother. I'm sorry that I worried you, but I'm up and about now."

"You don't want me there?" Balm's voice warbled. Again she had no idea of the emotion behind it. "A mother can't rush to her daughter's side, to see with her own eyes that she's alive and well?"

"You're the Balm of Gilead." She closed her eyes. Arguing with Balm was tough on the best of days; being off-line for two days left her with even fewer defenses against the head of the Commission.

She tried a different tack: honesty. "I'm fighting one of the Fallen. You can't be exposed to that level of threat. You need to trust us to do our jobs and stop this menace. You need to trust me."

"I trust you, Kira, but I don't trust what's around you. This is an entirely different level of danger than we've seen before. And for some reason, the Oracles have a large blank spot whenever they try to focus on you."

"Really? That doesn't happen."

"I know it doesn't happen," Balm snapped, a clear indication of just how upset she was. "This battle you fight is larger than Gilead's ability to track and predict. I . . . I'm afraid for you, Kira."

"I am afraid for myself." She had to blink rapidly

against the emotion that swept over her, threatening to pull her under. "I had a close call. I know that. It'll make me more careful, but not if I have to worry about the heart and soul of Gilead being so close to one of the Fallen." Her grip tightened on the phone. "Please, Balm. I need you to be in Gilead more than I need you here."

Silence, then a sigh. "All right, daughter. I'll return home. Make sure that you come to visit me this evening. I'll leave a pathway open for you."

"I will; I promise."

Her eyelids slid closed. She concentrated on simply breathing, too emotionally and physically drained to do much more than that. For Balm to be afraid, things had to have been really bad.

Khefar took the phone from her, and she whispered her thanks as she reopened her eyes. "You said it's been two days?"

He nodded. "This is late afternoon on the second day."

Zoo's magic and her own Chaser abilities usually made her heal faster than regular humans. She must have been seriously messed up to be out two whole days.

Her gaze roamed the room, taking in the twin-size bed with its plain white cotton sheets, the oak chest of drawers, the whitewashed door she remembered led to a bathroom. She looked to Khefar again, dressed in black jeans and a long-sleeved shirt she thought she'd seen him in before. Exhaustion pulled at his features, accented by the stubble shadowing his chin. Had he sat by her the entire time, holding her hand? "This is my safe room at Wynne and Zoo's house."

He nodded. "We decided to bring you here since none of us knew what protections you have on your place, and time was a factor."

Kira translated mentally: *I had probably been pretty close to biting the big one. It certainly would explain why Balm had been on the way to Atlanta and why I can't feel my extrasense.* The fact that she couldn't decide which of those terrified her more meant her batteries were in serious need of recharging.

"Here." He held a cup and straw for her. "You must be thirsty."

She was and eagerly sucked the water down. He returned the cup to the nightstand and without asking, gathered her hand again. It was nice. She shoved her free hand through her hair, wincing at the lingering ache. "Where are they? Wynne and Zoo?"

"When it seemed like you were starting to come out of it, Zoo went to his greenhouse to get some herbs for you. Wynne left a moment ago to get you some food."

Leaving her alone with the Nubian. That didn't make sense to her. In the handful of times that she'd gotten into serious scrapes, Wynne was always there to tell her—with much love and affection, of course—just how idiotic she'd been. Her friend wouldn't pass up an opportunity to remind her that they were all a team. What, she wondered, had happened?

"Okay." She wanted to sit up, but it meant letting go of his hand. Already she missed the contact. Her muscles protested as she tried to rise, causing her to grimace. Khefar moved to help her. She froze as his arms went around her shoulders, then forced herself to relax. "Someone had to carry me here. I guess that was you, huh?"

"Yes." So matter-of-fact, as unruffled as usual. "Do you need to go to the bathroom?"

Gods, he'd made her blush. She never blushed. "Yeah."

He stood. "I can carry you."

"No." Having him carry her would be more than she could handle. "No, just help me hobble over to the door. I can take it from there."

He wrapped a thick arm around her waist and helped her up. Going from sitting to standing was a dizzying experience and she leaned into him, inhaling deeply through her nose until her equilibrium returned.

She took care of business as quickly as her muscles would allow. Her empty bladder and stomach only compounded the sensation of something vital being missing. The Avatar had done something, worked some sort of magic to strip her powers away. Nico had done that too. Both had given her a liquid concoction that had scalded her senses and rendered her powerless. Maybe it was time to know what they had done so that she could find a way to reverse it. She never wanted to feel this level of powerlessness again. Never wanted to be without her magic again.

It was a fundamental realignment. Her extrasense was more than mental, more than psychic ability. In the Normal world, where magic was something acted out in epic fantasy movies or on Las Vegas stages, Kira was an anomaly. She'd always known things about people, at least since she was five and in the first foster home she remembered. Her earliest memory was of a ruler smacking her open palms, punishment for touching her foster mother. A five-year-old didn't have the social filter of adults, and she thought she was being helpful when she'd tell people what they were truly thinking and feeling. No matter how often she'd tried to suppress it, she could feel her power swimming through her veins gathering strength until it manifested itself as blue light when she reached puberty.

She'd hated her powers her entire life. Now that they were gone, she'd do almost anything to get them back.

Kira stared in the mirror, hoping to jog her memory. Her reflection was better than she'd expected but that was more a testament to Zoo's skills than anything else. Something was still off. She'd gone to confront the Avatar. She remembered it hadn't gone well, but she'd managed to fight her way clear.

No, that didn't seem right to her. She leaned closer to the mirror and blinked. Her eyes, normally a chocolate brown, had lightened to amber. Flecks of green caught the light as she turned her head.

Fingers curled around the lip of the sink. Memories swirled through her consciousness, indistinct but full of pain. Nico. Fighting Shadowlings. Screams and more screams. And colors, swirls of yellow, blue, and green. No, she hadn't left the Avatar easily. He'd done . . . something. What the hell had happened to her?

You belong to me, to Shadow, already. You just haven't realized it yet.

She whimpered as the words, the voice, slithered through her mind. No, gods, no. She was a Shadowchaser;

she belonged to the Light. She'd never give herself to Shadow. She'd rather die first.

"Kira, are you okay?"

She wiped at her mouth with a shaky hand, then opened the bathroom door, making sure to keep her gaze to the floor. "Yeah, just trying to get my legs back."

He helped her back to the bed, fussed with the pillows like a nursemaid. She considered it sweet in a way, but also concerning. She must have been in a really bad way to warrant this kind of attention from him. How had they found her? Where had they found her? Trying to remember only made her head hurt.

He wrapped his fingers around hers again, scattering her thoughts. It would have been nice, except for the fact that his frown was firmly in place. *The man could do eighteen different versions of dour.*

"So the Balm of Gilead, head of the Gilead Commission, creator of Shadowchasers, is your mother?"

She rubbed at her forehead with her free hand. At least he'd waited until she relieved herself to question her. "You know her, huh?"

"I know that it takes a formidable woman to be the Balm of Gilead. The brilliant mind of Cleopatra. The fighting spirit of Boadicea. The inspiring leadership of Amanirenas standing against the Romans. And she's your mother." He shook his head ruefully. "Now I know why you are the way you are."

She wasn't sure if that was a compliment or not so ignored it instead. "Balm did not birth me, but she took me in, forged me into what I am today. Anyway, she was about three hours from descending on us like a landslide, so thank you for letting me use your phone."

He gave a brief nod. "Seems like we averted another major crisis, then."

"You have no idea. Or maybe you do. I remember the day she gave me my Lightblade . . . gods." The reason behind the empty sensation finally dawned on her. "My blade. Where's my Lightblade?"

"You didn't have it when we found you. Anansi went back there yesterday but there were no traces of it."

"Gods, that means the Avatar has my Lightblade." She buried her face in her hands, trying to fight down her panic, her defenselessness. "How could he have it? He's Fallen. He's not supposed to be able to touch something forged of Light. How could I have let it go? Why would I have let it go?"

"What do you remember?"

She struggled to drag information to the surface, details fuzzed by whatever the Avatar had done to her extrasense. "I got a call from Gilead, saying that the sweepers had gotten a hit on Shadow-magic near the Fulton County Airport. She told me there was a special response team on site and when they went dark, I had no choice but to go in. They'd been put under the Avatar's control; that's how I got captured."

She remembered then that she'd left him at the Carlos. "I'm sorry I left you."

"No, you're not. The timing was just convenient."

True, she wasn't sorry, but he wouldn't appreciate that she'd left him behind as a safeguard. "Enig—the Avatar—told me he's been planning this move for years, moving up in rank and power in the Shadow-realm and of course, he's looking to make this world his new domain."

"He wants to destroy it?"

"No, not destroy, just take it over and create a new world order, the usual Shadow Shuffle. He seems to think your dagger will help him with that. He thought I would too."

"He wanted you to work for him?"

"Something like that." She looked away. "He tried to bribe me. Naturally I refused. It went downhill pretty quickly after that."

His anger broke free like a clap of thunder. She knew a curse word when she heard it, even if she didn't know the language. "What were you thinking, going off alone?"

"I was thinking that I was doing my job."

"It was a trap."

"I know."

"You knew it was a trap and you went anyway?" His grip tightened. "You could have been killed!"

She sighed. "I know that too. But I couldn't leave the Gilead team there and I couldn't take you since what the Avatar really wants is your blade. You're not the only one who's trying to save lives here. So I'm sorry if my actions threatened your karmic tally."

"My karmic tally." His jaw worked. "That's what you believe this to be about? That I'm angry because you could have cost me my afterlife?"

"Why else? This is my job. It's always been danger-ous and the unknown is even more so. It's why I give Wynne and Zoo an extraction time and why they have trackers on me. I've been a Shadowchaser for a long time and I've never been afraid of dying, especially if I take some of them out when I go."

Chapter 23

Wynne, frozen in the doorway, gasped, a distressed noise that sucked out all of Khefar's anger. Zoo stepped behind her, and squeezed her shoulder.

Kira turned her head on the pillow, grateful to postpone the argument with Khefar. "Hey, guys. Thanks for coming to get me. I'm thinking that was the closest call yet."

Khefar remained silent as Wynne and her husband entered the room. The other woman set a tray on the nightstand before stepping back, her gloved hands in front of her. "You don't remember?"

"He . . . the Avatar did something that blocked my extrasense," she said, frowning as she tried to remember. "Then we had the whole stupid good guy–bad guy back and forth, and . . . and he drugged me. He jabbed me with something that sent me on a serious trip. I went from zero to full power and had to fight my way out. It gets kinda fuzzy from there. Did Gilead's team get out? I don't remember seeing them. We were about a mile from the Fulton County Airport."

Her frown deepened. "You three keep giving one another strange looks. Somebody want to clue me in?"

"We didn't find you anywhere near the Fulton

County Airport," Wynne said. "Are you sure that's where you were?"

"Of course. I thought you said Nansee went back there looking for my Lightblade?"

Wynne shook her head. "We didn't go anywhere near the county airport when we were looking for you."

Her heart thumped. "Then Sanchez might have found it. Logistics directed me to a warehouse in the industrial complex there. I would like to know if the response team was extracted safely, but I'm not ready to talk to Sanchez yet. I spoke to Balm, but she didn't mention the team. Still can't believe Sanchez sent a team after the Fallen like that. She's the one who's always talking about protocol."

"At least there was more than one of them," Khefar muttered.

She ignored him. "If you didn't find me in the warehouse area, where exactly did you find me?"

"At Oakland Cemetery." Zoo moved to stand behind his wife. "We think they injected you with concentrated Chaos magic," he said. "I didn't know something like that was possible. Light and Shadow were basically duking it out in your veins."

"The Avatar wanted me to join him. When I refused, he promised to break me. Injecting a Shadowchaser with liquid Chaos would do it, I guess. I'll have to let Gilead know about this." She got a good look at Zoo, saw his right arm swathed in bandages. "What the hell happened to you?"

Wynne started to cry. "Oh, Kira . . . "

"What happened?" Wynne didn't cry. She was an

army brat from a family of army brats, and a combat vet to boot. Wynne didn't break easily.

Kira's fingers tightened on Khefar's as she thought about her new eye color, the holes in her memory, the nightmare landscape she'd dreamed about. Was it more than a dream? "Somebody tell me something here."

Khefar squeezed her hand. "They dumped you close to an abandoned warehouse not far from Oakland Cemetery, near where many of the homeless gather for the night. Some of them tried to help you. Others tried to hurt you."

"No, there weren't any humans around." Her brow furrowed. "There were halflings. He—the Avatar—let them taste me and t-touch me after he drugged me. All I could think of was escape, trying to make it through the commotion and the screaming. They kept touching me and it . . . it just felt wrong. I wanted them to stop. Gods, I wanted to get away as fast as I could."

She looked up at him, dread coiling in the pit of her stomach. "I thought they were attacking me," she said, her voice just a slice of its usual tone. "Their faces were all twisted and dark. Are you telling me that they weren't halflings, but human homeless people trying to help me?"

"You didn't know, Kira. You were going on pure instinct, the instinct of a Shadowchaser. It wasn't your intent to do them harm."

"Harm." She pulled her hands away from his, fisted them atop the sheets. "I was out of my mind, thinking I was fighting halflings, but in reality I was in the middle of a bunch of innocent humans. Did I . . . did I hurt people?"

Wynne's sob was answer enough, but she had to know. Her lips twisted as she fought to push the words out. "I . . . I did more than hurt people, didn't I?"

She looked at Khefar. She looked at him because she couldn't look at Wynne and Zoo, couldn't look in her friends' faces and see the condemnation there. She could look at the Nubian warrior and know that he would know, and understand, the burden of innocent souls weighing down her own—the guilt, the anger, the unrelieved heaviness that threatened to suck her under.

"How many?" She bit her lip to keep from screaming. "Tell me. How many people did I murder?"

"Kira . . ."

"How. Many."

Khefar held her gaze and when he spoke he didn't hesitate. "Eight died at the scene. Two more died on the way to the hospital, five others are comatose, and several were kept overnight. The media is claiming that they were caught in the factory fire."

A whimper of sound from Wynne.

"You somehow managed to get yourself to the cemetery. Nansee found your trail. That's how we located you," the warrior added.

She turned her head toward her friends but didn't dare look at them. "Zoo's arm. Were you trying to protect me?"

"I was careless and you got the jump on me," the witch said, his tone a forced brightness. "The Nubian took a hit too. You surprised us with that throwing blast thing."

"Blast thing? I hurt you?" Her world tilted crazily for a moment. "I attacked you?"

"Not your fault. You did try to warn me, even though you didn't know it was me."

She couldn't remember. Why couldn't she remember? "I didn't even recognize my own friends?"

"Hey, I'll survive. Good thing I'm left-handed."

"I'm sorry. I'm so sorry I—" She dropped her head, hiding behind her braids. She'd attacked her friends and killed innocent people. It went against everything she stood for, that Shadowchasers stood for. Slowly she pushed her hands beneath the covers, hiding them. "I'll make this right. I swear, I'll make this right."

"It's not your fault."

She wanted to believe Wynne. Wanted to believe that Wynne believed that. But she'd seen Wynne's expression as she looked at her husband. They all knew that he'd gotten injured trying to help her. Nothing could change the fact that if it wasn't for her, Zoo wouldn't have gotten injured and she wouldn't have seen the hurt in Wynne's eyes. But she had seen it, and knew it would take a while before it disappeared.

She'd hurt strangers, hurt her friends. No, it registered: worse than that, she'd murdered people, attacked her friends. She'd done what halflings had been doing for ages—attacking innocents just because they could.

You belong to Shadow. You just don't know it yet.

How much further could she stretch before she broke?

She fisted her hands. No. She knew she could not break. That was what they wanted, what everyone wanted. What the Avatar wanted. She was stronger than that. She would not break.

"I have to get home."

Wynne protested. "You can't leave yet—you're still injured!"

"I have to. I've been out of sight two whole days. The city—at least those I protect it against—will wonder and Gilead will want a report. I can't let them connect me to what happened—to what I did to those poor people. Not until after I stop the Avatar. Sanchez will think I've gone over and she'll send her Commission goons after me, no matter what Balm tells her. I can't let that happen."

"Okay." Wynne stood. Kira tensed, waiting for something, anything. *Take it. Whatever she says or does, take it. You almost killed her husband. You deserve whatever she decides to give you.*

Wynne backed away. "I finished the dagger."

It took her a moment to swim out of misery to realize what Wynne meant. *Her friend had backed away from her.* "Really?"

"Yeah. I needed something to do to keep my mind off—I mean, you know I always have to have something to do."

Kira winced, the flash of pain as quick and deep as a dagger strike. *I made my friends suffer and they helped me anyway. Zoo could have healed himself, but he'd used his magic on me instead. How do you repay people for something like that?* "Will you give it to Khefar? He needs to hold it for a while anyway to put some of his essence into it."

"I guess, but . . ." Wynne's voice trailed off.

"Khefar, do you have your car here?"

"Yes. What dagger do you speak of?" Khefar was clearly puzzled.

Right. She hadn't told him yet. She didn't want to tell him now, knowing that it would just infuriate him. "I'll talk to you about it later, I promise. Will you take me home?"

The Nubian nodded, his expression telling her that he'd hold her to her promise.

"Kira," Zoo said, "we can take you to your place as soon as we close up shop."

"No thanks. Got a ride." She tried to smile. "Besides, you need to rest up that arm." Kira didn't mention she didn't want them near her warehouse as it might expose them to more danger. They'd figure that out, too, soon enough.

"Okay. I guess you're right," Zoo said.

Wynne said, "I can't give you the dagger to take with you right now, Khefar. Zoo still needs to add some magic to it . . . ."

Khefar again nodded his assent. "I'm sure we can . . . make arrangements later regarding this mysterious dagger I know nothing about." His eyes darted to Kira. Was he judging her?

"Right," Zoo said. "I'll do my part tonight, then. Wynne?" He opened the door with his right hand. "Let's get back to the shop, let Kira get ready to go home."

She didn't relax until her friends left the room, closing the door behind them. *Were they still her friends? Would their friendship survive when this was over and done?*

Sudden, crushing loneliness gripped her. She was losing everything that had ever mattered to her, bit by precious bit. Bernie, her blade, her powers, her friends.

Even if she killed Enig, even if she recovered her blade and her powers, the loss of her friends would be too high a price to pay.

Khefar broke the heavy silence. "You should try to eat something."

She looked at the tray. Nausea, hunger, and dread churned in equal parts. "I can't. I know she used gloves, but I-I can't feel my extrasense. I wouldn't be able to cleanse it. I can't take the chance of touching it and finding out what she really thinks about me hurting Zoo—"

"You don't think she'll hate you?"

"I could handle that, if she hated me. But if my friends are afraid of me . . . "

A small sound escaped her. She stifled the rest of it, but it was hard and it hurt. Everything hurt. Thinking hurt. The darkness suddenly seemed more welcoming to her than this, better than this.

The Nubian touched her shoulder, and the darkness retreated slightly. "Do you need help to get up?"

"I think I can make my body obey me." She willed her legs to swing over the side of the bed and felt slightly surprised when they obeyed. Her feet and legs were bare, and she wore panties and a loose tank, both unbleached Egyptian cotton. So much skin showing, but not her hands, not yet. Those stayed tangled in the sheet, safely hidden.

She stared down at her legs. Memory flashed like a slide show. There had been blood and bruises and cuts, gone now. They had healed her, her friends, despite her having hurt them. It hadn't been easy letting them in to start with, allowing them to be a part of who she was and what she did. She wondered now if they regretted knowing her. But if she didn't have them, where would she be? Still in the cemetery with its memories of dead and grieving people? Dead herself? Or worse—targeted by local police and perhaps Gilead itself.

Again her eyes were drawn to her bare skin. No sheen of either yellow Shadow-magic or the blue of her own power. She hadn't even thought about it when she'd first awakened. Now she couldn't feel it, didn't dare reach for it. What if she tried and it didn't come? What if she'd permanently lost her power?

She'd dreamed of being without it, fantasized about being Normal. Even after losing Nico, she'd dreamed about it. But now, facing a reality without her extra-sense, it terrified her. She wouldn't be anything without her power except dead.

"Kira."

"There should be a change of clothes in the top drawer of the dresser there, wrapped in plastic." Her jaw tightened against the scream that bubbled deep in her belly, but she could feel it in her mind, deep in every fiber, desperately trying to claw its way out.

She'd killed innocents, hurt her friends. She asked herself: How much Shadow lurked in her soul now? Was she more Shadow than Light? Enig had said she belonged to Shadow. She'd denied it, but now she couldn't help wondering. Her eyes had changed. She had changed. Did that mean she was too far gone, so far beyond redemption that the Light had taken her power and turned away from her?

She started a silent prayer to Ma'at but stopped herself. She was afraid to test her relationship to the goddess in any way, yet knowing that if the Light had abandoned her, she was in major trouble. Despite being favored by the head of Gilead, Kira knew Balm would have no compunction about ordering containment if one of her Shadowchasers, even her own daughter, no longer walked in Light. Sanchez would throw everything she could at subduing Kira, and she'd resist. Her resistance would turn the town into a war zone.

"Anything else you need?"

"I should be capable of dressing myself." She tried dredging up a smile in his general direction. "If I can't, that would be a good argument for not going anywhere anytime soon, wouldn't it?"

Khefar left her, softly closing the door behind him before leaning heavily against it once outside the room. His heart ached for her. He couldn't be angry with her, not when she'd just been emotionally devastated. All he could do was promise to be there for her. He knew what it meant to have innocent blood staining one's hands. He also knew it never truly faded.

Kira was at her breaking point. He'd seen it in the slump of her shoulders, the tremor in her fingers. He couldn't press her about going off alone, question her about the dagger she'd had Wynne create—no doubt a replica of his. Those things could wait. What mattered now, more than anything, was making sure she stayed away from the shadows that threatened to consume her.

"Nansee."

The demigod materialized beside him. "Yes?"

"I need you to spin up a block around us and Kira's room. Quickly."

Thankfully the spider god didn't ply him with questions. Instead, he placed his palms flat against the door. Khefar felt the rush of power as it swept through him and down the hall. He pressed his forehead against the door and waited.

The first short shriek still caught him like the lightning-quick slam of a rifle shot. It was followed by another pain-filled wail, then another. Then more, blending into one long scream of agony.

His hands itched with the urge to open the door, to go to the woman breaking apart on the other side. She needed to excise the grief and she wouldn't if he went to her side. If she didn't get it out, the agony would fester and infect her entire being. That didn't mean he couldn't share it with her, endure it with her, even with a door between them.

Something stirred deep inside him, an emotion he'd thought long buried and gone. Revenge—the emotion that had consigned him to this eternity of rescue and redemption. Like a faltering ember it searched for fuel, found it in his growing regard for this young Shadowchaser, and began to burn.

Khefar vowed silently to himself that he would bring the Fallen to justice and save Kira—even if that meant saving her from herself. And if he enjoyed himself in the process, so be it.

Chapter 24

Kira leaned against the rear right passenger door of Khefar's Charger, trying desperately not to think or feel. Both options hurt like hell and she'd had enough pain to last a lifetime. Several lifetimes.

She'd hurt her friends. She'd killed innocent by-standers. It didn't matter that she'd been drugged and lost control. It didn't matter to her and it certainly wouldn't matter to Gilead. She'd have to atone some-how. Later. Right now, she had to find Enig. Then she'd have to destroy him.

"Kira."

She glanced up to see that Khefar had turned to face her from the front passenger seat. He said her name again, as if he'd been calling her for a while. "Yeah?"

"Do you want to stop for anything before you go home?"

"Uh-huh." She straightened, ignoring the pound-ing of her heart and the painful twinges shooting through her muscles. "I want to go back to where you found me. Not the cemetery, but the old factory where the homeless people were."

He didn't try to argue or overrule her, though An-ansi did throw a questioning look their way. Khefar ignored him, staring at her with his soul-dark eyes. He just asked one question. "Are you certain?"

"Not even a little, but I gotta do it. My blade's out there. I need to find it. A Shadowchaser without her Lightblade . . . " She shook her head. "Besides, I need to see the place where I . . . where I was."

"All right." He turned back around. For a stupid, fleeting, weak moment, she wished he sat beside her so she could reach over and thread her fingers through his. Even with her gloves on, just the connection would be enough. Just a touch, so she'd know she was still human. The hunger of it gnawed at her insides.

She thought she'd conquered it, the skin hunger. More than a decade's worth of Gilead training. Six years of living with the guilt of Nico's death. Then Bernie's death, Zoo's injury. Attacking Khefar. Innocents dying. She shouldn't want to touch anyone again, shouldn't want to take off her gloves ever again. But she wanted to touch the Nubian.

"We're here."

Lost in thought, she hadn't noticed the car had stopped.

Shoving aside her inconvenient neediness, she opened the door and pushed herself out before he could come to help her. Anansi wisely stayed in the car.

Yellow police tape ringed what was left of the old factory. A burnt smell still charred the fall air. She turned slightly to get her bearings. Oakland Cemetery lay a few blocks to the east, Grady Hospital just to the north. Her actions had sent people to both places.

"Remember anything?"

Khefar had an uncanny ability to pull her back

before her thoughts spiraled down. Then again, he'd been through this before. She'd killed ten people. He'd killed several thousand. Surely, she thought, he knew the emotion that strained her insides, fighting for a way out. Had experienced the strangling grief that welled inside her. After four millennia, did he still feel the weight of their souls, despite the lives he'd saved in atonement?

Did it matter? He'd had four thousand years to come to terms with what he'd done. She wouldn't even have a tenth of that.

"Kira?"

She shook her head. "I thought I'd be able to sense my blade, but it's not here. Which means it was at the other warehouse near the airport and it's probably long gone."

"Hopefully that means the police didn't confiscate it as evidence."

"The police would be the least of my worries." If Sanchez had recovered her gear . . . well, the phrase "public hanging" was too mild for what Sanchez would plan for her.

She concentrated on the scene, trying not to think of how vulnerable and off-balance she felt without her Lightblade. "You said you guys tracked me. Did I ping you from here or somewhere else?"

"No, it jumped from a location a little south of here, faster than you could have made it by car and not as steady as your path to the cemetery."

"The cemetery." Her mind instantly went to Zoo and Wynne. Her friends had risked their lives to save her and she'd returned the favor by trying to kill one of them. "I attacked Zoo," she said then. "He was trying to help me, trying to talk me down, and I zapped him."

"It was a stress-filled moment. You didn't single him out. Anansi and I took a couple of hits too."

That didn't reassure her. "So I attacked you, one of my best friends, and a demigod." She closed her eyes. "I must have been seriously fucked-up."

"You were drugged and the Veil was torn from you. You didn't even know your own name."

Memories slithered through her mind's eye, snakes and wraiths. "I attacked you. I tried to take your dagger."

"I think you were under a compulsion to take it," he corrected her. "As for the attack, it was the easiest way to disarm you. See?" He pulled at his collar, exposing the unmarred skin at his shoulder. "I sat in the sun and healed just fine."

"You kept me from hurting Zoo further, didn't you?"

He shrugged. "I'm immortal; he isn't."

So she'd attacked him. She would have killed him too, or at least tried. And Wynne—

"Thank you. For sacrificing yourself."

He nodded, but there was nothing he could say. You're welcome? No problem? Neither of those were true. The truth was, the Chaos magic had done something to her. Changed her. She had to pray that the damage wasn't permanent.

"What good does it do you to force these memories? None of us blames you, Kira."

Her shoulders bunched as she looked away. "You blame me for going off on my own."

"That's different. Regardless of what happened after, I would still be upset at you going off alone."

"Because I jeopardized your afterlife by making it impossible for you to protect me?"

He touched her shoulder, turned her around. "No, because we're a team. That means we decide and act together."

She wanted to argue that she was already part of a team. Not Sanchez and Gilead, but Wynne and Zoo. But the only reason their team worked was because she hadn't allowed Wynne or Zoo to override any of her decisions. She was the Shadowchaser; they weren't.

"Does it matter that I was trying to protect you?"

"Yes, it matters a lot." His expression lightened. "I don't think I can recall the last time someone acted out of concern for me. Thank you."

"You are welcome." She dipped her head. "That helps. But I think Wynne and Zoo will still blame me for a while."

"They don't blame you; you know that."

"Does it matter?"

"No. Not at the beginning."

She stuttered out a sigh, feeling scraped raw and totally out of her element. "I met them two years ago. They had a scrying mirror that had a nasty habit of feeding on souls and resisting their efforts to break it. I tracked it down, evicted the spirit inhabiting it, and confiscated the mirror. We've been friends ever since."

She turned away from the charred ruins of the warehouse. "They wanted to help me and I refused at first. Their friendship was more important, how normal they were. But they've got mad skills, you know?

I started relying on them for my gear, more than the Commission, and they came through every time. I thought they were adrenaline junkies or wanted some kind of fix for leaving their military life behind. Then I thought they were just crazy, especially when they stuck it out with me. But they're not. They're the bravest people I've ever met. They're human and so . . . so breakable. I go into danger all the time, but I've got my extrasense to protect me. What do they have? Kevlar and themselves. Their stupid, fragile selves. They could have been killed and I would have even more blood on my hands."

Khefar moved closer to her. "You know I know what you suffer. You think the blood will stain your hands forever."

She looked up at him. He did know. "You came through it. How did you do that?"

"Badly. I had to die to come through my anger and guilt. Even then I was basically a bastard for a century or two."

She felt a thin smile crease her lips. "Somehow I don't think I'll have the luxury of several centuries to balance my scales."

"Then don't think about next year, next month, or even tomorrow. Think about getting through the next minute, then the next one after that. You'll be surprised to discover that minutes become days and days become months and the hollowness becomes easier to breathe through."

He did touch her then, a hand on her forearm. "You're stronger than you know, Kira. I would rather you not walk the path that I did or learn your lessons as

I learned mine. But however you learn them, I'll walk with you."

She had to go up against Enig again. The consequences of not facing him were far worse than confronting him and failing to stop him. Yet the thought of going against him on her own filled her with a silent terror. She wouldn't ever ask Wynne and Zoo to back her on any missions again. But if Khefar wanted to help her, she would not refuse. "Thank you. Thank you for that."

"Come on." He guided her to the car. "We both need to refresh and regroup. Then we'll come up with a plan to stop this Avatar and get your blade back."

They made it back to her home in a much lighter silence than when they'd left Wynne and Zoo's. Still, two days had been lost. The only real bright spot Kira could identify in the gloomy scenario was that Enig didn't have the dagger.

Anansi slowed the car as they entered her neighborhood. She felt the Nubian tense before she noted the stiffness of his body, and she peered out the window to see what had caused the reaction. The distinctive grill of the Rolls-Royce Phantom gleamed in the sunlight in sharp contrast to the diamond black paint and tinted windows. She knew of only one person so ostentatious, but couldn't believe he'd endanger his neutral reputation by visiting her.

"I'm betting you don't see a car like that in this neck of the woods often," Khefar noted. "Friend or foe?"

"Depends on which way the wind blows." She released her seat belt. "But I need to talk to him. Something made Demoz leave his club. I better find out what it is."

She got out of Khefar's Charger, trying to move as if she hadn't been put physically and emotionally through the wringer. It was a challenge since most of her energy went to keeping her shields in place.

The woman she'd seen in the club a few days ago, the Light-infused one who had served them in Demoz's office, stood by the driver's side passenger door. The afternoon sunlight burnished her blue-white glow, making her appear almost like a Normal. For an inexplicable reason she reminded Kira of those cat-tailed servant girls in a bunch of Japanese anime, a shy and solicitous demeanor concealing the skills and temperament of an assassin.

The rear window rolled down enough for her to just make out the psychic vampire's bulk, a large shadow tucked in among other shadows. She wondered just how old he was. It was usually the older ones who had a thing against sunlight. Most of the younger vamps had their work-arounds, including mobile spray-on sunblock units.

She spackled on the sarcasm. "Demoz, I would invite you in . . . well, no, I wouldn't. What brings you here?"

"You. I had to see with my own eyes that you were still alive."

"Well, here I am." She spread her arms, sure her smile was as crooked as her stance. *Just fake it for a few minutes more.* "More or less in one piece. Hope that doesn't disappoint you."

"Surprisingly, it doesn't. It does disturb me, however. I have a reputation to maintain, you know."

"Far be it from me to do anything to damage your

reputation," she retorted, actually enjoying the back and forth with Demoz. "I would think venturing out in daylight might do damage to your brain."

"That's entirely possible. You have obviously recovered quite well, which means I can go ahead and give you this."

He gestured. The young woman opened the car's front passenger door and retrieved a case from the seat. Curious but cautious, Kira watched the woman lift the lid, then turn the open case to face her.

Kira couldn't control the surprised gasp or the shimmer of joy that immediately filled her eyes. Her Lightblade lay on pale raw silk, as beautiful as the day she'd first received it. Before she realized it, she'd raised her hand, her gloved fingers hovering above the hilt.

"It's all right," the young woman said in a musical voice. "It's been purified."

The girl was nearly Light-pure. Kira knew the woman couldn't have touched her blade otherwise and certainly couldn't have purified it. It made her wonder briefly who the woman was and why she was working for Demoz.

Before she could question anything further, she stripped off her glove and wrapped bare fingers around the handle. The familiar weight of it, the balance, the crispness of it, the absence of memories. She was nearly whole again.

A test to be sure. She called the blade, pushing with all her will through the Veil. Her extrasense responded with a pop of energy, flowing through her hand into the hilt. Her knees almost gave way. Until she'd tried, she'd doubted that she'd be able to call her power, but she couldn't take the blade into her house without testing it.

She refrained from clutching the hilt to her chest like a child who had grabbed the last piece of candy, sliding it into the new sheath instead. "Thank you. I suppose I owe you now." What the hell would she have to do to square up with him?

"You don't owe me, Kira." He paused. "What happened to you sent a shock wave through the psychic plane on par with the eruption of Krakatau."

Figures. He probably wouldn't have to feed for months. "I suppose you got your rocks off with that one, didn't you?"

"No." Something close to horror wrinkled his features. "It was a type of rape, of both you and of me. If I could undo what was done, I would. Since I can't, all I can do is ask that you never let anything like that happen to you again."

Demoz's apparently sincere concern nearly undid her. She bit her lip, needing the physical pain to push emotion back. Finally she gave him a jerky nod. "Can you put the word out that a certain Egyptian dagger will make an appearance at your club, to be auctioned off to the highest bidder?"

He stared at her. "Does this mean that I should make sure that my club's insurance policy is up to date?"

"You're always careful, Demoz. I'm sure your insurance is better than most."

"All right, Kira. Give me two days to get the information out to everyone who needs to know. I'll even make sure there are a few humans around."

"Not everyone needs to know. Make it tomorrow night."

"The club is closed then, so I suppose it could be done."

"I appreciate that." She paused. "I'm going to stop him, Demoz."

"I hope so, Kira. I hope so." He rolled up his window.

The young woman went around the car, opened the driver's door, then paused. A pale hand lifted, glowed. "The Light hold you, Kira Solomon."

"And you as well." She retreated to the sidewalk as the other woman got in the car, fastened her seat belt, then shifted the car into gear. She wondered again just what the woman was. A woman who could remain Light-pure working in the DMZ—obviously as Demoz's personal assistant—and who could purify a Lightblade. The mystery would have to wait for another day.

Khefar and Anansi, who had remained in the car during the encounter, joined her. "The psychic vampire recovered your Lightblade?"

"Yeah." Kira disarmed the biometric locks. "Forgive me for ever thinking it was right to keep your blade from you."

"No apologies are necessary, Kira. I'm glad you have reunited with your blade."

"Me too. You know the world's going to hell when Demoz shows concern for a Shadowchaser." Kira set about physically and magically unlocking the living quarters' door.

"I doubt he'd show concern for just any

Shadowchaser," Khefar said as he followed her inside. "Just you."

"Yeah, well, part of it was an apology for feeding off me. I got the feeling that he hadn't wanted to, but didn't have a choice."

Anansi shut the door behind them and she immediately sagged. Khefar made a grab for her, but she waved him off and sat on the sofa.

"I'm okay, I just—it took a lot of energy to act normal out there."

"You should have stayed with Wynne. I knew it was too early to move you."

"I couldn't stay there." Seeing Wynne's haunted expression had been a constant reminder of her failures, her crimes. She needed to be able to put the reminders aside for a little while, at least until Enig was stopped.

"Wynne and Zoo are good, but they can only do so much. I have stuff here that will help me heal faster. Besides, we both know I needed to send a message that I'm still functional. Enig needs to know that he didn't destroy me—and that I'm coming for him."

"We're coming for him," Khefar corrected.

"Right. We'll hunt him down together." She headed for the stairway. "I'll be back in a little bit."

"Are you hungry?" Anansi called. "I can make lunch. I can also start the kettle for the tea."

"Sounds good. Give me about an hour or so, all right?"

She needed to go visit Ma'at, to ask for forgiveness. The only problem was, she didn't know if it would be granted.

Chapter 25

After steeping upstairs in a bath filled with rejuvenating herbs, Kira made her way to the lower level and her altar room. Dread filled her as she stepped through the door and fired up the spirit lantern. She had to work to find a calm-enough center to begin the ritual, pushing through her fear and uncertainty. She wouldn't stand a chance if she didn't start in a clear state and she needed every advantage she could get.

She folded herself onto the large black silk cushion in the center of the tiled floor. Her sistrum and the gilded mirror waited to be used, the statue of Ma'at surveying all. What was going to happen? What would be the outcome of the ritual? Speculating wouldn't bring answers; only action would. She had to begin while she had the courage.

With her personal copy of the Book of the Dead balanced on her lap, she picked up the sistrum beside the mirror, gave the instrument a shake to start the ritual. As the sound of the instrument filled the room, the slick surface of the mirror wavered. She focused her extrasense, pushing through the Veil. Ma'at's scales rose up from the surface of the mirror, gleaming and golden, in perfect empty balance.

Kira centered her being, preparing for the most

important ritual she could perform, the weighing of her soul.

My heart, my mother; my heart, my mother! My heart whereby I came into being!

A single etheric feather appeared, poised on the bowl on the right side of the scale.

May naught stand up to oppose me at my judgment, may there be no opposition to me in the presence of the Chiefs.

A ball of pale light emerged from the center of her chest. The decidedly teal-colored cast of it worried her, and she almost called it back. It floated toward the left side of the scale, opposite Ma'at's feather.

For a moment both sides swayed. Then the scales tilted, the left side lowering.

Gods, no.

She fought a tremble as she scrambled to prostrate herself. *Do not reject me,* she prayed. *Sweet Mother of Justice, do not turn away from Your daughter. Not yet. Allow me time to balance my scales. Please, Lady of Truth, hear my plea.*

With her forehead pressed against the cool golden tile, she waited for a sign. Would the goddess acknowledge her? Would her prayer be answered? Was she too late, too full of Shadow to be worthy of Her favor?

A soft touch, the merest whisper of sensation at her cheek. She lifted her head. The scale rocked slightly, up and down, not balancing. The final judgment was yet to be rendered.

Relief flooded her system, bringing tears. She still had Ma'at's blessing, still had time to make things right. "Thank you," she whispered, her voice quavering. "Thank you, goddess."

With a quiet word and wave of her hand, Kira cut the flow of extrasense to the scales. The feather dissipated and the ball of light floated toward her, settling into her chest. The glow dimmed around the scales as they slipped back into the satiny surface of the mirror.

Pulling her gloves back on, she shut the Book of the Dead, then placed it and the sistrum back into the ornate wooden chest. It was only after she'd extinguished the light and secured the door that she allowed herself to ponder the ramifications.

She'd felt the change, the way one could feel an approaching thunderstorm. Her insides tightened with the knowledge she'd gained.

The scales didn't lie.

Her soul had been weighed and found wanting. Enig had accomplished what he'd set out to do. *You belong to me, to Shadow, already. You just haven't realized it yet.*

Shadow had wanted her for a long time. Soldiers deserted from both sides, though never with any frequency. Usually Chasers were sacrificed before Shadow could use them, taken out by highly trained units of the Gilead Commission that Chasers weren't supposed to know about. Shadow, of course, didn't let anyone go willingly.

The ones who lived in the gray area, the ones who slipped so subtly into Light or Shadow no one detected it, those were the ones most coveted by Shadow. It was one of the reasons why the Fallen were so powerful and so dangerous. They knew exactly what it was like to be on either side of the Eternal Struggle.

There was still time, of course, time to do good deeds before Final Judgment. Time to do the right thing, to push her soul back to Balance . . .

Except there was no time. She had to stop Enig. Facing down the Shadow Avatar, stopping him before he caused more destruction, would have to suffice. If it wasn't enough . . . she'd have to hope that Ammit the Devourer claimed her before Shadow did.

Unless she had a fail-safe. A fail-safe she trusted, not one sent by Balm or controlled by Sanchez.

She sealed the corridor and the office, then made her way back upstairs. Khefar sat in the sling chair, leafing through a book on Mesopotamian societies. A panda-shaped teapot and two mugs waited on the coffee table and she wondered if it had been a deliberate choice on Anansi's part. The panda was her favorite teapot, so he might have chosen it for her. But she couldn't imagine Khefar using it, so Anansi might have chosen it for him, simply the whimsy of a trickster demigod. The spider god, of course, was nowhere to be seen.

Khefar balanced the opened book upside-down on the chair's arm. "I thought maybe you'd fallen asleep."

"No, I had other things to do." She poured herself a mug of tea before sliding back onto the couch. The fragrant aroma wafted up with the steam and she inhaled it gratefully, wishing the simple pleasure of tea would be enough to soothe her. "I got sidetracked. Besides, I think I've had plenty of downtime to last me a while. Where's the spider?"

"He went to market about half an hour ago," he said, leaning forward to lift the panda-shaped teapot. "I don't suppose he ever really *needs* to go shopping for food, but he often does so anyway. The process fascinates him. Knowing him, he'll get distracted and it will be another hour or so before he returns."

She looked at him, the silly panda teapot in his hands but no distaste on his face, and had a moment of realization. He could do it. So many things he did and had done without complaint, completely unflappable. He had honor and integrity. How many people would be able to shoulder the burden he had, and work tirelessly to see it through? She could ask him to be her failsafe and he would do it. He was the only one who could.

She pulled her feet up on the couch, balancing her mug on her knees. She told herself she was trying to find the right words to make the request, but really she just wanted to prolong the moment. She wasn't sure how he'd react to her idea and this quiet camaraderie was like an oasis in the middle of the chaos that her life had become. She had an immortal warrior in her living room and a spider god out shopping for lunch, but it felt . . . nice.

"I have a favor I need to ask you."

He looked up from adding honey to his tea. "What sort of favor?"

Smart man. Most people would have said 'sure,' then asked what the favor was about. "Actually, it's more of a promise, like a pact, I guess."

He returned his mug to the coffee table, then settled back into the chair, his posture open and relaxed. He was back to a white T-shirt again, and his feet were bare beneath the frayed hem of his well-worn jeans. "What sort of promise do you wish me to make to you, Kira Solomon?"

She had to look away from him for a moment. He was just too damn touchable. "I don't know what your plans are after we deal with Enig and I know you have more lives to save before you get to move on, but if you're still around when it happens—if it happens—I'd like for you to be my fail-safe."

"Fail-safe?"

"Yeah." She unfolded from the couch, then placed her mug on the table before beginning to pace. Movement helped her think, to decide what to say. "Sometimes, when I'm fighting or pulling Shadow out of artifacts, sometimes a little of it sticks. Most of the time, my work with the Gilead Commission balances that out, balances me out. Keeps me from sliding too far into Shadow."

She turned to face him. "There are people out there who are waiting for me to lose the Balance, waiting to capitalize on that opportunity. I can't let them. So I'd like to make a pact with you, that if I become Unbalanced, you'll make sure that Shadow doesn't get its hands on me."

He rose, then folded his arms across his chest. "You want me to kill you."

"No." She lifted her chin. "I want you to uncreate me."

"Uncreate you?" His eyes widened. "You mean, use the power of the Dagger of Kheferatum to erase your existence?"

She winced, then nodded. "Basically, yes. I can't ask Wynne or Zoo to help. I don't think they'd be able to do what needed doing when the time came. I can't let anyone in Gilead know, and if they were sent after me, I'd probably fight them and . . . and hurt them. I've had enough of hurting innocent people to last me a lifetime."

She dragged air into her lungs. It felt like inhaling shards of ice. "It has to be you. You're the only one strong enough. You're the only one I'd let get close enough."

"And you believe that you deserve this?"

"It's not a question of what I deserve. It's a question of what's going to keep people safe. I might wait too long, think I could fight it, or think I'm not too far over the edge. My judgment would be impaired and I wouldn't be able to make the right call."

"How do you know your judgment isn't impaired right now?" he demanded.

"I don't. That's why I need you to be the one who decides."

"I can't believe you're asking me for this—this thing that goes against the very vow I made to Isis." He made a cutting gesture with his hand. "I am here to protect you, not bring you to harm!"

"You're here to save my life," she corrected, willing him to understand what she wanted and why. "But I'd rather that you save my soul. What if . . . what if instead of keeping me alive, you save my eternity by preventing me from hurting other innocents? What if by taking my life you save it, and dozens of others in the process?"

His frown deepened. "What if I refuse?"

She hadn't considered the possibility that he'd refuse, that she couldn't persuade him. Desperation plucked at her nerves. "Please don't."

"Why?"

"Because I'm close." The admission shot from her mouth like a projectile. But here, with him, she could say it. "I'm closer than I've ever been. When I was captured, he . . . Enig did something to me. He damaged me. There's Shadow living inside me now."

"You don't know that. Zoo and Anansi, they healed you, they got it all out."

"Look at me." She stepped close to him, wrapped her fingers around his wrist, and brought his hand up to her face. "Look at my eyes."

He glared at her, even as his fingers moved gently along her cheek. His hand spasmed a moment before his eyes widened. "Gods, Kira."

"Told you so." She tried for a smile but couldn't make her lips curve. "They didn't get all of the Shadow out. You can see it in my eyes. The color's changed and not because of the magic they worked to heal me. I-I think there's a permanent taint on my soul."

He shook his head in denial. "You don't know that. The Balance is in constant motion. You still have a chance to swing your soul back to Light."

"Khefar, I don't have that kind of time." She gripped his hand that was cupping her cheek, then confessed, "When I went downstairs, I weighed my soul. My soul . . . it was heavier than Ma'at's feather. You know what that means."

His expression dimmed. "I do. Your soul would be fed to the Devourer."

"Ma'at has blessed me with a little time, but I can't trust that I'll be able to do the right thing when the point comes to choose. I can't trust that I won't flip out and murder more innocents. I can't trust that I'd die and go straight to judgment. Shadow would find a way to prevent my soul from being given to the Devourer. So I need to know that I have an option, a trustworthy option. I need to know that there's an out. I need that bit of hope to hold on to. I can't let Shadow take me. I just can't."

She was shaking. She didn't realize she was shaking until he knelt in front of her, then wrapped his hands around her fists.

"I will do this for you, Kira Solomon. I failed you once. I will not fail you again. If unmaking you will save your soul, then by my hand you will die. Know also that if letting you live will save your soul, then by my hand you will live. This I swear."

The calm returned. Staring down into his strong features, she knew she could count on him. He'd spent four millennia saving lives and souls in a variety of ways. He would do this for her. She'd be able to take on Enig without fear, secure in the knowledge that if she lost, if Enig infected her again, Khefar would stop her.

As long as he was there, she'd never hurt innocents again.

"Thank you." Relief liquefied her knees, forcing her to sit on the coffee table, the nearest surface. Her voice quavered beyond her ability to control it. "Oh, thank the gods you agreed. Just knowing that, I can breathe, I can do what I have to—gods, what is wrong with me?"

He leaned over her, hands outstretched. She immediately shrank away. "Don't touch me."

"Why not?"

"Because I want it too much. Because I don't deserve it, not after I—I don't deserve—" she broke off, groaning as a tremble shook her body.

"Kira." Slowly, carefully, he wrapped his arms around her, drew her closer.

She wanted to resist. Wanted to pull away, wanted to be stronger, more capable. Wanted to at least wait until she was in the privacy of her own room before she gave in to tears that had become all too frequent. But he was warm and he smelled of leather and cardamom and maleness, and he just tucked her head against his shoulder and waited.

Another shudder spasmed her body, causing her to gasp for air. Then another, and another, until the gasps became sobs, tearing out of her like rapid-fire torpedoes. She cried for Nico, for Bernie, for the unnamed innocents, for her friends. And she cried for herself, for fear that her goddess would turn away from her and leave her to Shadow.

Her hand knotted on his shoulder. "I don't think I'm going to be able to balance this. They might think I'm too far gone to make it."

His thumbs brushed at the tears running down her face. "As long as I am here, I'll help you."

She turned back to face him, reading the resolution in the darkness of his eyes: he meant it. He would do whatever it took to protect her, to protect others. Thank the Light he'd been sent her way!

She shocked herself by reaching up, pressing her lips to his. His body froze for a moment, no doubt he was as shocked as she was. Then his fingers slid into her braids, pulling her closer as he began to return her kiss with hungry, ferocious kisses that fired every synapse in her body.

With a whimper of need, she threw her arms

around his neck, pressing closer to him. He felt incredible, like the perfect summer day, his kisses better than any wine.

"You're glowing," he whispered against her lips. "Should I be worried?"

Her eyes popped open. Sure enough, her exposed skin emanated a turquoise sheen. "Ah, I don't know. This hasn't happened before."

"Reason enough to stop, then." He kissed her once more, then stepped back. "Other than the fact that Nansee will return soon and we need to come up with a plan."

"Plan, right. The plan." She took a couple of steps away from him, and it became much easier to think. "Yes, we need to plan, you and I. And if the trickster can give some advice, I'd appreciate it." She gave him a watery smile. "You wanted me to try this whole teamwork thing. I think I'm ready to give it a shot."

Chapter 26

O kay, I'm ready to talk about the dagger now."

Both Khefar and Nansee looked up from their third bowls of harvest soup, matching chunks of bread in their hands. Nansee had returned within moments of their kiss, providing a much-needed distraction as they helped him prepare the meal. If the spider god noticed the new, different sort of tension between them, he didn't ask about it, for which Kira was extremely grateful. She had a feeling Nansee's amusement would be more than she could handle.

Kira's body fairly hummed. Khefar had given her his promise, and the relief she'd felt had ramped up her appetite. So had the kiss. The meal had been delicious, the spider god an excellent cook. She'd matched them for two bowls, wolfing down chunks of chicken and root vegetables with relish.

"What dagger?" Nansee asked, perching on his stool. Somehow, along with groceries, he'd managed to procure four cane stools. Thanks to the spider god her worktable had been returned to its original purpose as a dining table. Next he'd probably want to remodel her kitchen.

Khefar focused on the remnants of his soup, using his bread to sop up the broth. "Apparently Kira asked

Wynne Marlowe to forge an imitation of my blade, a blade she now plans to use to trick the Fallen."

The demigod's gaze swung back to her. "You asked the metalworker to forge another Dagger of Kheferatum?"

"Something like that but not exactly," she said, noting the shock and worry on Nansee's face. "I asked her to create a fake dagger to thwart whomever was coming for the blade. It's taken just about three days, but she said it's ready now."

"Three days." Khefar's tone was even, but only a fool would think he was unruffled. "That means you asked her the day you and I met."

He was back to angry or being offended, and she didn't understand why. "Yes," she replied. "I figured it was the easiest way to get Bernie's killer while making sure the original dagger was safe."

Khefar gathered their bowls and the now-empty soup pot, then rose. "Were you going to try to give me this impostor blade?"

She watched him take the dishes to the kitchen. "You have your real blade back, so that's a moot point. But the Fallen wants the Dagger of Kheferatum, and he's expecting me to bring it to him. How else do you propose I get close enough to kill him and still protect the true dagger? A fake dagger is the best option."

"Not you, us," Khefar pointed out as he came back for more dishes. "You are not facing the Avatar alone."

The finality in his voice came through loud and clear. "Us, then," she said. "If we show up, he'll know I didn't kill you and we have no intention of turning over the dagger. I'll be the first to die. The fake dagger will give us the diversion we need."

"A fake dagger that you've had Wynne and Zoo work magic into," Khefar pointed out as he came back for more dishes. "And you want me to hold it to impart some of my energy to make it something more than ordinary. Something powerful enough to fool the Fallen."

"Exactly. It needs to be good enough to make Enig think he has the right one. But I also asked Zoo to put some extra magic into it so the false dagger will be a trap as much as a decoy."

Nansee looked at Khefar. "And you agree with this?"

Khefar's lips thinned with disapproval. "How could I agree to something that hasn't been discussed yet?"

"We're discussing it now," Kira pointed out, injecting every bit of sensibility she could muster into her voice. "I'm hoping we can agree on a plan tonight."

"By creating another Dagger of Kheferatum?" Nansee's voice rose along with his eyebrows. "There's a reason why there's only one in existence. It's a god killer. The only reason it hasn't been destroyed is because the attempt alone could unmake everything!"

"I'm not planning to kill any gods, just this Fallen."

"Kira, you're not dense," Nansee snapped, surprising her. Though his outward elderly appearance didn't change, she suddenly felt there was more of the demigod in the room, as if he'd been suppressing his power before. "You know very well that we all come from the same source. Fallen, god—our only difference is where we stand on the Universal Balance and the power we gain from those who believe in us. Most deities don't take corporeal form because it makes them vulnerable. That dagger is one of the few things guaranteed to not only destroy our corporeal forms but our eternal essence as well. And you want to reproduce it?"

Stunned, Kira turned to Khefar, who looked from her to the demigod with a curiously neutral expression. She wondered then if Nansee had befriended the Nubian out of self-preservation as well as companionship, and if Khefar thought the same. She'd made a mistake in assuming the charming and amusing storyteller was all there was to Nansee.

"It is not a true re-creation of Khefar's dagger and was never intended to be anything other than a decoy. Nevertheless, you have my solemn vow that I will destroy the impostor dagger as soon as we defeat Enig."

That seemed to soothe the demigod. "You've made a vow to me. Know that I will hold you to your word."

"You should." She changed the subject. "I've taken on more than a few hybrids and Shadow Adepts, but I've never faced anything on Enig's level. We need to find some way to neutralize him that doesn't result in the destruction of half the city."

"You need to separate the Fallen from the Avatar shell," Nansee said. "The Fallen can not remain in this existence without that body."

Kira considered the demigod's words. "But can't the Fallen simply take up residence in another Avatar?"

"It takes time to prepare another shell. Three days minimum for the Avatar to be transfigured."

"Three days . . . transfiguration? But that sounds like—"

"Part of a very good story," Khefar cut in as he rejoined them. "But it still doesn't tell us how we can push the Fallen out, what to do with the Avatar, and how to keep the Fallen from moving into another body."

"There are ways to separate Light and Shadow from the bodies they have chosen to inhabit," Nansee said. "At times it can be as easy as David using a slingshot and stone against the Avatar Goliath. Other times you'll need the skill and luck of Perseus confronting Medusa."

Khefar barked out a laugh. "Somehow I don't think a slingshot and a rock will take down this Avatar."

"It would need to be a pretty big rock . . . wait." Kira leaned forward. "Demoz has a huge slab of clear quartz in his office. He uses it as a table, but I know that particular stone can also be a huge energy amplifier, among other things."

"Reminds me of a story I once heard." Nansee looked thoughtful. "A village was being plagued by an evil spirit. No matter what the villagers did, what offerings they made, the spirit was not appeased. One day a strange magic man came along, and the villagers asked him to rid their village of the evil spirit. Being a poor village, they had little they could offer the man. One of the chief's daughters offered herself, and the magic man agreed.

"That night, the evil spirit returned to terrorize the village, only to find the magic man waiting for him. The magician had a staff atop which sat a large magic stone—he called it a shaman stone. With a voice booming like thunder, he pointed his staff at the spirit. Power like lightning sparked from the stone, wrapping around the spirit, trapping it. The magic man spoke again, and the evil spirit was drawn into the large stone that topped the magician's staff.

"The chief's daughter gave herself to the shaman who had saved her village. The next morning, the magic man was gone. All that remained was his staff—and a child, for the chief's daughter became pregnant. She gave birth to a son who grew up with knowledge of magic and the ability to control the staff his father left behind. That child became head of the village when his grandfather died. And so the village continued, peaceful and protected."

Kira stared at the demigod. "That's a good story. So I suppose the moral I could take from it is that one gifted in magic or the ability to draw off energy should be able to boost their power using a stone and trap an evil entity."

Nansee nodded. "That is how the story goes. If it be sweet, if it be of use, if it pleases, take it with you."

"Thanks for your help, Anansi."

The spider god smiled. "I'm prevented from helping, remember? All I did was tell a few scraps of stories. If you're inspired by my tales and decide a course of action, well, that's your free will at work, isn't it?"

Kira smiled. "You're right. Then let me say thank you for your stories."

"You're welcome, Kira Solomon." The demigod reached out, gave her a clearly affectionate pat on the shoulder. "Your graciousness and strength serve as inspiration and your courage makes us all better than we were before. Good evening."

Bemused, Kira watched the spider open the door leading to the garage—except the view beyond the doorway wasn't her garage. Rather, she caught sight of a beautiful sunset, the ocean, and a hammock strung between two palm trees before he stepped through and closed the door behind him.

"Must be a nice way to travel."

Khefar stood. "He says it is, but he doesn't get frequent flyer miles."

Kira leaned against the table. "Are you happy with the plan?"

"The plan is incomplete. What if Enig brings a full team with him? What if he wants to disarm you before you meet face-to-face? What if Demoz decides not to side with you? What if there are innocent humans working in the club? How are you going to get them out if Enig decides to use them as bait or punishment for you not bringing him the real dagger?"

"All right! All right!" She thumped her hands on the table. "I already said I'd try this teamwork thing. You obviously have some ideas. Let's hear them."

"You need to bring in Sanchez and her team. You also need Wynne and Zoo."

Her heart jumped hard in her chest. "No."

"No to which part? Sanchez or the Marlowes?" He stepped closer to her. "You need them; you need all of us. Gilead can provide tactical cover, and a pretty damn big distraction. You need Zoo to put specific magic into that other dagger to help pull the Fallen out of his Avatar. Both Wynne and Zoo can be under the radar, your ace in the hole to help get you out if it all goes to hell."

"Khefar, come on, I can't do my job with all those people there. Sanchez has already lost a response team—she'll be gunning for anything and anyone not for the Light. And Wynne and Zoo—"

"Wynne and Zoo are your friends." He clamped his

hands onto her shoulders. "They care about you and they want to help you."

"I don't want their help." She bit her lip. "I don't want them in the line of fire."

His hands shifted, moving up to cup her cheeks. "The Marlowes are soldiers. They know what being in the line of fire is all about. More than that, you know if you don't assign them something to do, they're going to show up anyway. Much better to have them where you want them than have them crashing in with guns blazing, right?"

He had a point. "You're good at this."

He smiled. "Well, I've got a little experience with military tactics."

Military tactics, my ass. "Distracting me and making me agreeable by touching me, that's a military tactic?"

"No." His eyes darkened. "That's just me enjoying touching you."

She covered his hands with her own, reveling in the sensation. "And this is me enjoying you enjoying touching me. Or something like that."

"How about something like this?"

He brushed his lips across hers, once, twice, again. That was just as good as the touching, maybe even better. She leaned against him, her hands sliding down to settle at his waist, her fingers slipping into his belt loops.

With everything else pressing down on her, she wanted to grab this moment, this feeling, and hold on to it as long as she could. This bright glittering need was an oasis in the bleak desert her life had become, amid the losses that chipped away at her soul. She wanted more of it, even though it scared her. She wanted more of it, even though it wouldn't last.

He pulled away before she did, regret filling his expression. "Kira . . ."

"I know. I know." She took a step back, then another, shoving away the hunger. "Bigger things happening right now, fate of the world and all that. I'll talk to Sanchez and to Demoz. Will you call Wynne and Zoo, let them know the plan and what we need on the dagger? I'll let them know what time to show up at Gilead tomorrow as soon as I talk to the section chief."

It was the most motley crew she'd ever seen and that was saying something.

Everyone she'd contacted sat at Sanchez's oversize mahogany conference table, the view of Midtown Atlanta clear in the oversize windows beyond. Everyone that is, except Demoz. Not only would he have not made it into the building, just being sighted near it would have caused trouble for the psychic vampire. He was too valuable to both sides. Besides, the less he knew about the plan, the less information he'd be able to share.

She surveyed the people who'd come in response to her calls. Only Sanchez looked as if she belonged there, serene in her gray suit and position at the head of the table. The handpicked Special Response Team—four men and two women—flanked her, formidable in their black combat gear.

Kira sat midway down the oval table on the left side, Khefar beside her. Wynne and Zoo, the latter happily without his arm sling, sat across from them. Wynne's hair was now an incredibly deep purple and she seemed to have recovered most of her natural ebullience. At the foot of the table sat the four members of Inviolate, the band that regularly played at the DMZ. She knew the others wondered why the band was there, but if there were any contingencies, some of the band members had skills that would prove useful.

She rose. The disparate groups instantly quieted. "First, I want to thank all of you for coming here today. I know this isn't the most comfortable place for some of us, but right now it is the most secure."

Zoo coughed. Wynne smirked. "Second, what I'm asking you all to do is probably the most dangerous thing you'll ever attempt: face one of the Fallen. This Fallen, Enig, says through his Avatar that he's been making his moves and planning for more than twenty years. That makes him even more clever and dangerous than most Fallen. So if any of you want to back out of tonight's confrontation, I won't blame you. But you should leave now."

No one moved. They were either all crazy or adrenaline junkies. "Okay, here's how we play it. The band will already be in place onstage when I enter the DMZ through the front door and make my way to Demoz's office. Enig will probably already be there with most of his people scattered throughout the club levels. Khefar will give me ten minutes, then follow with the Gilead team."

"Are you sure Demoz will turn off the club's protection?" Zoo asked.

"I'm betting that Enig will make that a condition of

meeting," Kira answered. "And if he doesn't, then we'll have two layers of hackers working on the system."

"I still object to the use of civilians," Sanchez said.

Kira dipped her head at the section chief. "I understand." It was an old argument, begun when Sanchez had first learned of Kira's relationship with Wynne and Zoo. Kira hadn't had time for it before and she certainly didn't have time for it now. It had been good enough for Sanchez to allow her to gather everyone in the section chief's offices and lead the planning; she couldn't expect a Charles Dickens miracle to transform the woman.

"Wynne and Zoo are ex-military and their idea of a romantic weekend away is to go base jumping in South America. They can handle themselves." Especially since she had no intention of putting them anywhere near the line of fire.

"Lambert is also former military and has a wealth of experience." And that was all that Sanchez needed to know about Khefar, at least for right now. They already knew from the building's security scans he was not exactly a Normal. Just to get him into the place she'd had to request special clearance for his "personal weapon similar to a Lightblade." She'd eventually have to figure out what to tell Sanchez. For now, even the section chief understood the imperative was dealing with the Fallen.

Sanchez pursed her lips. "I understand why you use the Marlowes. They have impressive skills and considerable experience. While I don't know anything about this Kevin Lambert person, his records check out, but—"

Kira briefly wondered how a four-thousand-year-old warrior managed to have a paper trail valid enough to pass Gilead inspection, but she suspected he had the help of a certain demigod who claimed to have invented the World Wide Web.

"—what I don't understand is your plan to use these musicians," Sanchez continued.

Good. She wasn't pursuing questions about the warrior. "These musicians, Chief, are just about the only people other than staff who can enter the club without any suspicion," Kira explained. "Besides, only one of them is human. They have skills we can use if we have to."

"Skills like what?"

Kira sighed. "Smoke, do you mind?"

The drummer smiled. He was as nondescript as one could be: average height, average build, mousy brown hair and eyes. He looked to be somewhere between nineteen and thirty, though Kira knew he was actually close to the century mark.

He rose, then took his time walking down the length of the table to the section chief. Tension ramped up in the room as the SRT tightened their grips on their weapons.

Smoke paused, looked at Kira. "Section Chief," Kira said quietly, "you said you wanted proof."

"So I did." She looked at her team. "Stand down."

Smoke continued to Sanchez's side. He put his hand on her shoulder. Almost immediately, gray haze flowed up around them. They disappeared, only to reappear in a gray haze at the far end of the room.

"Thank you, Smoke," Kira said with satisfaction.

The drummer grinned widely, ducking his mousy head in acknowledgment as he rejoined his band mates.

Sanchez straightened her suit jacket with sharp precise tugs as she strode back to her seat. "That was impressive. What about the others?"

"K.P., the lead singer"—she gestured toward the diminutive Asian woman, who bobbed her head—"specializes in sonic dissonance. You don't want her to demonstrate unless you feel the need to buy new windows. The redhead is Bryon, the bassist, and he's descended from a fire elemental. The blond one is Chris, the guitarist. He's human, but that's probably a good thing. If he combined superhuman speed with his mad martial arts skills, he'd be a superhero."

Kira glanced around the table. "Inviolate will be emergency backup only. If the crap hits the fan, they'll get all the innocents out of the club first. If it's safe, you come back for us."

K.P. stirred at that. "But Kira—"

"No buts, K.P.," she told the singer. "Enig is high up on the Fallen food chain and he has way too many tricks up his sleeve. I don't want you guys to be retaliated against without reason."

"And you don't think getting you out if things go wrong is reason enough?"

"I will see to it that Chaser Solomon makes it out of the DMZ," Khefar stated as if no one would disagree. No one did.

Miracles could occur. She'd been surprised that everyone had agreed to come together in the first place. But considering they all had good reasons for wanting a piece of the action, perhaps it was not illogical. Gilead wanted Enig destroyed and was willing to participate in the assault in hopes of recovering the special response team he had captured and turned. The band—well, halflings that straddled the Universal Balance, were always interested in proving their loyalties. For Kira and Khefar, it was both a mission and a path to personal redemption. As for Wynne and Zoo, they had more than proven that Kira's work and person were integral to their lives.

Now all Kira had to do was hope luck and the gods would stay with them long enough for Enig to become history.

"Okay. Section Chief Sanchez will run time and communications from Command Post One. Wynne and Zoo, you'll work on hacking the DMZ's security system from Post Two. The band will monitor us and will get any staff to safety. Khefar and I will take on the Fallen. All we're after here is stopping Enig. Understood?"

"Understood."

"All right then, people. Let's synch up and then head out. We've got a big night ahead."

The meeting was over. The band members exited. Kira, the warrior, and her friends stood and moved toward the door. Sanchez looked up from a sheaf of papers she shuffled on the conference table. "Solomon."

Kira paused at the door, steeling herself for whatever comment the section chief felt the need to make. "Yes?"

"Good job bringing everyone together. I have no doubt that everyone will do their best giving tactical support." She gave Kira a sharp nod. "Good luck."

Completely surprised, Kira returned the gesture. "Thanks, Section Chief."

Kira and her friends left the conference room, heading for the elevator. Wynne stepped up next to her. "Hey, Kira—"

"Not yet." She made a vague gesture to encompass all of Gilead. "In the van."

Minutes later, Wynne pulled the van out of the parking deck and onto Peachtree Street. Concern filled her features. "This is going to work, isn't it?"

"It has to," Kira answered. "We don't have any other options."

"Not any with a better probability for success, at least," Khefar added.

"We're going to come through this just fine," Zoo said with his eternal enthusiasm. He'd recharged enough to finish healing his arm, but enough stiffness lingered for Kira to use that as an excuse to have them on tech duty.

Kira glanced out the window. It was a beautiful fall day, the kind that inspired poets and painters. What would tomorrow look like? Would she even see it? "Of course we will, and we'll commandeer the upper deck at the Vortex and gorge ourselves on Tater tots to celebrate."

Zoo laughed. "Now that sounds like a plan."

They spent the rest of the drive to Kira's debating which of the Vortex's burgers were the best. It was a light-hearted moment that Kira tucked away in her memory. She'd need moments like this, memories like this, to combat the hold Shadow had on her.

The van slowed to a stop before Kira's front door.

"Hey guys, thanks again for taking part in this," Kira said as Khefar slid the side door open.

"Like we'd do anything else," Wynne said, rolling her eyes. Then her expression hardened. "Besides, we owe the bastard for what he did to you."

"What he did to all of us," Zoo added quietly.

Kira's throat tightened. She stepped onto the sidewalk, blowing out a sigh. "Khefar will give you guys a call when everything's a go. Take care of yourselves, all right?"

"Back at you." Zoo passed a wooden box through the window to Khefar. "Here's the dagger. If anything's off with it, let us know. Otherwise, we'll see you guys in a little while."

Chapter 27

Kira and Khefar made their way inside as the Marlowes drove away. They headed for the reclaimed dining table. "You ready to take a look?" Khefar asked, placing the longish oak box on the tabletop.

At her nod, he flipped the brass latch, then lifted the lid.

She blew out a sigh, then turned to Khefar. "So what do you think?"

Khefar looked down at the dagger. "I think Wynne Marlowe is a genius."

The replica Dagger of Kheferatum was as breathtaking as the original. The bronze and ivory gleamed with a combined sheen of age and magic. It looked just like the real one, so much so that it was eerie.

Kira smiled. "There's a reason why she's the best metalworker in the country. Go ahead, pick it up."

He did, testing the weight and balance. "Amazing. If I didn't have the real one on my hip expressing its outrage at the impostor, I'd swear it was the same blade."

"With Zoo's skill, we put a little attitude into the new dagger. We wanted it to think that it's the Dagger of Kheferatum."

"You certainly did that right. I'm very impressed. It just needs one more thing."

Before she could say anything, he slashed the blade across his left bicep, drawing blood. "Now they'll believe you didn't take it away from me without a fight."

"Goddess." She ran into the kitchen, grabbed the first-aid kit, then ran back to him. She tucked his arm close to her body as she dabbed at the gash with a sterile wipe. "Do you think you could warn someone before you do that?"

"You know I'll heal from that, right?" Amusement lined his tone.

"So? We put extra levels of surprises into that blade," she exclaimed, wiping at the blood on his arm. "You could have made sure it wouldn't be dangerous for you before you did something like that."

"What can I say?" He smiled at her. "I guess I have a reckless demeanor at times myself."

"Not funny."

"You're becoming more at ease with touching me."

She stopped dabbing at the cut. He was right and it left her flustered. She applied a butterfly bandage with more force than necessary. "Well, don't get used to it. It's not like it means I'm getting used to you hanging around or anything like that."

"Of course not." Khefar shook his head, sliding the replica into his own sheath he'd taken from his waist. The real dagger was safely housed in a new rigging just under his left arm. "Are you good with this?"

"It's a plan concocted with a guy who's fought in thousands of battles large and small and perfected by a trickster demigod. Everyone who needs to be on board is ready to go, and all I have to do is make it through a meeting with a Shadow Avatar who's already mind-raped me once. I'm as ready as I'll ever be."

He held the blade out to her. "I don't have to tell you to be careful, do I?"

"No, you don't." She took the blade, shouldering into the harness and settling the sheath into the middle of her back. Her own Lightblade lay at her hip. "Besides, you'll be right behind me."

"Remember that." His hands settled on her shoulders. "It's okay to be a hero. It's not okay to be a superhero."

"Really? And I just put a shiny new cape on order."

"I'm serious, Kira." His grip tightened. "We stop Enig and we both walk out of the DMZ more or less in one piece."

"I understand." She briefly covered his hands with her own. She appreciated these easy gestures more than she dared to let him know. Since her run-in with Enig, Khefar had been a literal and figurative lifeline to her, his touch and his understanding a healing balm to her psyche. She still felt the heaviness in her soul, but as each moment passed, the burden became a little easier to bear.

"Nothing is more important than stopping Enig."

"Good." He squeezed her shoulder. "I have a feeling that once we get this done, a certain demigod is going to produce one heck of a feast."

"I think that scares me more than facing down the Fallen."

She looked around her home, at the comfortable clutter, the subtle changes that had occurred in the week since she'd met Khefar and Nansee. They'd warmed the place with their presence, and she was glad for it. "I want you to know, I reworked the magical protections around the place this morning. Everything but the standard alarm will vanish once I'm no longer around, and you already know the code for that."

He stared down at her with the most absolute self-assurance she'd ever seen. "I have no intention of losing you today."

"I know and I appreciate that. You're the one who said to plan for any contingency, so I'm planning." She looked up into his strong features, the implacable resolve. "Wynne and Zoo have access to my safe deposit box and my will. Everything is accounted for except my Book of the Dead, which is in my altar room and recoded to allow you entry. If you have to unmake me, I want you to take my book and the contents of that room."

"Kira . . ." Now he looked uncomfortable.

She squeezed his fingers. "It's just in case, right? I know of everyone, you'll appreciate those things the most, and it makes me happy to think of you having them."

"Very well. I'll consider it an honor." He dropped his gaze. "Kira?"

"Yeah?"

When she turned around, he hooked one hand behind her head, dragged her close, then kissed her. Just one sharp, quick, potent press of lips that she felt all the way to her toes.

He broke away. "If you didn't like that, you can punch me later."

"What if I did?"

He smiled. "Then you can punch me later. But for now, it is time to prepare for the rendezvous."

With the duplicate dagger strapped to her back, Kira took her second loaner SUV to the rendezvous at the DMZ, trying to keep her mind on anything but what she was about to face. Difficult to do when she was equal parts scared shitless at facing Enig again and unnerved by Khefar. It had probably been a deliberate tactic on his part, to distract her from the worry of trying to eliminate someone she'd already underestimated once before. Worry weakens and allows fear to seep in. Fear can destroy.

She had to do it. They had to do it. The Avatar had to be stopped. There was no alternative. Khefar couldn't just disappear with the Dagger of Kheferatum and hope to stay off the Fallen's radar. If they didn't stop Enig here, now, more and more beings from Shadow would come after Khefar and his dagger. Since destroying the dagger was out of the question, they had to take a stand. And it was much better to make a stand on their own terms.

The club looked more bleak than industrial-cool by the light of day. The place looked its worst at dusk though, when the metal structure glowed the burnished red-orange of the setting sun. Or blood.

She parked the SUV and got out, preparing to take the first of many gambles. The DMZ's security system had, she hoped, been turned off. Her bet was that Enig would insist and that Demoz would comply. She hedged the bet with the thought she wouldn't be able to take the blade inside anyway with the system activated. Another reason for Demoz to have it turned off. She'd keep her extrasense on a low flame as a matter of course.

No line of patrons was strung along the sidewalk outside of the club. No lizard-eyed coat-check girl unable to identify her as a Shadowchaser. Just the bouncer with the large-sized plugs in his ears.

His attitude was different this time around. Her new reputation as a Shadow-touched Chaser had obviously preceded her. "Chaser," he said with a quick acknowledging nod of his head. "The boss is waiting for you."

"Where?"

"The main office."

She pushed through the Veil long enough to verify the metaphysical security system was truly deactivated.

Her nerves stretched tight as she pushed open the double doors. Same bare-bulb T-shaped corridor, same choice for Light or Dark. Just as before, she swung through the Shadow side, moving swiftly down the corridor.

Music wasn't blaring as it would when the club opened, but she could hear Inviolate practicing. She bit back a smile. *Good. Another key component in place.*

She skirted the Pit, then made her way up the back stairs to Demoz's office. Two sets of halflings waited just outside the office. They grinned as she approached.

"Oh, I remember you," one said.

"Yeah, you taste really good," the other added.

She stopped. "Really?"

The first halfling stepped closer. "I'd like to taste that again."

It took a moment for her to realize that he meant they had been at the warehouse near the airport when Enig had injected her with Shadow poison. They'd been among the ones who'd touched her, triggering her defenses, before releasing her among the homeless like a fox in a henhouse.

She crashed the heel of her hand, spiced with a solid dose of her extrasense, into the halfling's nose. The resulting crunch was satisfying. So was his crumpling to kiss her boot. "Next time, say please."

She sauntered into the office. Demoz, who had been sitting behind his desk, rose as she entered. More halfings and one Adept held up the walls. The Shadow Avatar sat in one of the two chairs flanking the gigantic cluster of clear quartz that served as a table and energy amplifier. Goody, the gang was all there.

Demoz stared at her with a good impression of a questioning look on his face. "Welcome, Chaser. But I must admit . . . I don't think I've ever seen you do anything so . . . not you, Kira."

"Well, I'm not the same person I was a few days ago," she said, nodding to the Avatar. "Am I, Enig?"

The Avatar steepled his fingers, his white suit brilliant against the black chair. "You came alone?"

"In the end, aren't we all alone?"

The hybrid she'd punched hobbled up to him. "She came alone, Master."

"Go clean yourself up. You embarrass me." Enig turned back to her. "I must say that when our host told me that you would arrive today with the Dagger of Kheferatum, I was tempted to discount him. And yet, here you are. Why did you change your mind?"

"Kinda had my mind changed for me, didn't I?" She allowed her real anger at the Avatar to bubble to the surface as she took the chair opposite his. *Use the true fury to fuel the deception.* "Whatever you did to me was, pardon the expression, enlightening. The clock's running down on my time at Gilead, I already knew that, and your little display a few days ago left a permanent stain on my soul. If I am no longer worthy of my goddess's favor or walking in the Light, what else is there left for me?"

Enig looked at Demoz, who looked at her. The vampire's midnight face dripped sweat. He actually looked worried and more than a little uneasy.

He pulled out a handkerchief, blotted his forehead. "She means every word," he said, his voice tight. "She's telling the truth."

"So you have it? The Dagger of Kheferatum?"

She reached for the sheath nestled between her shoulder blades, the dagger singing softly as she pulled it free. She held it across her body, the glyphs catching the light. "Is this what you've been looking for?"

Enig leaned forward, preternaturally beautiful face tarnishing with greed. "How were you able to get it away from the Nubian?"

"There's blood on the blade," Demoz said, his voice hushed.

"Yeah, about that." Kira let a grin pull at her lips. "It's amazing what you can do to people when they make the mistake of trusting you."

"Too true," Enig murmured. "For example, I do not trust you, Shadowchaser."

"And I really don't care." She rose. "You want the blade or not?"

Enig rose. "Try to leave and I will kill you."

"Dude, I'm dead already. The Nubian's going to be pissed when he resurrects and Gilead's not going to be happy with me either. All I want are the answers you promised me."

"And you shall have them." He held out his hand. "Give the dagger to me."

"Sure." She twirled the dagger so that the hilt pointed his way. "If you think that the dagger will accept you, go ahead, take it."

He reached out.

"But I have to warn you—if the dagger doesn't like you, it will definitely let you know."

His eyes fixed on hers. She maintained the stare, her arm steady as she held the dagger out. Movement out of the corner of her eye as she noticed his hand come up, wrap around the dagger's hilt.

His face split into a grin. "I knew sparing your life in Venice was the right thing to do."

"Wh-what did you say?"

"I told you, Shadowchaser, I've been planning this for a long time, making plans, gathering weapons. I discovered you in Venice. How do you think your precious Nico acquired the serum that stripped your powers? You do remember that, don't you? It was such a beautiful night."

Blood pounded in her ears. "You killed Nico."

"No, my dear Chaser. I didn't make you take the potion. You willingly gave up your powers, even though you knew the consequences. And I knew then that a Shadowchaser so willing to part with her blade and her powers would be a perfect weapon for me to use one day." Enig's smile widened. "And so you are."

He pulled the dagger out of her limp hand. "The Dagger of Kheferatum is mine!"

"I don't think so."

Khefar stood in the doorway, blade in one hand.

"What is this?" Enig hissed.

"Call it an intervention." She pulled her Lightblade, called her power.

Both she and Khefar leaped at the same time. Just as she hoped, Enig hopped onto the slab of quartz. As Khefar kept the Avatar distracted, she slapped the slick surface with her bare hand, flooding it with power. It triggered the spell Zoo had buried into the hilt of the fake dagger. A prism of blue-white light shot up from the gleaming slab of stone, encircling Enig.

He screamed. Energy crackled and hummed, lifting her hair. Kira channeled more power into the slab, supercharging the giant crystal, counting on its properties to amplify her ability and literally separate the Fallen from its Avatar host.

Yellow light flared as Enig threw Shadow-magic at the metaphysical sieve. Kira grimly held on, hoping that Zoo's second spell had kicked in and the impostor dagger was on its way to deteriorating. Hoping too that Khefar had her back and was making short work of the Shadowlings stupid enough to stay around.

Sweat stung her eyes, pain throbbing through her body. "Separate, damn you!"

Pressure built like a tornado was approaching, filling every crevice of the room. Enig shrieked, throwing raw Chaos at the prism trapping him as his two selves finally began to separate into a human husk and a twisting boiling darkness. *Now.* She focused her intent again, trying to channel the Fallen into the quartz. A sonic boom ripped through the office, shattering the soundproof windows overlooking the club, followed by popping that sounded like gunfire. Was that Gilead's team making their presence known or the quartz overloading?

Kira blinked rapidly. Either complete silence had fallen or the boom had deafened her. She couldn't hear the ceiling crashing down around them, couldn't hear the crystal cracking beneath her hands, couldn't hear Khefar shouting as he tried to reach her. Couldn't hear anything until the Avatar, bits of the Fallen still clinging to him, slammed into her, the remnant of the impostor dagger sinking deep into her shoulder.

The momentum carried them through the now-glassless window overlooking the club floor. She reacted on pure instinct, swinging her Lightblade up, her blade gleaming blue-white as she gathered her force. Screaming with effort, she swung, slicing diagonally through the Avatar's throat and collarbone just before they crashed into the Pit.

Chapter 28

"K ira!"

Khefar vaulted over the railing, landing in the Pit beside her. The remnants of the Avatar were already beginning to disintegrate, but enough of it had been beneath her to break her fall. Unfortunately, breakage was the least of his worries.

Carefully, carefully, he turned her onto her back, ignoring the people rushing around them. A large welt had been carved into her vest, but the thick leather seemed to have deflected most of the brunt of the blow. A portion of the imitation dagger stuck out of her right shoulder. The blade glowed a sickly yellow color.

Khefar muttered a curse. The Fallen, before complete separation, had charged the knife with Chaos magic before the Avatar stabbed her.

He decided against warning her, pulling the blade free before she could tense up or he could change his mind. It didn't matter that the blade had missed vital organs or veins. The purpose had been to infect her again with Shadow magic, to poison her already compromised system.

"Gods, it burns." She clutched at him, her skin burning blue as her body tried to fight the toxins invading her system.

"I know, but you have to fight. You've got to be strong for a little while longer."

She grimaced on a wave of pain. "Did I slow him down?"

"Yeah." He held her close, but not close enough, never close enough. He pressed his hand against her wound in a futile effort to halt the inevitable. "You killed the Avatar, but there's no sign of the Fallen controlling it."

"It . . . will have to be enough. The Fallen is at least weakened if not annihilated. The crystal . . . all the pieces need to be gathered up. Take them to Gilead so they can be stored away in a barrel of purified salt, just in case."

"I will."

"Khefar." She coughed, sweat beading on her forehead. "You have to do it, Khefar. You have to unmake me."

Holy Mother Isis, had she intended to die all along? "Why did you do it? Why?"

"Scales . . . had to balance my scales. Maybe now the Light will take me, Ma'at willing. But if the poison is too much . . . you need to use your dagger on me."

"No! You're not going to die today. Do you hear me?"

She smiled up at him. "It's okay, Khefar. This is a good way to go. If you unmake me, the Fallen won't get me. Just sorry you couldn't take me off your total."

The rattle. He heard it, the sound of death filling her body. "No!"

She couldn't die. Not this one. Not this one, most of all. Khefar slashed his dagger across his wrist, opening the large vein. He pressed the wound against the puncture in her shoulder, mingling his blood with hers.

"Live for me," he whispered, drawing her close to him once again. "By the Light, you must live."

He did not know if this crude transfusion would work or not. His blood had been circulating in his body for four millennia; surely it was part of the key to him surviving his most grievous wounds. If it could fight the poison, if it could keep her here, he would gladly give every drop of blood he had.

Anansi materialized beside him. "My boy, what have you done?"

"Help her," he demanded. "We may not worship you but we believe in you. Do something!"

Lethargy settled into his limbs as he slumped against the stone column. He could feel his soul struggling against the bonds of his body, wanting to break free. He longed to do just that, if only to find Kira's soul and return it to her shell.

The darkness brightened, a pearlescent gleam piercing the Veil of Death. The light began to take shape and form, flowing locks from the top of it, then a face, then the hint of limbs. A representative of the Powers of Light, sent in the form of a crone.

"Kira," the being said without moving its lips. "Come, child. It is time to take you home."

As near to the dying as he was, Khefar could see Kira's spirit hovering just above her ravaged body, trying to join with it again. "No," he protested, a feeble sound of voice and soul. "Do not take her. Please don't take her."

"Why not?" the being asked. "You would deny her the rest she deserves?"

"Never. But I would keep her here for now."

"There will be another life for you to save, Khefar," the crone said with compassion. "Even now it can be revealed to you. Your journey will soon be at an end."

"My journey could last another millennia," Khefar declared, "if it would keep her here with those who love her. I have never asked the Powers of Light for anything in the last four millennia. I would ask this of them."

The being drew closer, hovering between him and Kira. "Why this life?" she asked. "Of the thousands you have saved and the dozens you have lost, why does this life matter so greatly?"

"Because she's special. I know it and you know it."

The being remained silent for a long moment, eyes closed. Khefar waited, staying conscious with effort of will until the dark spheres opened once again. "Would you sacrifice your quest for this one, my child? Would you turn from your existence to grant this wish?"

Kira's spirit opened its mouth, but no sound came out. Khefar knew she would not want him to sacrifice himself for her, but he knew he would do it anyway, anytime, anywhere. He dropped a kiss to her cold forehead. "I would," he whispered. "She wants to stay. She wants to return to her body. I give of myself gladly so that it may be so."

The crone bowed her head once. "Then let it be done."

She stretched out a hand, engulfing Khefar in a blanket of light. He felt his spirit draining from his body and smiled. Even if he would know only darkness, it was a sacrifice he was willing to make to give Kira her life back.

Chapter 29

Kira knew this place.

The Hall of Souls, lined with thrones gleaming gold in torchlight upon which sat the gods and goddesses of the Two Lands. She saw the jackal-headed Anubis, the Great Mother Isis, Her Consort Osiris . . . and so many more. Before her were the gilded scales, standing as tall as she, with her patron goddess, Ma'at, beside them.

Kira's legs could not hold her. She hit the ground, hard. Of its own accord, her body pitched forward until her forehead pressed the ground as if to hold it in place. *Ma'at, protect me.*

"Lord of the Dead, Great Osiris," a voice intoned. "Two souls—a new soul and an old soul—are come before us."

The import of the words struck her. Two souls? Who else would be here at this time, with these gods, with her? She became aware of another presence, muted by the majesty of the gods, kneeling beside her.

Khefar. He stretched out beside her, as still and silent as she. They were both to have their souls weighed.

Fear drove out every ritual spell and prayer she'd memorized for this day. Her Book of the Dead was nowhere to be seen, still safely ensconced in her altar room. She could hear the growling hunger of Ammit the Devourer. She could not let Khefar's heart be lost.

"The old soul has endured much," the god—she realized it must be Anubis, guide and friend of the dead, speaking—continued. "Is there one here who will speak for him?"

"I will speak for him," a feminine all-voice intoned. "He is My child and he has done what I have asked of him, willingly and without complaint, and at great personal cost."

Though Kira didn't dare look up, she saw the beautiful golden light brighten, felt the presence of the goddess move closer. She trembled and felt Khefar do the same.

"Speak, child of Mine. What is it that you wish of Me?"

Khefar spoke. *"Nutjert en Ankh, sat Nut, sat Geb, merit Auser . . . "* The words pressed against her, then into her, translating through her soul. "Goddess of Life, daughter of Nut, daughter of Geb, Beloved of Osiris, hear one unworthy of your blessing. If it be Your will to grant the wish of one such as I, I would wish that Kira, faithful servant of the Light, handmaid of Ma'at, be returned to her life."

Shock locked her muscles. *No, Khefar. Don't ask this. Not this. Ask for yourself.*

"What of the vow you made, My child? If she is sent back, your vow to fail-safe still holds. You will remain, denied entry to the Field of Reeds until she leaves the world. Is that your choice, My son?"

Move, she begged her frozen muscles. *He can't give that for me. I can't ask him to sacrifice his afterlife for mine!*

"I follow Your will in all things, Goddess of Life," he said then. "I will hold to my vows."

"It is not just My will that determines this day. What say you, Mistress of Justice?"

Kira shuddered as another presence, a familiar one, joined Isis. "I will speak for the new soul, for she is My child, My fierce and zealous daughter who has served Justice faithfully. Speak now, beloved one, the truth of your heart."

Gratitude trembled through her pores, the gentle presence bringing words to the surface. "Ma'at the Great, Goddess of Justice, Mistress of the Sentences, She of Order and Rule. May I shine each day in Your presence, doing Your will in all things. I would not ask another to sacrifice for me. He has served faithfully. If it is his time to rest, please allow him to join his family in paradise. I would not deny him his reward, not for my sake. I live and die by Your will."

Silence, during which she could feel Khefar's soul vibrate in outraged reaction: *You have done so much for me, Khefar, so much in such a short time. I'm grateful I met you, and you have touched me in more ways than you know. Have your peace now. I'll be content with that.*

Ma'at's presence washed over her. "My will is this: you will return to the living land to be My instrument in this world. You will serve Me as you have always done, secure in My blessing as you stand against Chaos."

She was more than goddess, She was a Universal Truth, Mother of Order and Function, the foundation of everything. "You honor me; I will abide by Your will."

"As Justice has spoken, so shall I," Isis said then, her

voice nowhere and everywhere. "I am Isis. Mother of All. Do I not have power over life and death?"

Khefar stirred. "Yes, Great Mother."

"She is Ma'at's child, but you are Mine. You are needed in this world a while longer, Khefar, son of Jeru, son of Natek."

"You honor me, Lady of the Words of Power."

"Will you return?"

"I will, Great Goddess."

"As We speak, so let it be done."

The light around Kira intensified. "You may stand now, child."

At the gentle urging of the goddess, Kira's body unfolded, pushing to her feet. The Hall of Thrones had vanished, as did Khefar, Isis, and the other gods. The embodiment of Truth and Order stood in her shining glory, beautiful and pure and golden. By contrast, Kira felt dirty in body and mind and soul.

Ma'at smiled and Kira's heart leaped in response, giddy. "You are My daughter, the Hand of Justice."

She removed the white plume feather from her headdress. It balanced in the palm of her hand, gleaming blue-white and golden with power. Then it began to dance, as if caught on a current of air, lifting away from the goddess and toward Kira.

She instinctively raised her hands. The feather settled against her cupped palms, humming and nearly insubstantial. Light and heat emanated from it, brighter and warmer until it consumed her vision and seared her soul.

The goddess spoke one final time. "Go forth into the day, My child. Your friends await."

The golden light faded.

Kira opened her eyes to find Wynne's worried face leaning over her. "Oh, thank God!"

"Goddess." Kira trembled. "I saw Her. Them. I saw it all. It was so beautiful . . ."

"I'm sure it was beautiful for you, but it was scary as hell for us. Think you can space out these superhero action sequences a little more?"

"I'll work on it." She looked around the room. An espresso-colored lowboy sat against the far wall, a plum-colored orchid sitting atop it. It was the minimalist Zen-like style she preferred, but it wasn't her house or her safe room at Wynne's. It didn't feel like a hotel room and she didn't think her friends would take her to a bed and breakfast to recuperate. "Where are we? Where's Khefar?"

Wynne bit her lip. "Well, see, that's the thing—"

"I'll answer her."

Kira blinked in surprise. "Balm? You're here?"

The head of Gilead took the chair Wynne vacated. She wore a beige cowl-necked sweater, tweed slacks, and dark brown boots, a far cry from her usual turn-of-the-century garb. "This is my safe house in Atlanta. You didn't really expect me to go home, did you? Abandon my daughter when she faces the greatest challenge of her life?"

"No, I suppose not." She sat up, appreciating the soft cotton gown and bed sheets, the simple impression of blue sky and warm sun she felt from them. She had no idea Balm had a house in Atlanta, but she found it didn't bother her. At that moment, little could. "I feel like I should apologize to you."

"For what? For doing your job and sending one of the Fallen back to Shadow? No. If, however, you mean dying and scaring me half to death, then yes—you damn well need to apologize."

Kira gazed at the woman who'd shaped her life, noting the strain about the eternal woman's eyes and lips. "I'm sorry, Mother. I didn't mean to cause you worry."

"You never do, and yet I worry." Balm reached out a gloved hand toward Kira, then drew it back. "You've never had to face anything like this before."

"No. This was the worst. It was almost too much, what the Fallen did. He got into my head, dangled the promise of information about my past, my family. He promised to tell me who I am and why I am."

Balm sighed. "You didn't believe him, did you?"

"Of course not. You should know me better than that." She looked away. "He's the reason Nico is dead. He supplied Nico with the serum that blocked my powers. He used the special team to dart me with it, to trap me."

"Oh, Kira." In a surprising move, Balm slid onto the bed beside her. "I'm sorry you had to endure that, daughter. I know it doesn't ease the pain, but perhaps you can take some comfort in knowing that this Fallen can no longer hurt you and yours."

It was cold comfort, but it was all she had. "I'll take what I can get at this point. And we did win one for the Light."

"That's the spirit." Balm gave her a smile as soothing as her name. "I've worried every day since you left Santa Costa, knowing that the day would come when I'd have to let you go, let you walk your path without me."

"What are you saying?"

"There are places even I cannot go, paths I cannot take. You, my dearest daughter, walked with the gods, the Guardians of Light, and have now been taken into direct service." Balm adjusted her sleeves. "You've always chafed under my authority, and now you'll answer to a higher one."

"So it wasn't a dream?"

"No. You were claimed by Ma'at Herself."

Kira leaned back against the pillows, trying to absorb Balm's news. "Are . . . are you saying that I'm no longer a Shadowchaser?"

"You will always be a Shadowchaser," the head of Gilead retorted. The harshness eased from her voice and features as she returned to the chair. "You remain a weapon of Light to push back Shadow. You're just more now. Can you not sense it?"

Kira closed her eyes, trying to find confirmation of what Balm had told her. She had no idea how long she'd been unconscious, how many days had passed since she'd fallen out of Demoz's office window with a poisoned dagger in her shoulder. Lying prostrate in the Hall of Gods, feeling Ma'at's blessing and Isis's grace? It felt as if it had just happened.

An image took shape in her mind's eye, the glowing form of Ma'at's feather. Its light warmed her, spreading through her like heated brandy, making her feel almost giddy. Yet she felt something slide along the edge of her senses, a hint of Shadow just beyond the brilliance of Ma'at's truth.

She was still tainted. Her burdens hadn't disappeared just because she'd been called by her goddess—not that she'd expected them to. Now she knew why the Mother Goddess had told Khefar that he'd have to come back. He might still have to keep his promise to use the Dagger of Kheferatum to unmake her. And surely he still had one more life to save?

Her eyes popped open. "What about Khefar? Uh, the man who fought the Fallen with me?"

"Ah yes, the immortal Nubian." Balm arched an eyebrow. "You've been holding out on me, daughter."

Kira dipped her head. "I know. It was just—it got real complicated real fast."

Balm smiled. "Men can do that."

Heat crept up Kira's cheeks, but she studiously ignored it. "Is everyone else okay? Was Sanchez able to retrieve the first Special Response Team? We didn't lose anyone else, did we?"

Balm handed her a pair of thin gloves. "Why don't you get out of bed and come see for yourself?"

Kira pulled on the gloves, then levered up off the bed. "Where is this place?" she asked, changing into the dark gray trousers and lighter gray sweater waiting for her at the foot of the platform bed. She wondered how Balm had known that she liked Zen decor for her sleeping quarters. Her rooms on Santa Costa had been austere out of necessity, not choice.

"Ansley Park, not far from the Atlanta Botanical Gardens."

She followed Balm out into the hall. "You're so old-school, Balm. I'm surprised you're not in one of the mansions near the governor's place."

"Too much space in those enormous houses. However, at the moment, I could use a little more space. My formal dining room is crowded right now."

"Crowded? What do you mean . . ."

The dining room was indeed filled with people. Zoo and Wynne, Khefar and Nansee, Sanchez, even the members of Inviolate. They sat at an ornate Queen Anne cherrywood table overloaded with food, laughing as Nansee spun one of his stories.

Her gaze rested on Khefar. He looked as if he'd come through the ordeal completely unscathed. She remembered what he'd done for her, the sacrifice he'd been willing to make on her behalf, and almost choked on the gratitude that welled up in response.

He stood up as soon as he saw her. The others fell silent as he crossed the dining room to Kira and Balm.

"Khefar."

He inclined his head. "Balm."

"As always, we could use you in Gilead."

"As always, I must refuse. Especially now."

Kira looked from one to the other. "How far back do you guys know each other?"

"Our paths have crossed a few times over the years," Balm explained, which really didn't explain much of anything. "I'm sure you two want to talk for a moment. It's warm enough that the verandah should be comfortable for a while. Don't stay out too long. This feasting is in your honor, after all." She joined the others in the dining room, smiling as Nansee gallantly held her chair.

Khefar led Kira through the sitting room and out the front door. The house really did have a verandah and not a porch, running the length of the front of the house before bending along the right side. A swing hung from one of the beams to the left of the front door.

"How long has it been?"

"Three days this time around," he answered. "Wynne said that someone tried to re-engage the DMZ's shields after I went in, but she and Zoo were able to keep them down. Sanchez's team exchanged some light gunfire with some of Enig's men, which provided enough of a diversion for the band to get all the staff members out of the club. Sanchez took all the shards of the crystal as you suggested and they're now safely locked away. Demoz is fine, repairs are ongoing, and he expects the club to reopen this weekend."

Kira nodded. She wanted to ask him about the sacrifice he'd made. Wanted to ask why he'd done it. Was he still immortal? Didn't he still have another life to save?

He sat beside her on the swing. "I heard what the Fallen said about your former handler. I'm sorry."

"Yeah. I should have known something that would negate a Shadowchaser's powers would come from Shadow-magic."

"You were just out of training. There was no way for you to know."

"Thanks for saying that." It was something she'd have to carry with her, just like all the other regrets and mistakes she carried. She leaned into him and the regrets and mistakes didn't seem as heavy.

"What you did . . . what you've done all along . . . "

"I did what I had to do, as did you." He set the glider to swinging. "I would do so again, if I had to."

So would she. "I saw . . . I saw amazing things while I was . . . well, dead. Did you see . . . ?"

"The hall, the gods. Yes." He smiled. "Definitely amazing."

He'd seen what she'd seen, experienced what she'd experienced. But he was supposed to move on, not stay behind in this world. He'd petitioned the goddesses for the right to return to the world of the living, to continue being her fail-safe. Yes, he had one more life to save, but that wasn't the reason he gave them. He'd wanted to save her life. Save her. She wanted to ask him why, but she wasn't sure she really wanted to know the answer. Not yet.

She asked a different question instead. "Isis sent you back and Ma'at sent me back. What do you think it means?"

He touched her throat, the mark of Ma'at's feather imprinted there, then pulled down the collar of his shirt to show her the Isis knot just below his Adam's apple. "It means that we've been blessed by our goddesses. It means we still have a lot of work ahead of us." He regarded her. "Are you prepared?"

"Prepared? No. Shadowchasing and the Gilead Commission have been a big part of my life. I don't know how to live without them anymore. But I'm ready to do whatever Ma'at asks of me."

He stood, held out his hand to her. "At least you know how to be a team player now. Sort of."

"Sort of? What do you mean, sort of?" She let him pull her to her feet. "I think I've done pretty well with the teamwork thing."

He coughed, clearly to cover a laugh. "Why don't

we go inside, grab some food, and ask the others how well you've got the teamwork thing down. I think we'll get some interesting answers."

"See, now you're not playing fair. Maybe we should ask them if you've learned any humility in the last four thousand years."

Khefar responded with a wry smile.

She stood and headed inside. The ancient Nubian warrior followed her.

There were still tons of questions that needed to be answered, decisions that needed to be made. As long as Ma'at guided her, she'd face whatever the Universe wanted to throw her way.